THE AFFAIR

CLAIRE ALLAN

B
Boldwood

First published in Great Britain in 2024 by Boldwood Books Ltd.

Copyright © Claire Allan, 2024

Cover Design by Head Design Ltd

Cover Photography: Shutterstock

Every effort has been made to obtain the necessary permissions with reference to copyright material, both illustrative and quoted. We apologise for any omissions in this respect and will be pleased to make the appropriate acknowledgements in any future edition.

A CIP catalogue record for this book is available from the British Library.

Paperback ISBN 978-1-83533-422-5

Large Print ISBN 978-1-83533-418-8

Hardback ISBN 978-1-83533-417-1

Ebook ISBN 978-1-83533-415-7

Kindle ISBN 978-1-83533-416-4

Audio CD ISBN 978-1-83533-423-2

MP3 CD ISBN 978-1-83533-420-1

Digital audio download ISBN 978-1-83533-414-0

Boldwood Books Ltd
23 Bowerdean Street
London SW6 3TN
www.boldwoodbooks.com

For
Joe & Luka

PROLOGUE
OCTOBER 2023

The first bite of the icy water always stings. It brings a sharp inhalation as the waves rumble towards the shore and over neoprene-clad feet. The cold seeps through anyway; the water coats their ankles.

'Just breathe,' she tells herself, as the bitter cold of the salt water causes every blood vessel in her body to constrict, making it feel as if her lungs have been vacuum-packed. Her now-shallow breath leaves her mouth in puffs through quivering lips before she tries to inhale deeply. Her entire body shudders.

'Are you okay?' her companion asks as they proceed, hand in hand, holding on to each other in an unspoken pact to just keep walking. The water's now lapping at their knees. She wonders if this is the coldest the water has been. It feels colder than last time – than all the other times. The blood in her veins is already chilling. The numbness will come in time. She longs for the dissociation that comes with the drop in body temperature. That's what has kept her doing this time and time again.

'Are you okay?' her companion repeats and she feels the grip on her hand tighten. She realises she hasn't answered, but right now she doesn't have the ability to speak. Not yet. Her whole body is shaking and fighting the urge to break free and run from the sea towards the shore. Towards a warm towel and a cup of hot chocolate and the radiator on full blast in the car as she drives away from here. She reminds herself the temporary discomfort and fear as her body adjusts to the water is just that – temporary. Her body will adjust.

But the comfort and courage she normally finds in holding the hand of a fellow swimmer as they march forwards into the biting cold waters of the Atlantic isn't materialising today. Something is off. Maybe it's just because she slept badly last night – it has knocked her form off – but then again, she'd struggle to remember the last night she slept well. Normally it doesn't matter.

There's a different energy tonight, she thinks. Tonight she's felt that something has shifted with her companion. Maybe on the drive down, or maybe it was once they reached the beach, but it is definitely not as it normally is. It's not how she expected it would be. They'd changed in near silence, pulling on their warm beanie hats and neoprene gloves – preparing themselves for the deep cold that only a night sea can bring.

Her least favourite part of wild swimming has always been the initial walk into the waves. That's the part that requires the greatest willpower, and it never gets easier. That's what she put her companion's silence down to – listening to the self-talk that's needed to propel yourself forward versus the urge to back out. But this is more than that. It isn't just the cold that is making her shudder violently. She can't pretend any longer.

Putting all her energy into breathing as steadily as can, she gasps as the water laps at her chest. It forces her to her tiptoes, as she tries to find her balance against the shifting sand beneath her feet.

They are out further than normal. Usually they stop just past waist height and drop down under the water, keeping themselves on a decent footing. The Atlantic tides can move fast – they can knock you off your feet and pull you under in seconds. Especially on nights like this when the water is choppy and the wind is up. It just takes one big wave.

She tries to stop walking, tries to let go of her companion's hand. 'I think we're out far enough,' she says, her teeth chattering, but her companion doesn't appear to hear.

Her heart is thumping now, only just distinguishable from the roar of the water and the wind. This is not safe. She is not safe.

Her feet bob up and down off the seabed and she is buffeted by the waves. A mouthful of salt water makes her gag. She needs both arms to be able to right herself, and to swim closer to shore. Again, she tries to pull her hand free, tries to tell herself she is panicking for no good reason. But her companion just holds on tighter as rain starts to fall, water on water, and it feels like the world is turning upside down. Rain falls in fat, heavy drops, like icy bullets pummelling her skin, and she isn't sure if she noticed it before now, but the moonlight has dulled, lost behind the sudden influx of clouds and cold rain.

She calls again, forcing a lightness into her voice that she most certainly does not feel. 'I think maybe it's time to get out?' But her voice is carried off on the wind and her companion appears to be doing their best to pull her deeper into the water. She pulls back, twisting her arm to try to break free.

Her companion knows she's not a confident swimmer. She doesn't like to get out of her depth. She needs to be in control, and she isn't. She glances to the shore to see if there is anyone there, anyone at all, who can see them and can help them. But as the light on her hat flickers and dies, she can't see much beyond the end of her own nose.

Panic rises in her as she feels her arm twist back, propelled by the angry energy of her companion.

'No!' she says, though it comes out like a strangled scream. 'Let go!'

And that's when she sees it. The fury as her companion's illuminated face comes into focus. The hate that has always been there but has been hidden so well. It's there now.

She realises then, only one of them is coming back out of the water alive.

1

CHRISTINA

June 2023

All it will take is a click of a button and my life will change. Even I can click a button. I don't even have to get dressed. I can sit here in these well-worn, now shapeless cotton pyjamas with my mouth still furry with morning breath and my hair sticking out at angles. I can do it in the stale confines of my bedroom where the curtains have been pulled tight for the last three weeks, keeping out the glare and heat of the summer sun.

The only thing that would require less effort from me at this moment is breathing. This is just clicking a button – just tapping the screen to do something positive for my future. To stop me marinating in my own misery any longer. Maybe.

Clicking that button doesn't leave me obligated to do anything. It doesn't commit me to actually leaving the house but it's a start. It's what Una Doyle, my therapist, would call a 'positive step in the right direction'. It's an expression of an interest to do more. To be more. To be among people.

For all her expertise, Una doesn't seem to realise that being a chronic introvert with a limited social battery isn't something that can be cured with exposure therapy. She doesn't understand that while I want to be a part of the world, I find it incredibly hard. It's something that has always turned out to be better in theory than reality. When I have forced myself to try and be the kind of person who joins in, I have more often than not found myself on the sidelines feeling lonelier than before I left the house. But I do need something more in my life. My world is shrinking with every month that passes. There are days when I stray no further than the bathroom or the kitchen, then back to my desk in the living room to work from home like a good little minion.

I have to go into the office two days a week now, and there are weeks when those two days are the only times I leave the house. I know myself it's not good enough. I don't need Una to give me that sympathetic but clearly disappointed look she does so well over our weekly Zoom therapy session to know I need to try a little harder.

And I am trying. I have been following this Facebook group for a long time now. Maybe eighteen months. I started not long after it was set up – and I've watched these women share their stories of great new friendships, and book clubs, and cinema trips and the 'craic being brilliant' – and I've felt a sense of longing to be among them.

I've read them talking of their friendships and new-found confidence and I have felt pangs of jealousy. It's not unreasonable to want to have friends. To be part of the in crowd, even just once. I know it will require effort – and a leap outside of my comfort zone. I know the journey of a thousand steps starts with just one. It would make Una so happy. And it would make Shaunagh – my oldest friend who left Derry to follow the love of her life to Edinburgh and who is now swept up in the madness of new motherhood – worry less about me too. Not that I believe she worries about me all that much any more. Baby Thomas takes up too much of her time for that. But she says she does, when she implores me to just 'put myself out there a bit more'.

All I have to do is tap my phone screen. Just once. And I'll be the latest member of the Soul Sisterhood – a 'community of women empowering ourselves and each other to overcome life's challenges and support our mental health goals'.

The slideshow of pictures moving across the top of the screen shows smiling faces, women clad in bright colours, their hands curled to make the outlines of hearts. It shows yoga classes, people lying on mats, eyes closed in meditation, and a group of women walking hand in hand into the sea for their daily wild water swim.

The pictures offer so much more than this nothing existence I have, here in my bed in this stale room. It offers more than doomscrolling through umpteen social media platforms, each offering a different presentation of lives that are more 'perfect' than mine could ever be.

Sorcha Hannon appears next on my screen as I scroll. The leader of the pack and Social Media Influencer of the Year according to this latest video clip, recorded last night at the Irish & Influential awards.

She oozes class, with her sleek chocolate-brown hair, sprinkled with caramel highlights, her form-fitting but tasteful black gown and the adornment of a simple silver chain with a letter S pendant as her only jewellery. Sorcha doesn't need to be showy. Her brand is built on her authenticity – showing the good and the bad of her life. Of course her bad isn't quite the same level of duvet dwelling as some of us experience, I think as I haul myself up to sitting and feel the crinkle of a Wispa wrapper brush against my leg. I try to remember the last time I ate a Wispa...

'This award isn't just for me,' Sorcha says on screen as she casts her eyes over the solid silver statuette in her hands and back at the sea of smiling, perfectly groomed faces in front of her. 'It's for every woman who stands up and asks to be given the recognition and respect she deserves. It's for every woman who chooses to take back her own power.

'We all work together to help each other create a life we can be proud of and happy in.' She grins, her perfectly white veneers sparkling brightly. The sound of applause fills my ears before the video cuts off and I am left staring at a still of a beaming Sorcha.

I want to be that Sorcha-level of happy. I want to feel as if I'm living a life I can be proud of and happy in. I don't want to let these demons win. I've not felt brave enough to do it alone, but maybe with help I can. Una says I can, and she hasn't given me any reason to doubt her yet. My heartbeat quickens and I'm not sure if it's fear or excitement. Maybe it's a bit of both.

I close my eyes. I'm not in my bedroom any more, in these pyjamas that are stale with sweat and should probably have been thrown in the laundry yesterday, if not the day before. My hair is not messy and in desperate need of deep conditioning. I'm there, among them. I'm on the stage beside Sorcha and she is grabbing tightly to my hand, squeezing it in a silent show of friendship and solidarity. She's telling me, 'We've got this!' I'm smiling at her, feeling like the cat who got the cream in my slinky dress with hair that is silky soft and full-bodied. Shaunagh is smiling and waving at me from the audience and I can see pride written all over her face. Pride, and maybe relief that she doesn't have to worry about me quite so much any more.

When I open my eyes again, hauling myself back to my reality, I look back at the screen, and her face. It feels as if she's inviting me personally. As if she knows what my life is like and she genuinely wants to help me create a life I can be... How did she say it again? A life I can be proud of and happy in? Something like that.

Sorcha Hannon wants to help me be happy.

Taking a deep breath, I tap the screen and just like that, I've taken the first step to a new me.

2

There's a coffee morning today. The kind of thing I'd normally avoid like the plague. I don't do small talk. It makes me incredibly uneasy. Once I exhaust the limited script of talking about the weather, what people do for work and offering enough compliments on their hair/clothes/earrings to appear friendly but not creepy, I am done.

There have been too many times when I have sat, mouth flapping open like a fish, willing words to come out that will show me to be an interesting person to get to know, only to eventually find myself dropping my gaze and wandering off while someone else takes charge of the conversation. Then, of course, I have to build up my nerve once more and start all over again, approach a new person or a new group and hope they accept me enough to talk to me and don't just give me the side-eye that is universal sign language for 'this is a private conversation, weirdo'.

My hand shakes as I try to apply some mascara. It's shaking so much I manage to accidentally brush my eyeball with the mascara wand, which hurts like a motherfucker. Watery-eyed tears course down one side of my face, cutting through my painstakingly applied foundation. I don't wear make-up often – not beyond a quick dusting of pressed powder to take the shine off my face and some Burt's Bees tinted lip balm.

But Sorcha always wears make-up. Even when she's doing yoga or going for a swim, or having a cry about the breakdown of her marriage and how it spurred her to reclaim her life and her happiness.

People say she is so brave to expose her deepest feelings and insecurities online for everyone to see. That she makes women whose relationships failed feel less like failures. That she empowers them to leave behind the shame they may carry on their shoulders from the dissolution of their happy ever after.

Even in her raw and honest state, she always manages to be beautiful. Sorcha Hannon has never ugly-cried in public, I bet. I wonder for a moment if it's easier to be brave when you look like Jennifer Aniston's younger, hotter sister? Or does she feel pressure to weep in a dignified and elegant way? Tears like crystal droplets, cascading down dewy skin. No red nose and sniffles. No contortion of her face into something grotesque. No howls of mangled grief. No garbled swearing and pleading. Dignity, at all times. I wish I could be as refined, but pain has a habit of pouring out of me like molten lava – destroying everything in its path.

Has she ever cried like that? Like her heart would break? When her perfect illusion of a perfect marriage caved in around her, did she feel as if her world was ending? Did she have moments of self-doubt and self-hate? Moments that aren't curated for the cameras, aren't lit perfectly and don't show the unflattering reality of heartache?

Does she have moments of intense self-loathing – where she glances in the mirror and makes her body rigid with anger at her own flaws? Not that she has many, if any, physical flaws. Unless it's all filters and face-tuning.

Sorcha says beauty comes from within and isn't dependant on what 'product' you use on your face or have on your dressing table. It's easy to say that when you're beautiful. But I don't feel beautiful and I absolutely don't want to show up looking like the broken slob I have become. I want to make a good impression. I don't want to fuck this up. It's all about preparation. If I feel confident, maybe I'll act confident.

I've watched eight YouTube tutorials on foundation application – some of them several times – and they have helped me to achieve a look that's supposed to say 'effortlessly natural', even though it has taken seven layers of different product to achieve. I feel as if I'm wearing a mask – which isn't far from the truth in fairness. Maybe that's why these influencer types love make-up so much. It's the modern equivalent of a Greek theatre mask. A face they wear to perform.

Today, I've ploughed my way through serum, primer, concealer, liquid foundation, bronzer, highlighter and finishing powder. I had to buy everything new bar the concealer and liquid foundation. I've never been particularly high-maintenance – and especially not lately. My make-up bag would at best be described as 'minimalistic'.

But today, as I get ready to be among all these women I've never met before, I feel as if I have to at least try to look 'put together'. And try hard. I'm pretty sure I've applied everything wrong, despite the YouTube tutorials. I don't see the point of half of it if I'm being honest, but Sorcha says we should 'trust the process' when applying skincare products or make-up. The look always comes together in the end. Unless we stab ourselves in the eye during said process with a mascara wand, presumably.

Once my eye stops watering quite so much and I'm able to open it again without the stinging pain overwhelming me, I wash my now streaked make-up off and start all over again. Thankfully I factored the possibility of unexpected errors into my timekeeping and as long as I don't mess it up again, I'll still be able to make it on time.

My hand, however, is still shaking and there's a risk I'll take my other eye out if I don't steady it. I'd take a shot of something alcoholic to steady my nerves but I'm driving to the coffee morning and I never, ever drink and drive. It's one of my absolutes.

Instead, I practise my deep-breathing exercises – something else I've learned from Una and TikTok, along with meditation and affirmations. They don't work most of the time, but I'm hoping this time will be different.

I tell myself, out loud, that I have nothing to fear from this coffee morning. Everyone in Sorcha Hannon's Soul Sisterhood Facebook group is lovely. They've been so welcoming since the day two weeks ago when I tapped on my phone screen and joined. They've made me feel one of their gang already. I've had sixteen hug emojis and ten heart emoji clicks in response to my post about being lonely and wanting to reach out to meet new people. I had thirteen ordinary thumbs-up emojis too, which I know aren't as good as hugs or hearts, but at least it means people cared enough to click. Maybe it's sad to count them or use them as an indicator of anything of importance but they must mean something. Even if it's just that they give me courage to walk into a room full of women I've only seen before on computer screens.

Shaunagh says I'm overthinking things. But it's hard not to overthink things when you've been hurt in the past.

'Just be yourself,' she told me. 'But maybe not all yourself, all at once, in the first five minutes.' She'd laughed. Of course, I'd laughed too even if I didn't find it all that funny. I've tried to take her advice.

I haven't lied in any of my posts but I've also been careful not to give too much of myself away. I don't want to come across as desperate and needy. I don't want them to brand me as 'too much' before they've even met me. I've made that mistake before and opened myself up from the get-go. Shaunagh says I've given people who don't like me sticks to beat me with.

Taking a deep breath, I look in the mirror to assess the damage. My now bloodshot eye is still watering. It itches as if there is grit stuck in it, my eyelid puffy and slightly swollen. Even with all my new make-up at my disposal, the vivid blood red of my sclera stands out like a warning beacon.

Maybe I shouldn't go today after all. What kind of a first impression will I make walking in looking like I've been punched in the face? What if they want to take one of their big group photos and it captures me looking like a domestic violence survivor smiling awkwardly at the camera?

Slumping onto my bed, I grab my phone and click into the Sisterhood group page. There's a post, of course, asking who is coming along to the coffee morning and promising a selection of home bakes, fine coffee and great craic. There is much excitement. Looking around my room, I want more than anything to get out of this space and out of my head for a while, but I'm scared. More so now that I've Quasimodo'd my own eye. What if I don't fit in? Or Sorcha takes one look at me and forms an instant dislike?

A heaviness settles in the pit of my stomach – one I know is neither a sign of fear nor excitement but the deep belief that I am not good. I am not enough. This has all been a bad idea. I don't know what I was expecting to get out of it. My finger hovers over my phone as I wonder whether to call Shaunagh to ask her to talk me down from this ledge – but then I remember how she sighed from the pit of her soul when we spoke last night and told me I need to put my big girl pants on and just do it. I don't want to hear that sigh again.

I type into the group:

I don't know if I can make it. I'm so stupid – I managed to stab myself in the eye with my mascara wand while I was getting ready and I look like I've done ten rounds with Mike Tyson. *cry emoji*. You'll be wondering who the weirdo with the red eye is! Ha ha! I'll catch you next time.

If there's one thing I've learned in my life it's that if I call myself the weirdo, or the bore, or the stupid one first, people tend to be more understanding of my faults. The key to fitting in is beating everyone to the punchlines with some well-timed self-deprecating humour. Pressing send, I curl up into a ball on top of my unmade bed, anxiety making my head pound. I listen out for the ping of any notifications in response. Maybe none will come? Maybe I don't matter. Maybe I should've put my phone on silent or switched it off.

But, before long, a series of tinny chimes alert me to new activity in the group. Hauling myself back up to sitting, I straighten my spine, take a few deep breaths and start reading.

My post has earned three hug emojis, which is a good sign. There's one laughing-face emoji. I'm not sure how to read that. It could be a bad thing. The person might be laughing in sympathy, or maybe they think it's funny that the strange new girl would think anyone would care about her sore eye. Maybe it's funny that I'm clearly so stupid that I can't even manage to get ready without hurting myself.

My stomach clenches, and I tap at the screen to see the emoji was sent by a woman called Becca O'Reilly. Scooting down my bed, I grab the notebook and pen I keep on my dresser and write her name down on my list of 'Ones to Watch'. It's always helpful to keep lists. Mostly I use them as an aide-memoire so that I have a starting point for conversations with people. It helps me feel more in control. On other occasions I use them to remind me not all people are my friend.

More tinny chimes announce more replies. There are a few written responses now, my screen refreshing as each new one arrives.

Kathy is *sad to hear* I won't make it, but tells me *maybe next time?* Fiona writes:

Ouch! You poor love. I hate that! It stings so much! But unless it's very sore, would you not come along anyway? We're all a bit weird so don't worry about a sore eye putting us off! *laughing emoji*

Joan writes:

Don't worry about how you look! I look like I've been dragged through a bush backwards this morning. Absolute state of me!

And then there's a new message and this time it is from Sorcha herself. My heart quickens. It means she has noticed me and, holding my breath, I read:

Christina, please come along anyway. I've read your other posts and it seems you could do with a friend or two, and some laughs. Besides, Fiona is baking her chocolate brownies and you absolutely don't want to miss those! I'll make sure to save you one. Just say you'll come?

I exhale with a sob that I didn't realise I'd been holding in. Sorcha Hannon has replied to me. She is keeping a brownie for me. Beautiful, confident, caring Sorcha says she knows I need a friend. Sorcha who has made a success of her life despite the challenges she has faced. Sorcha who has fought her own battles, and reinvented herself as a strong, independent influencer not afraid to reach out to other women and help them empower themselves. Sorcha who has grabbed life by the balls and lives it unapologetically.

I long to be just like her. I don't want to sit on the sidelines of life any more. I'm fed up existing in a never-ending cycle of working or doom-scrolling on TikTok, and occasionally ordering beautiful, fashionable clothes I will never wear because I've nowhere to go and no one to go with.

The shoebox that has been lying on the floor beside my bed for the last nine days taunts me. The lid is open and a pair of bright green strappy heels poke out from under pastel-coloured tissue paper. They're beautiful. Vintage. Real leather. I had to have them, even though I already know I'll forget I even own them in a few weeks. They'll just blend in with all the other boxes I have stacked on top of each other, all filled with beautiful, unworn 'going out' shoes.

An idea flashes through my mind. I click heart emoji responses to the replies to my post before typing a response to Sorcha's comment. *You had me at brownie!* I type, before I delete the exclamation mark, and retype it, repeating that process four times until I decide to leave it in. This is the kind of group where exclamation marks are overused with abandon. Everything is worth celebrating in this world.

Then I type:

You're right – I really could do with a friend. I'll see you all there!
I'll be the one with the eyepatch, maybe! *laughing-face emoji*

With a smile on my face and a new-found lightness in my heart, I flip my phone over so it doesn't distract me while I reapply my make-up and get dressed into a pair of brand-new dark denim wide-leg jeans, an also-brand-new floaty kimono-style top that is very much not my usual style and very much something Sorcha would wear.

I slip my feet into the strappy green sandals. When I look in the mirror, I'm disappointed to see I don't look quite as good as I hoped it might – I think my legs might be too short to really carry off wide-leg trousers – but it looks better than the pyjama bottoms and worn-out T-shirt I've been living in for the last forever. I don't have time to get changed anyway. I want to be there precisely five minutes after starting time so I don't look too eager, but I'm not so late it appears rude.

Reading Sorcha's message one last time, I take a deep breath before grabbing my keys and heading out the door.

3

Sorcha Hannon is even more beautiful in real life than on the screen of my phone. The version of her that is unfiltered, smiling as she chats to her friends, brings her beauty to a whole new level. I'm paralysed by it for a moment, until I'm forced to move out of the way to let someone else in through the door. Mumbling an apology, I step to the side – keeping my distance from the group of women drawn like moths to a flame around Sorcha. There is much smiling and hugging. High-pitched hellos punctuate the admiration of each other's hair/clothes/make-up.

I press the now sweaty palm of my hand flat against the very centre of my stomach to try and quell the anxiety-induced nausea that's bubbling up inside me.

Maybe this was a mistake. I don't know why I thought I could do this. Here, I am, on the outside looking in, just like I have always been. Always watching, and longing to be brought into the fold, but never being enough. It's too much like hard work to try.

A cold sweat beads and breaks on my brow, even though I know this room isn't too warm. The room is light and airy, floor-to-ceiling windows offering a view of the frost-covered gardens outside. It is not too crowded. At a rough guess, there are maybe forty or fifty people here. It's a tiny representation of Sorcha's online following. We are not packed in like sardines. There are enough seats – chairs and chintzy covered sofas dotted around the room – that everyone has room to move around, to sit and chat to friends, to feel connected but not overwhelmed.

Yet, I feel overwhelmed and now self-conscious about the trickle of nervous perspiration I've just felt running down my neck. Although I'm doing my best to take deep, calming breaths it feels as if the air is being sucked from my body with every inhalation. The feeling is so clawing, a part of me wonders if it's possible for a body to forget how to breathe properly.

'Just breathe in.' I hear Una's voice in my head. 'Just to take one, long, steady breath inwards. You've done it before, and you can do it again.'

But it feels as if there is no air to be had.

Another bead of sweat rolls down from my hairline. It tickles like a fly buzzing at my ear as it slides further downwards before coming to rest in the dip just above my collarbone. Raising my hand to brush it away, I realise more beads are following its path as well as carving new ones on my skin – careering down my neck, and behind my ears. I cringe as I feel sweat pool at the base of my spine and in the dip between my breasts. Of all the sensory triggers that make me nauseous, the feeling of sweat, of clammy damp skin is close to the top of the list. People will notice. They'll look at me and judge. Dirty. And greasy. And smelly. I feel dirty, greasy and smelly. Disgusting. No doubt my carefully applied make-up is now on a one-way journey southwards. My chest feels tight.

I've no idea how or why I thought this would be a good idea. Jesus, maybe I am as defective as I've been led to believe. Too sensitive. Too fussy. Too odd. But this is supposed to be me trying to do better. To be better. This is my new start.

Head bowed, I try focusing on the fifty-six steps that I need to take to get me out of this place and back onto the street where there is air, and a breeze and anonymity in a crowd. Fifty-six steps is not very far. Escape is within reach.

It took me twenty-four minutes to get here from the moment I left home, and that means I can be safe again in twenty-four minutes. I can be back in my cocoon, with my curtains closed and my duvet over my head in less than half an hour. *Just* half an hour. Even I can do half an hour.

Once I get home I'll leave the Facebook group and never think of being so stupid again. I am not Sorcha Hannon. We may share certain life experiences but I do not have her poise and confidence. That should have been obvious from the very start. That I thought that I could exist in the same space as her and not mess up is ridiculous and naive – another of my stupid ideas.

Muttering 'excuse me' and 'sorry', I push my way back through the groups of people who are just arriving, already buzzing with energy and excitement. Snippets of their conversations ring in my ears. Someone is 'dying for a pee'. Someone else is 'hanging like a bat' – cue uproarious laughter. These women they hug, and cling to each other. They enthuse about how 'amazing' the other looks. How 'pure gorgeous' each of them is. I just wanted to be a part of this inner sanctum of female friendship, but I should've known that would be impossible.

The world does not work this way for people like me. I'm not one of *them*. I'm not witty, or funny. I don't know the perfect things to say to the right people at the right times. There are no pearls of wisdom rattling around in my head, ready to be dispensed when needed. I don't always notice when it's my time to talk, or my time to shut up for that matter. I don't always keep the thoughts that should stay in my head to myself, blurting them out in a shameful word vomit instead.

I've taken just eighteen steps towards my escape when I feel the warm weight of a hand grabbing mine – the unmistakeable ick of clammy skin on skin makes me pull away so violently that I manage to dig my elbow squarely into the ribs of a woman who was just trying to walk past me. Spinning, I apologise profusely to her, but I can't bring myself to look up and see her face.

Adult me knows, of course, that the old 'if I can't see them, then they can't see me' belief that many a child holds so dear isn't real, but still I hide my face.

I'm making myself small, Una would tell me. Not just because interaction with other people often makes me uncomfortable, but because, she says, I have never really embraced my right to take up space in this world. We're working on that one. We've been working on it for a long time.

The hum of the room around me is just increasing in volume, and the woman I've apologised to is replying but I can't distinguish her voice from the others clamouring for attention from each other around me. Then the same warm hand is grabbing mine again, and another hand is gripping my forearm and I hear my name.

'Christina?'

The clarity of her clipped, media-savvy voice cuts through the noise and I recognise that it is Sorcha herself who is speaking to me. Glancing at the hand holding mine, seeing a perfectly tanned wrist, bedecked with a myriad of fine silver bracelets, coloured strings and glass beads, and 'Still I Rise' tattooed in Courier font, my suspicions are confirmed. I recognise that arm from a multitude of Instagram photos.

Without thinking, I look up and am met with the sight of her pale blue-grey eyes wide with concern. Her perfectly sun-kissed features – blemish-free bar for a smattering of freckles across the bridge of her nose – all exude compassion and curiosity.

So this is Sorcha Hannon, I think, as words fail to form. I wonder how she manages to get it so right.

'You're Christina, aren't you?' she asks. 'I recognise you from your picture on Facebook.'

I nod, feeling incredibly self-conscious, and shy, and racked with nerves. I'm acutely embarrassed that I also feel... sort of star-struck. I know the face in front of me. I have seen it every day on my computer screen and my phone screen. I have looked at her pictures, watched her TikToks and her Reels, joined in with her 'Live' chats. In her bio, she describes herself as 'just an ordinary girl, keeping it real and promoting sisterhood', but in this moment in front of me she doesn't look like 'just an ordinary girl'.

She is the woman I wish I was, with the life I'd love to have. 'I'm Christina,' I stutter, repeating my own name back to her as if she hasn't just said it to me first.

'Well, it's lovely to meet you,' Sorcha says, a soft smile illuminating her face. I can't help but notice how perfect her teeth are. Even more so than they look in her pictures. I wonder if they're veneers. They probably are.

Running my tongue over the uneven ridges and edges of my own teeth, aware of their imperfections, I keep my mouth firmly shut and just nod, again. Why am I behaving like a stupid fucking nodding dog? This is not the first impression I wanted to make. She'll be thinking there's a want in me.

'You weren't trying to leave, were you?' she asks, but doesn't leave me any time to answer before speaking again. And yet somewhere in the breath between that question and her next words, I am able to run through multiple negative scenarios in my head. She's judging me. She's angry with me for leaving. She thinks I'm pathetic for not being able to hack a few minutes in the company of strangers. 'Because you absolutely have to stay, at least until you get a brownie, or one of Joan's scones,' she continues, cutting off my self-hatred at the knees. 'They're fresh-baked this morning and still warm, so let's get in there quick before these vultures eat them all,' she adds with a wink.

With a smile and a gentle tug she leads me back through the crowd and towards a trestle table where a selection of home-baked treats has been set out on brightly coloured paper plates. Women are busying themselves pouring teas and coffees, spooning sugar from a white Tupperware container into cups before adding whatever variation they take on 'just a splash of milk'. I can't take my eyes from the same spoon dipping in and out of the sugar bowl, still wet, leaving tannin traces as the sugar congeals around the spoon. I shudder.

'Tea or coffee?' Sorcha asks. I mutter 'tea' even though I'm not really a fan of tea. However, I find it more palatable than coffee so I can fake my normality better with this option, even if it's over-brewed and will be much too strong for my taste.

'Milk and sugar?' she asks.

'Just milk,' I say, not daring to risk cross-contamination from the spoons.

'Just a splash or are you like me and prefer some tea in your milk?' she asks with a broad smile, which I find strangely reassuring.

'I'm like you,' I tell her, even though I am quite obviously not at all like her. Life would be so much easier if I was. If only I was able to carry myself with her poise and confidence. If only I was able to look even a fraction as gracious and beautiful as she does. Things would be so very different. Then I think of her troubles and remind myself no one has a perfect life.

I stand, mute and a little in awe, as she tops up a cup and hands it to me before asking if I'd like a brownie, or one of Joan's scones, and then if I'd like butter and jam.

'Coming to something like this can be really intimidating,'

she says as she slices a scone open and slathers on a thick layer of butter. 'You should be really proud of yourself. You'll get to know everyone quite quickly and find out we're all just the same.'

I nod, impressed at how easily she navigates this scenario – how she acknowledges the other women in the room and their bond but keeps her attention focused on me. 'Everyone has their reason for coming along here,' she says as she hands me my buttered scone, wrapped in a paper napkin. 'Some are here just for the craic. Some because they've realised life has become lonely despite all this social media connectivity nonsense we have at our fingertips. Some of us have been through the mill and need a little gentle encouragement to find ourselves again. But no matter the reason, we're all here for each other. We all know life can be tough sometimes.'

Seamlessly, and without my even really noticing, she guides me away from the food and drinks towards a small group of women seated around a table and already deep in conversation.

'Girls,' Sorcha says, 'this is Christina, and this is her first time here. Can I trust you all to look after her while I go and make sure to say hello to everyone else?'

The 'girls', who all appear to be at least in their thirties and forties, look up at me, taking me in from head to toe.

'Of course!' a woman with a friendly face and bright pink hair, which I immediately covet, says. 'How's your eye, Christina?' she asks, and it throws me off guard. I don't know who she is and even though I know I mentioned my eye in the online group earlier, I feel disarmed by her familiarity.

'It's... well, it's fine now, I think. No lasting damage anyway,' I say, hovering near them, afraid to sit on any of the available chairs in case I choose the wrong one and fail some unknown test.

'I'm so clumsy like that,' the pink-haired woman says. 'So I really felt for you. Here, have a seat,' she says, shifting over to create space for me. 'I'm Aoife,' she says.

'And I'm Joan,' the woman sitting to her left says. Joan looks like the kind of woman who can never sit still – who always has to be doing something. Like baking incredible scones for example.

'You're the scone lady?' I say, and sit down.

'I've been called worse.' She smiles. 'And, this is Fiona – known for her incredible brownies – Carla and Mags.'

The three women all nod and smile as she says their names. They look friendly and I so want to relax and join in, but I'm not ready to drop my guard just yet.

I give a rather pathetic wave, which I immediately regret. It looked so geeky. 'It's nice to meet you all,' I say and wonder, does my voice sound weird? Too high? Too posh?

'It's nice to meet you too,' the woman identified as Carla says. She has a warm, welcoming smile and I instantly take to her. 'We always like to meet new people.'

'So,' Joan says, as I take the smallest sip I can from my still too-strong and too-hot tea. It seems I'm even less like Sorcha than I thought, her definition of 'tea in your milk' being dwarfed by mine. 'What brings you here, Christina? What's your story?'

My eyes dart quickly across the room to Sorcha, then back to Joan, a tall, willowy woman with the kind of silver-grey hair that definitely comes from an expensive salon and isn't solely down to the passage of time.

'This might sound really pathetic,' I say. 'But I suppose I just wanted to meet some new people. No one tells you how lonely your thirties can be. Especially if you're single and have no kids.' I force a laugh I certainly don't feel because I don't want them to think I'm the weird kind of lonely. 'And Sorcha, well, I've been following her account for ages now. She seems so nice online and, you know, inspirational. How she bounced back from' – I pause, then drop my voice to a whisper – 'the break-up.'

They nod and I can see they hold her in high regard. I watch their faces for any hint that they might feel different – that there could be something about Sorcha and all this that might be unpalatable, but there's nothing there.

'I saw how she was bringing all of you together and this just seems like something I would like to be a part of,' I add, and they smile.

'You won't regret it,' Aoife says. 'This is the best thing I've ever done for myself and I know a lot of the girls here feel the same. It has given so many of us a new lease of life.'

Fiona nods vigorously. 'It really has,' she says. 'Before this I was just either at work, or looking after my wains, or cleaning the house and I didn't do anything for myself. This has been a game changer. Everyone's just so nice.'

Statistically I know it's unlikely everyone really is just 'so nice'. That's not how large groups of humans work together – and certainly not large groups of women, no matter the common goal. All of us are equal, but some are more equal than others, after all. And Sorcha, for all her niceness, is the most equal of everyone in this room. But I smile anyway and allow myself to believe that people can really be entirely good even though I know without a doubt that isn't true.

4

When I'm back in my car, I think about how I relaxed into the company of these women. Not enough to take the lead in the conversation or challenge anyone when I didn't agree with their views but enough to laugh, nod and not feel like an intruder on their fun.

I was happy to be in invisibility mode and able to sit and listen and gather snippets of information that will help me in the future.

I was happy because Sorcha Hannon spoke to me herself – and not just when I arrived. Before I left she approached me once again without me having to find the courage to wait in some sort of unofficial queue to see her, or hover close by looking expectant in the hope she'd spy me out of the corner of her eye and feel obligated to come and chat.

The event had just been wrapping up when I'd felt a hand on my arm. When I turned around, there she was, smiling beatifically in my direction. The woman practically radiated with confidence and friendliness. That was such an incredible relief to me.

'Did you get on okay?' she'd asked. 'I'm sorry I didn't get back round to you before now. Lots of people wanted to talk today.' She gave a little roll of her eyes as if she couldn't quite believe anyone would want to talk to her. Was she, a woman who shares almost every detail of her life online, really that shocked that people wanted to talk to her? She spends her days creating video content of her morning routine, her evening routine, her self-care hacks, and of her ongoing journey through divorce. People view her as a friend because they know the intimate details of her life. She even lets her followers know when she has her period, for the love of God.

But at the same time she did seem very genuine today. There were no obvious red flags on display. She gave me no signs that I shouldn't trust her or that I've been stupid to like her. Then again, as I've learned in the last few years, when it comes to judging the character of other people, I don't always get it right.

Still, I'd told her I'd enjoyed myself. 'It was lovely. Joan and Carla kept an eye on me. Everyone is just so lovely,' I'd said, and instantly hated myself because lovely is such a nothing word. It's bland. Vanilla. Boring. Just like boring and vanilla old me. If the only word someone can use to describe a person is 'lovely', you better believe that also means 'dull and inoffensive'. It's just a polite way of saying it. I should know. I've been described as 'lovely' often enough.

'Everyone was very friendly and the scones were to die for,' I'd babbled to Sorcha as she walked me towards my car. I was rewarded with one of her full-beam smiles.

'They are, aren't they? I have to watch how many I eat or I'll be the size of a house!' she'd said, before patting her perfectly toned stomach and puffing out her cheeks in an effort to look fat.

'Never.' I'd forced myself to laugh, hyper aware of my own size, of the size sixteen label I'd cut from my jeans earlier as if removing the offending tiny piece of fabric would undo all the hatred I hold for my own body. While a size sixteen isn't particularly big, and the world tells me I should be body positive, it's hard to undo a lifetime of self-loathing – especially when thin, gorgeous women like Sorcha talk about getting fat as if it would be the worst thing that could ever happen to them.

'Well, I hope you enjoyed yourself enough to entice you to come back another time?' Sorcha had asked. 'Social media is great and all, but sometimes I think it makes it too easy for us to hide away from the world and miss out on actually living,' she'd said. 'And the only way out of that is to be proactive, you know? Check the group page anyway and you'll see what everyone is up to. We've different activities on most days. You know what, I think you'd love wild swimming. A group of us go three days a week, so there will be lots of chances for you to join in. Why don't you come along and give it a go?'

'I'm not much of a swimmer to be honest,' I'd told her, not wanting to admit that there is something about the swell of the sea that terrifies me. Some people feel grounded standing in front of the ocean. I just feel irrelevant, and pointless. One tiny grain of sand means nothing against all this vastness. One tiny grain of sand could be washed away in a second.

'If you don't feel able to swim, you can just dip in the water instead,' she'd said, undeterred. 'You'll get all the benefits of the experience. It's the cold water that works its magic – that and being in nature. It has all sorts of amazing benefits. Natural dopamine release, Vitamin D, a sense of accomplishment...'

'Frostbite?' I'd blurted, thinking of the bitter cold waters of the North Atlantic. I'd seen pictures of the Soul Sisterhood swimming in the waters alongside a number of Donegal beaches – be it Lough Swilly, which is just twenty minutes' drive from Derry, and definitely the calmer option, or another twenty minutes across the Donegal hills to the bracing Atlantic shoreline. Both scare me more than I'd dare to admit.

'You get over the cold quickly,' Sorcha had said with a laugh. 'Honestly. After a minute or so, you don't even feel it. And you feel amazing when you get back out. I won't push you, but you'd be most welcome to come along if it suits you work wise et cetera.'

'I'll think about it,' I'd told her, my stomach immediately knotting at even the thought of willingly walking into the sea, wondering if there were any dry land activities I could do instead.

'Do! And if you want to give it a go, send me a message first and if you want, we can travel down together. We always try to carpool to spread the cost for everyone. I'll even hold your hand while we walk in. That's the hardest part.' She'd smiled.

So I know I have to do it. I just need to find the courage to take that step.

Looking in my rear-view mirror, I see my eye is a little bloodshot but it doesn't look quite as angry as before. My make-up has survived the torrent of nervous sweat. I still look intact. And normal.

I have survived the first challenge – actually, I think I've won this first challenge. I've made it out of the house and met new people. I didn't make a show of myself. I didn't say or do anything obviously wrong and while I haven't made concrete plans to meet with the group again, I have laid some groundwork. Sorcha has invited me to go swimming. She's offered to drive down to the beach with me. To hold my hand as we walk into the water. You don't do that if you hate someone. No one is that much of a saint that they give their time and energy willingly to people they just don't like. Are they?

I feel a sense of motivation that wasn't there before, not even this morning. It's almost as if a weight is lifting from me. There is less pressure piled on top of my head. I don't have the same urge that I normally have after time among people to run home and hide under my duvet to wait for my social battery to recharge. I don't have the urge to play the last hour over and over in my head again and pick myself apart for the way I spoke, or sat, or ate. I don't have to berate myself for the tone of my voice, or the timbre of my laugh.

When my phone pings I see I have new follower requests on my largely dormant Instagram. Joan and Carla and Sorcha herself. I'm resistant to accept them – and it's not because I don't want to connect with these women. It's more I wonder what they will think when they see my almost empty Insta grid and read my twee bio. It's not quite 'Live, Laugh, Love' bad but it's not far off it. 'In a world where you can be anything, be kind,' it says. I immediately wipe it, replacing it with: 'Here for the craic. Proud Derry girl,' and leave it at that.

I scroll down the half a dozen photos I posted before I forgot I even had an Insta account and check them for the cringe factor. It's pretty safe. Two clichéd shots of food, taken on a night out. A picture of me holding a friend's new baby – who is probably four or five now. It's taken from above me as I cradle the tiny newborn, my head bowed to take in her beautiful features. My own features are largely hidden. Two pictures of glasses of ice-cold wine, beads of condensation forming, and finally, an oddly angled shot that just about captures the essence of me hiding behind a pair of sunglasses and a novel. It's not all that arty or worthy of showing to the world but it's not atrocious either. I let it stay, and then before finally accepting the requests decide to have a little nosy at both Joan's and Carla's accounts.

It's quite clear that Carla is very active in the Soul Sisterhood, and her account is flooded with pictures of different activities, different swims, although there are also plenty of pictures of nights out with Sorcha which, I see, go back more than a few years. Scrolling through, I come across a picture of a younger Carla, dressed in a pale green bridesmaid dress and smiling broadly with a very photogenic and exceptionally happy-looking newly married Mr and Mrs Hannon – the caption reads: 'Throwback Thursday: To 2009 and the best of days with the best of people. Happy anniversary, Sorcha and Ronan, my favourite married couple!' All three look ridiculously happy.

In each subsequent picture I look at, Carla is smiling and surrounded by friends. She seems like the kind of person you'd want on your side. I can't see any obvious evidence of a current partner or children and I wonder have I found someone like me – or at least like the me I want to be. Single, without ties and enjoying every ounce of her life. I accept her request.

Next, I look at Joan's page and it's clear she's a much less prolific poster than Carla. There aren't all that many pictures and it can be months between them. Her page gives little away save to say she works as a manager for a healthcare trust. In the few pictures there are of her she is staring directly at the camera, a hint of a smile playing on her lips but nothing more. The pictures seem at odds with the woman who welcomed me into the group earlier today. Her Instagram profile is quite reserved and officious, but I see she follows both Sorcha and Carla and they follow her too. She may not post a lot of her own updates but she comments regularly on Sorcha's page and seems to be a one-woman cheerleading team. I like women who support other women, so I accept her request. It feels good to see my follower count increase, even if only by a few.

With some newly found confidence I do some more reciprocal following. A couple of 'was lovely to meet you' messages pop into my inbox and I smile, pushing down my fears about my sad little Insta account. Today has been a good day.

I don't feel judged and that's a thread I don't want to pick at any longer because I have found that if I pick at things for long enough they will inevitably come apart at the seams. *I* will inevitably come apart at the seams. And I don't want to do that...

5

I wake the next morning feeling hopeful and grateful my confidence hasn't leached from my body while I've slept.

Today, I think, as the kettle bubbles to life beside me, I'll finally start putting some order on this flat. If I have a new friend in Sorcha, I have to make sure this place won't embarrass me if she calls round for a cup of tea, or a glass of wine.

It won't ever rival her Insta-perfect home. My kitchen is small and dated – no match for the sleek gloss finishes in her *Grand Designs*-worthy space. I've no kitchen island or instant boiling water tap, no plumbed-in fridge freezer with in-built ice dispenser and most certainly no bifold doors to a luscious garden.

But it's mine and it can be cosy. I know that. It has been a sanctuary to me at times when I've needed to hide from the world. Like me, it has character and it has its quirks. The walls are not perfectly straight. There is a knack to opening the windows that requires both patience and strength. Draught excluders are essential in the winter to stop an arctic breeze blowing through. But at night-time, when I'm listening to the sound of the rain beating off the dormer windows, in the soft glow of candlelight, it feels untouchable from the rest of the world.

Or it did – before I let someone in who left an unwelcome and painful echo on every surface they touched.

I've not been great at keeping house lately. Una tells me that's common with burnout – which is her diagnosis after months of therapy. Burnout sounds more glamorous than it is. As if it happens after working in a high-pressure environment or living an adrenaline-fuelled life. No one really talks about the people who just find themselves unable to cope with normal life because they've never quite fit in. Add to that a major 'trauma' – another of Una's diagnoses – and it's no wonder I've slipped into a depression to boot.

At least I know why I'm sad. I know what hurts. And I know that only I can work through it, so that's exactly what I'm going to try to do. I've lost enough time to grief and self-loathing. I need to give myself a good shake.

Shame nips at me as I take in the sight of the dirty sheets on my bed, the floor that needs vacuuming and the dust-covered surfaces cluttered with the detritus of my disorganised life. The air around me is stale, and there's a vague hint of dampness to it as a result of my hanging my clothes on the radiators because I don't have anywhere else to dry them.

Empty cups and bottles clutter my nightstand and unwashed dishes fill the sink. In its current state, it's hard to imagine how this was ever a place that felt warm and welcoming. It looks very much like a place that has been through the wars, which I suppose it has. Just like me. It's still my safe place, but only in the same way that Satis House was a safe place for Miss Havisham, I think wryly.

Opening Instagram to check Sorcha's updated stories, I'm greeted with a picture of a perfect breakfast served on a perfect sage-green chalk-painted tray, resting on top of a perfect soft sage-green knitted throw, which adds texture to her starched white Egyptian cotton bedding. On the tray there is a delicate china teacup and saucer, a one-person cafetière filled with rich dark coffee. A matching china bowl with yoghurt, granola and berries and – according to the caption – a drizzle of local honey, sits beside a small glass of orange juice. The pièce de résistance is a tiny china vase filled with a few wildflowers. It's perfectly curated – perfectly Sorcha – and infinitely classier than the Maltesers mug I got with an Easter egg sometime in the early 2000s and into which I've just thrown a teabag. Breakfast for me will not be natural yoghurt and local honey. It will be a slice of white bread toasted and spread thick with Flora margarine, washed down with a mug of milky tea.

Looking at her aesthetically pleasing offering, I can't help but feel pathetic that on the average day I still eat like a student who's prioritising beer money over nutrition.

Maybe if I ate like Sorcha I would feel properly nourished, have extra energy. Maybe I'd be slimmer, and sexier. Maybe I'd have a body that screamed health and fitness. Maybe I'd be enough...

Resolving to put an online grocery order in later, I decide to ask the Soul Sisterhood group chat for hints and tips about healthy eating. I might even ask Sorcha directly. I'm sure she won't mind telling me. There isn't much that she keeps to herself. Apart from, of course, the real reason behind her marriage break-up.

It must be hard for her all the same – sharing her life online, but knowing where to draw the line when things start to fray at the seams. People who she has never met and wouldn't be able to pick out of a line-up speak with her as if they are her best friend. They believe, I think, that because Sorcha is open that she really is a friend to all.

Of course, the truth is, if they stopped to examine, with any sort of intelligent eye, why they keep coming back to her content day after day after day, they'd find that it's because they don't see her as a real-life just-like-you-and-me person. Sorcha Hannon is the star of her own soap opera and her fans view the ups and downs of her life as little more than entertainment. They crave the drama of it all. I imagine Sorcha has to watch her every move and reaction. She can't allow herself to appear rude – especially not when she's advocating a 'Be Kind' culture. The constant fear of being cancelled must weigh heavy. One wrong word is all it would take and all of it just ends. The fame and the fawning could not so much as fade away as vanish.

Reading the rest of her Insta caption I see she's planning on a 'chilled one' today – 'a walk in nature then lunch with the girls'. Her children, she says, are with their daddy for the weekend. The house, she adds, is too quiet without them. She's not used to having the place to herself. She has used a sad-face emoji and I feel a pang of sympathy for her.

It must be hard to have a full life together torn from you, forcing you to be alone and to be a part-time parent to the children you'd planned to raise with your significant other. Especially when your life was so exceptionally picture-perfect as it was. A happy couple, parents to two beautiful, photogenic little girls – twelve-year-old Ivy and five-year-old Esme. That perfect family provided a perfect backdrop for a world that was showcased online. Sorcha's life was enviable. It was aspirational. It was blessed.

Then it changed.

She doesn't involve her girls too much in her content now – citing their right to privacy among other reasons – but on the rare occasion they do appear they beam angelically at the camera. They don't look like the kind of children who have ever had a full-on meltdown in Tesco. Nor do they look like the kind of sisters who would tear the hair from each other's heads in a fight about a borrowed top or toy. They are perfect, just like everything about Sorcha is perfect. Apart, that is, from her romantic life.

I take comfort in that failure. Because no one really deserves to have it all and have it so easily. Not even Sorcha with her bright smile, perfectly toned lowlights and flawless complexion. If things can go wrong for her – with all she has to offer – then it's a comfort to me. If Sorcha couldn't make her relationship work, then there's no shame in my failings in that regard either.

My finger hovers over my phone with the urge to send her a message just to say I know these weekends must be tough, and that I'm sending my support. Is that the right way to approach this though? I've only met her once and don't really know her but then I'm not asking for an invitation to lunch. I'm just trying to be friendly.

But navigating social norms isn't something that has ever come easy to me. I have a tendency to go in too hard, I think, as the toaster pops. I get so overexcited at new friendships that I throw everything I have at them and inevitably, and quickly, become 'too much' for other people.

I don't want to fuck this up the way I have fucked other things up. There are only so many times I can land myself at rock bottom and haul myself back out again.

Fuck it, I think. I'll send something. I'll let her know I'm thinking of her, and thank her for being so welcoming yesterday. That should do the trick. It should be enough. This is a marathon and not a race after all. I tap a few lines into Instagram and hit send before taking a bite of my now cold and soggy toast. The claggy consistency sticks to the roof of my mouth, making me gag, so I dump the rest of it straight in the bin.

To distract myself from thinking about the message I sent Sorcha, I tie my hair back in a messy bun, open my curtains for the first time in weeks and throw open the windows to let some fresh air circulate around the flat.

Grabbing bin bags, I start to sort through the clutter and mess that has been festering on every surface. I pick up dirty clothes from the floor and haul the dirty sheets from the bed. Sticking on a wash, I decide I'm going to buy myself some two-thousand-thread-count Egyptian cotton sheets, in the same crisp hotel white Sorcha has.

I want my room to be Instagram worthy, just like hers. Grabbing several boxes at a time, I carry the shoes that I will probably never wear to my spare bedroom and stack them against the wall. Maybe I'll get round to wearing them, or maybe I'll sell them on Vinted. Use the cash to treat myself to new things.

This room has been a sorry excuse of a space for too long. There was a time I'd hoped I'd maybe rent it to a flatmate, or organise it into a perfect work-from-home space. When I'd moved in, I'd decorated it as a chic and stylish place for my friends to come and stay during a weekend of brunches, spa treatments and nights dancing in darkened bars. But that had never really happened. My friends were getting promoted, settling down, becoming partners and parents who spent their weekends at swimming lessons, or baby yoga, or opening a bottle of wine in front of the TV with their special someone.

Then the pandemic hit and any potential overnight visitors disappeared into the mists of lockdowns and changing times. For the last couple of years this room has been more of a reminder of what could've been – what I'd lost – rather than what I wanted. It has become a dusty storage space, a place to dry clothes. It has become a visual representation of my depression.

It could be a really lovely dressing room, I think, my mind wandering to the gorgeous space Sorcha has created in her home with built-in storage, inspirational quotes on the walls and Hollywood lights on her mirrors. There's a long way to go before this room looks anything like that but at least it's a start. Giving this room a purpose instead of it just being another part of my sad story is a positive thing. I set myself a goal of transforming it from its depressing current state into something worthy of 'the 'gram', as I've seen the young ones call it.

I carry through the packages of new clothes I've ordered but not yet worn – keeping them for when I lose a little weight, or when I have a special occasion or any occasion to leave the house outside of my two days a week at the office. I'll unpack them and sort through them later. For now it's enough to see the clutter start to disappear from my bedroom. The floor is clear and I can start cleaning properly. In my head I'm already composing the perfect captions for when I'm done.

I know I should pack everything away that brings a bad memory to mind, like a twisted reflection of the Marie Kondo method. I manage to part with a few things – a book, a perfume whose scent will always remind me of that night. But when I come to other things, including the picture of him – the heartbreaker who shall not be named, my own personal Voldemort – on my nightstand, I don't know if I can bring myself to pack it away just yet. I'm certainly not ready to throw it away.

It's not even a brilliant picture. He's not quite looking at the camera. It's as if something off to the right has distracted him. He looks uncomfortable while I am grinning at the camera like the village idiot. It's like a bad pap photo, but it's the best I have from a man who claimed he hated having his photo taken but seemed to particularly hate having his photo taken with me.

Asking myself, 'What would Sorcha do?', the answer becomes immediately obvious. She'd pack it away. Or burn it. Maybe have some cleansing ceremony with sage and crystals and a handful of positive affirmations. She would absolutely not hang on to it, and the bad memories it conjures.

But my problem is that along with the bad memories, there are good ones too – moments of hope and incredible love – and I'm not ready to let go of those. This particular chapter of my life did not end well, but it is still a huge part of my story and one I will never be able to let go of fully.

I hold the picture in my hand, unable to choose between keeping it or letting go when my phone pings to life with a reply from Sorcha.

Hi lovely Christina. Thank you for your message! It's lovely to know people are thinking of me. Yes, I'm feeling sorry for myself at the mo. I know it's stupid – the girls will be back 2morro night and I'll be wishing for peace and quiet again! (Joke, of course.) Have you thought any more about joining us for a swim? Please say you'll come? We're going to Tullagh Bay tomorrow if you're free? I can pick you up if you want. It's always easier to go to these things with a friend.

A friend? She called me a friend! I know I shouldn't be so excited by it. Not at my age. I'm thirty-seven for goodness' sake – hardly a schoolgirl – but I do feel a frisson of excitement that she has used the 'friend' word.

My eyes darting once more to the picture on my nightstand, I make my decision. I open the drawer and slip the photo inside, under the cards and letters and other detritus that make up my poorly organised life. Maybe one day I'll forget it's there. I long for that time – when the 'him' part of what happened will fade away to insignificance. Maybe the key to making that happen is living more boldly?

I think I'll give it a go. And a lift would be great,
thank you.

I tap the message into my phone immediately, not allowing myself the chance to change my mind. Then, reinvigorated, I plan the rest of my day. I'm going to need to buy a new swimsuit, I think, realising the last time I swam was at least three years and eighteen pounds ago.

I can pick up new sheets when I go into town to buy one, and whatever else I might need for my first walk into the water with Sorcha – my new friend. I screenshot the message she has sent me and save it with the others we have exchanged. Social media is too often much too fleeting and I want to remember this.

6

Sorcha is smiling as I walk towards her car. She waves and reaches over to give me the most fleeting of air kisses on my cheek as I climb into the passenger seat. 'I'm so glad you decided to come.' She smiles. 'You're going to love it. And today is the perfect day because it's always quieter. Most people are at work.'

I smile and push down my unease. Technically I am at work too. Or at least I'm on the clock, on one of my work-from-home days. I've set Teams to Do Not Disturb, which isn't that unusual. As a project accountant, getting a fresh file of numbers to crunch requires my full and undivided attention and there are a number of fresh files I should be working on so my status shouldn't raise any red flags.

Of course, I'll have to double down and work extra hard this afternoon and into the evening to make up for skiving off now but I'm sure it will be worth it. That is, it will be worth it if I can manage to behave like a normal fucking human being for the next couple of hours. The pressure to be witty and entertaining – to be great company for Sorcha – is weighing down on me. I know I should be making conversation but I'm sitting here like a useless lump thinking of possible responses and then dismissing them as pathetic as she chatters.

'I see you're well prepared,' she says and glances away momentarily from the road to look at me – sitting there in my Dunnes Stores version of a dryrobe. I feel like I'm wearing a duvet and, as it's June and fairly temperate, I'm starting to overheat a little.

She probably thinks I'm a sad case – not having even tried wild water swimming once, but making sure I have all the gear already? Wearing a changing robe when I'm still fully dressed and the breeze is warm screams try-hard.

'Yes... well, I thought... might as well give it my best shot. You know... if I've got the full kit I'm less likely to find something I hate about it,' I stutter.

'Apart from the icy water, that is.' She laughs, and I'm not sure if it's just her sense of humour or if she's mocking me. I feel her hand on my knee and she gives it a squeeze. 'I'm joking,' she says. 'You're exactly right to be prepared. I hadn't the first notion what to expect the first time I came down to do a swim. I brought an old beach towel and my favourite swimsuit and just went in. I'd have given my right arm for a changing robe when I got out of the water. And a hat, and my neoprene gloves and boots. I suppose you've those all packed in your bag too? It might be June but the water is still nippy enough.'

I think of how I ran around like a blue-arsed fly yesterday to make sure I had all of the above. How I had scanned website after website for hints and tips as to what to wear and what to bring. How not only do I have the items Sorcha has mentioned packed in my bag but I've also brought a flask of hot chocolate. Enough for two people so I can offer Sorcha some after we're out of the water. Along with my swimsuit, I bought and packed a rash vest and swimming shorts – so a lot of my wobbly bits will be well hidden. The thought of my dimply thighs displayed alongside Sorcha's toned legs made me feel queasy with nerves. I've brought thick woollen socks and fleece-lined joggers to slip on when I get out of the water, and a pair of Uggs. I've tried them all on to make sure none of them challenge me on a sensory level. All the websites I looked at said to bring clothes that are warm but don't require tricky buttons, zips or laces in case your hands get numb from the cold. I *think* I've everything I need.

I give a small shrug and laugh, mocking myself for being so organised because – again – if I mock myself other people are less likely to. I have become quite adept at self-deprecating humour even if I don't always understand how or why it is funny. 'You were so brave to just go for it,' I tell Sorcha. 'I'd have chickened out if I were you.'

I don't tell her that I might still chicken out even with all my fancy new purchases. I've taken the labels off everything but not thrown them away, so maybe I could still return everything to the shop, get my money back, and abandon this whole idea altogether.

'I don't know if I'm brave or just stupid,' Sorcha says and there's something in her tone of voice that makes me think she is talking about much more than swimming.

'I think you're brave,' I tell her. 'In everything. Look how much you've achieved. You're raising your two girls, working for yourself. How many followers do you have now?' I ask even though I know that Sorcha has just over a million followers and is gaining more day by day. I know her following has spread far beyond the confines of our city, or indeed Northern Ireland. The launch of the Soul Sisterhood has catapulted her from being a fairly run-of-the-mill influencer to one being booked for major talk shows, and mental health conferences. Brands are falling over themselves to work with her. Branches of the Soul Sisterhood are organising, informally, in multiple countries and Sorcha has spoken of her hope to formalise the organisation so that 'women everywhere have a voice'.

'I'm not sure it takes bravery to have people watch you online,' Sorcha says, brushing away my compliment. 'But not everyone who watches is a fan. There are a fair few people who hate-watch. Can you imagine that? Actively watching people you dislike, and who wind you up, is now so popular they've come up with a name to call it. Hate-watching. It's hard to think people have the time and energy for that,' she says, with a bitter laugh.

I find it strange that her immediate response to my compliment is to comment on the negative side of being a social media personality. I wonder if something has happened that might have knocked her confidence a little today, but I'm not sure I should ask. Yes, she's said we're friends, but we're not properly, really friends, are we? Not yet, anyway. Deciding I must not push too hard, I opt for showering her with reassurance and positivity instead.

'People who behave like that towards you... well, their actions say more about them than they do about you,' I tell her. 'All the people who watch you, and love what you do – they're the ones you should give your attention to. But the fact you keep putting content out there anyway for the people who love you, knowing you'll come up against hate-watchers? Well, that proves you're brave,' I tell her.

'Or stupid, but all I can do is my best to rise above them,' she says with a shrug of her shoulders, her eyes firmly on the road ahead. I doubt she'd give any of it up though. The influencer life provides her with quite a good income. It provides for her daughters. She's doing great things making the Soul Sisterhood a brand. There may be haters but there are many more fans.

'I think we're all a little guilty of stupidity from time to time,' I tell her. 'None of us are perfect. I'm certainly not.' I know she won't contradict me or tell me I'm being silly. It's obvious to anyone with eyes that I, sat here in my over-the-top swimming uniform, struggling to make anything resembling intelligent conversation with Sorcha, am about as far from perfect as it comes.

'No one should want to be perfect,' she replies. 'It's not achievable, and if it was we'd all be boring as hell. Life needs a little drama, and drama doesn't come from perfectionism,' she says, as she flashes her perfect smile at me, her perfectly manicured hands on the steering wheel and her hair swept up into a perfect 'messy' bun. Some people can do that. They can pull off that effortless chic she does so well. It looks low-maintenance but it's not. Looking that good takes time.

My skin prickles with jealousy. Without thinking, I raise a hand to my scalp and scratch hard under my hairline. I have to force myself to stop scratching before I start looking like I have head lice or I break the skin and start to bleed. I need to be careful. My crazy is starting to show.

'Sorry,' she says. 'I said that in my best influencer voice, didn't I? I have to remember I'm not in Instagram mode here. But you know what I mean, I hope. I think it's an achievement in itself if we all just do our best and try not to be dicks to each other,' she says with a laugh.

There's a beat while her words sink in. Is it really that easy? Do your best and don't be a dick? Are those the modern-day commandments? Forget about coveting this, and forsaking that. If Moses was coming down from the mountain today would the tablets simply read 'Do your best' and 'Don't be a dick'?

'So, Christina,' she says, breaking the silence before it becomes awkward. 'We didn't get to talk too much on Saturday. Tell me a little more about yourself. What's your story? What inspired you to look us up?'

I take a deep breath because I know what comes next has to be a lie.

7

Lying has never come easy to me. I'm not a spiritual person but like most people of a certain age in Northern Ireland, I was raised under the glare of religion.

From the moment I was born I was marked out as a sinner – carrying the shame of Adam and Eve's original sin on my newly birthed shoulders before I'd so much as taken my first breath. Life from that point on has become a process of sinning and seeking absolution, and all the while feeling a deep, deep shame for my human failings.

Shame is built into our DNA in this part of the world.

Even though I have long since turned my back on religion, letting go of those feelings of guilt and shame that come from any wrongdoing – even the telling of a white lie to save the feelings of someone else – has been next to impossible.

And this is a white lie, I suppose. It's intended to protect Sorcha's feelings. I readjust myself in my seat, wondering whether it would be okay to open my car window and let some fresh air in. Instead I pull down the zip on my robe.

'It's not very interesting,' I tell her, meaning of course that I'm not very interesting. I hope she keeps her eyes on the road ahead instead of looking at me. Surely one glance would let her know I'm hiding something.

'I suppose I just wanted to meet some new people. All my friends are married and/or procreating,' I tell her. 'I'm just a sad old spinster, with not a single child to my name.' I fake a laugh and pretend my reality doesn't hurt. 'So when I see them – which isn't very often at all because they're always busy, or like my closest friend Shaunagh, they've moved away – well, all talk tends to focus around their children. I understand that. I get how having a child would be mind-blowing and of course they become the entire focus of your world, but it does leave me feeling as if I'm sitting on the sidelines just watching everyone living their best lives. I thought meeting new people and trying new things might move the focus away from all that, you know. It might expand my horizons. I suppose I just wanted to make some new friends too.'

Sorcha makes a kind of sympathetic, reassuring noise and nods her head, but she doesn't speak. She waits for me to continue but I know this trick. Leave a gap in the conversation and someone will blink first and start to speak. Conversational chicken. I've seen it used in interrogations in true crime documentaries. But this is not an interrogation, I remind myself. As far as anyone knows it's just a chat between two women getting to know each other. I have to do my best to act like a normal human being.

'So, have you never been married yourself?' she asks before apologising immediately. 'Oh God, I'm sorry. Maybe that's too personal a question. Don't feel you have to answer it! Not everyone overshares their entire existence like I do. Sometimes I forget that,' she says with a wry smile.

'It's okay,' I reply. 'And no, I've never been married.' This part isn't a lie so it's easy to let the words trip off my tongue. But as I speak the words that follow, I become acutely aware that they are half-truths. 'I've never even been close,' I tell her, my eyes firmly on the road ahead. 'I've just never met the right person – you know, a person I'd look at and think, "I wouldn't mind spending the rest of my days with you"?'

It sounds like such an obvious lie to me that I half expect her to call me out on it, but of course, she doesn't.

The truth is there had been that someone I had looked at in that way. I could have happily spent every hour of every day with him, but unfortunately for me, in the end, we couldn't make it work. I'm still trying to wrap my head around that. I'm still trying to forget the man who charmed me, spoiled me and loved me so intensely there were moments when I felt as if I would combust trying to hold all those feelings inside.

Even now the realisation that he will never kiss me again can threaten to derail me.

'There's time for you yet,' Sorcha says, cutting into my memory of his lips brushing against the side of my neck. 'And there's nothing wrong with staying single either. Sometimes I wish I had.' She laughs again – that same brilliant burst of noise that I'm starting to wonder if she is just making to detract from something that makes her uncomfortable. Maybe I'm not the only person hiding my truth to make myself more socially palatable. No one wants to watch a heartbroken woman sob online at the injustice of her break-up.

'It must have been very hard for you,' I say, choosing my words carefully. 'I can't imagine going through a break-up so publicly.'

Sorcha exhales and I watch her knuckles whiten just a little as she grips tighter on the steering wheel. 'It's not something I'd recommend,' she says, forcing a lightness into her voice that doesn't quite hit the mark. 'If I was reviewing the experience it would be a straight zero out of ten. Absolutely would not do again. But what can I say? We weren't working any more and it had to end. I was already doing my videos and my following was already substantial. I realised I had two choices, I could pretend everything was hunky-dory and just not mention my marriage ending at all, but you know what this place is like for rumours and gossip. It would've got out there anyway and people wouldn't like that I kept it from them. So, the other choice I had was to be open about it – and maybe even use it to my advantage. A divorce wasn't in my life plan, but without it I'd never have started the Soul Sisterhood.'

'I admire you,' I say, hoping I don't sound too cringe. 'You've a strength there that a lot of us don't. I fell to pieces when my last relationship ended and it wasn't like I had to worry about the legalities of getting divorced, or dividing up a house, or making custody arrangements. I just hadn't seen the break-up coming and it pulled the rug out from under me.'

Of course that's a sanitised version of what happened. I'm not ready to tell Sorcha the full story yet. The consequences would simply be too extreme.

'Don't get me wrong,' Sorcha says, 'people might have seen me continuing to put new content out there and assumed I was doing okay. But off-camera I was falling to pieces. I needed the Soul Sisterhood when I started it. I needed to build my own support network. Maybe it would've been more authentic if I'd shared the full absolute train-wreck version of myself, but people want aspirational content – not me on my second bottle of wine calling my husband a rotten bastard. Nobody wants to see the before without knowing what the after looks like.' She grimaces. 'Screenshots last forever. I've said it a million times, Christina, don't trust what you see online. You don't see the real person or their real life. It's all smoke and mirrors! I gave them just enough of me. I cried for them enough, but then I became a queen at faking it 'til you make it.' There's a pause. 'But look, here we are. Both of us, out the other side of it and living life as two independent bad-ass women.'

I smile, and hold back my truth. That I don't really think I'm out the other side of it at all, and this... all this 'new me' is just my way of coping with the unfairness of the situation.

Because it isn't fair. That some people get so much and others are left with nothing.

8

A short time later, we're parked at the side of the road at Tullagh
Bay in Donegal, part of what has now become known as the Wild
Atlantic Way – miles and miles of road running the full length of
the west coast of Ireland.

'Grab your bag and follow me,' Sorcha says, jumping from the
car. Stepping out, I catch sight of the expanse of ocean stretching
off into the horizon in front of me, and am met with the rhythmic
noise of the waves rushing to shore. All there is between us and
America now is this body of water – bigger than I can compre-
hend. More than three thousand miles of sea and all she holds. As
I walk through the reeds and seagrass, towards the beach, I'm
unable to take my eyes off the waves gently lapping at the shore-
line. My breath catches a little in my chest.

'It doesn't matter how many times I come here,' Sorcha says as
she walks a couple of steps ahead of me leading the way, 'it always
hits a reset button somewhere deep inside me. I don't know if it's
because I can see how insignificant we all are in the grand scheme
of things, or if it's something else, but I always feel more grounded
when I'm here. It puts things in perspective.'

I nod, even though I'm not sure I share her feelings exactly. I'm blown away that something which can look so calm and beautiful as it gently rolls over and bubbles onto the shore also holds dark, dangerous secrets. That no one has ever reached or explored her deepest layers. That she still has the ability to surprise. The ocean both terrifies and enthrals me – and that mix of feelings unsettles me as does the thought of wading in through the cool June waters.

'It tends to be quieter down here than some of the other beaches,' Sorcha says as we walk along the brow of the dunes until we find a path onto the sand. 'Off-season, anyway. It's busier in July and August, obviously with all the holidaymakers staying in the caravan parks. But this time of year, it's more remote so we often get this place to ourselves. So don't worry if you have to scream and swear.' She laughs as she turns to reach out to me, helping me take the last few steps down the soft sand dune onto the beach.

In the distance, huddled close to the edge of the dunes, there is a small group of women – maybe five or six of them at most. I blink against the hazy early summer sunlight to try and see more clearly. Their hum of their chatter carries across the air to us though I can't make out what they are saying. The urge to turn and go back to the car is strong now. I could be a safe distance from this challenge in under a minute. Surely Sorcha will understand if I give in to it and just decide this isn't for me. Not everyone will like it after all.

It's almost as if she senses my hesitation and I feel her squeeze my hand tighter and pull me along behind her. 'You can't back out now,' she says. 'You've not come this far to only come this far!' It's another Instagram cliché, but this one hits where it's supposed to and where I need it to. She's right. I haven't come this far only to come this far. I'm not going to give up now, so I force myself to keep going even though my legs are heavy and every nerve and sinew in my body screams at me to stop and go back to the car. By the time we reach the group of five women already on the beach, I am sure I must look like a truculent toddler being hauled out of the play park by a mother who has had enough of my shit.

There isn't time to think about it too much though as I'm pulled into some sort of constant motion group hug as these women, who clearly are all the very best of friends, greet each other warmly. Among the melee I spot Joan, Aoife and Carla, who I remember from the coffee morning. Aoife smiles broadly and pulls me into a hug. 'It's great to see you here,' she says in my ear. 'And don't be afraid! We're all here to support each other.'

For a moment I allow myself to revel in the warmth of the embrace – in the fleeting feeling of being held by another human being. The urge to cry that rises up inside my chest is unexpected and I push it back down, muttering a quick 'thank you' to Aoife and taking a step backwards to take a deep breath.

'Because you're a first-timer,' Sorcha tells me, 'I don't want you in the water for anything more than five minutes at the very most.'

Five minutes? Have I gone to all this effort and expense for less than five minutes in the water? Yes, I know at the moment even the thought of one minute is daunting but come on... 'Is that all?' I say. 'I'm sure I'll be grand to stay in longer than that.'

'We take safety very seriously,' Sorcha says, and Carla nods solemnly beside her, before starting to fidget with her watch.

'I'll set a timer,' she says.

'And I'll come out with you after five minutes.' Sorcha smiles. 'So you don't have to do it alone. Trust me though, on your first go, five minutes will be more than enough.' The others nod sagely, bonded in their shared experience of a first-time swim.

Nodding mutely, too nervous to speak, I follow the others' example and begin peeling off my layers of clothes, wishing I could keep the stupid oversized changing robe on.

I feel exposed in my swimwear. The others don't have as much to cover as I do, and I feel every single extra ounce on my body.

Closing my eyes, I try to quiet the internal monologue that tells me I'm fat and ugly and worthless. But it's hard to quiet something you've heard all your life and it's hard not to pre-empt being judged when you've been judged your whole life.

I'm pulled out of my negative self-talk by a touch – her touch – and I realise I'm already starting to recognise it. 'Everyone is concentrating on themselves,' Sorcha says in a near whisper. 'And everyone felt just like you do the first time they did this, but look, they're all here again now. You focus on you, on breathing and on getting through this.'

'Okay,' I say, both dreading what's to come and desperate to get going so I can get it over and done with as quickly as possible. I need to prove to Sorcha I can do this. That I can be brave and strong and worthy too. I need to prove it to myself.

'Okay,' she says. 'Let's get this done.'

I pull on my neoprene gloves, and start to walk towards the shore with the others.

'Just keep breathing and you'll be fine,' Sorcha says.

'I wasn't planning on stopping, to be honest,' I say through teeth that are already chattering. Sorcha throws her head back and laughs. It's a full, throaty laugh – one she means.

The other women are chatting excitedly, clearly hyped for their swim. There's an energy – an electricity almost – in the air now and I allow it to help carry me forward even when the first icy chill of the sea makes me want to scurry back to dry land.

'Just keep walking and just keep breathing,' Sorcha says, her grip on my hand tighter than ever. 'Keep your breath measured.'

I nod because I'm not sure I can speak. My focus is on not allowing the bite of the cold water to trigger a fight-or-flight response as it reaches my knees.

'That's it,' Sorcha says, her voice low and soothing. I imagine it's how she talks to her girls when she's trying to encourage them to do something difficult or unpleasant. 'You're doing really well – just keep breathing.'

I count my breath in for four and out for four just like Una has taught me, and I'm relieved to find it helps take my mind off the chill of the Atlantic waters.

'Now don't worry about going out of your depth. Yes, there's a big shelf in the seabed not far out but we won't be going near that,' she says and I look at her, eyes wide. Does she know exactly where it is? What if we accidentally go too far out? Could we not have come to a beach that doesn't have a sudden drop in depth?

'I'm not a good swimmer,' I stutter, which is an understatement and a half.

'Well you won't need to swim, trust me. We don't take risks,' she says, her voice still soothing. I glance around to the other girls, to check that they're still smiling and laughing – that their high-pitched yells are just from the cold water hitting their thighs and their waists and not from fear. They seem okay so I try again to focus on counting my breath in and out.

'Okay,' Sorcha says as we reach the point where the water is just over my waistline. 'From here we can just dip down into the water. Just drop down fast and keep your shoulders under the waterline. Move your arms around if you want to – it can help. But stay down.'

My eyes are wide and I don't know if I can do this. I'm already much too cold. As I start to shake my head, Sorcha grips tighter. 'You're doing it,' she says, her voice firm. 'Don't overthink it. Just dip down with me after three...'

My heart is thumping now and every part of me screams that this is not safe. This is not right. I don't like it. I don't want to be here.

'Okay,' Sorcha says, her gaze fixed intensely on mine. 'One... two... three...'

And she dips down, pulling my hands as she does so, forcing me to drop down and, as the cold water encases me, I feel as if every drop of air of in my lungs is expelled from my body and I can't breathe. I can't get air into my lungs. They won't expand. I am frozen in shock and I cannot breathe.

'Breathe,' I hear Sorcha shout over the thumping of my heart and the lapping of the water around my shoulders, and I try. I do my best. I look at her and suck air into my lungs, watching her face for cues because my body seems to have forgotten how to do this.

My chest expands and I breathe out. The cold bites and my head is spinning just a little but I keep my eyes on Sorcha, and I breathe in and out again and follow her lead. After a moment I'm aware of Joan beside us, watching me and glancing at Sorcha before turning her head back in my direction.

'You're doing so well, Christina,' she says. 'You'll be addicted to this soon, like the rest of us.' All I can think is that I don't understand why anyone would choose to put themselves through this time and time again.

The cold is dispersing, being replaced by a numb sensation. I dare to take my eyes from Sorcha and Joan and look up at the sky – the clouds are thickening above us in the same shades of grey as the vast ocean. Summer has yet to arrive. Water laps at my chin, and as I take my next breath in, I accidentally swallow a mouthful of the salty sea and feel it catch at the back of my throat. Spluttering, the foul taste bitter on my tongue, I pull myself to standing, my stomach turning, and I pray I don't throw up. Not here, not in front of everyone.

'You're okay,' Sorcha soothes, and she's standing beside me again. 'Let's go and get a drink of water. You're okay. You've done really well. You did the full five minutes.'

I nod as I cough and lurch forward in the direction of the shore. My limbs pull against the weight of the water, and when I reach the shore – still trying to rid my mouth of the salty taste of the water – I'm shocked to find I no longer feel cold. I don't feel a chill in the air. The skin on my legs has turned a vibrant, fiery red, and they feel light. Weightless. I feel like I'm floating as we walk up the beach, my brain trying to make sense of the discordant sensations in my body.

'It's mad, isn't it?' Sorcha says, as we reach our bags and she scrabbles in hers for a bottle of water. 'How you don't feel the cold when you get out? It's the weirdest, best sensation.'

Fresh, clean water washes the bitter taste of sea away and I catch my breath. This is good. I expected to shiver and shake, and be desperate for my fleecy joggers and Uggs.

'Don't forget,' she says, 'your body might not feel cold now, but it is cold. Your core temperature will have dropped. Get changed as quickly as you can into dry, warm clothes. We don't want to risk hypothermia setting in!' Sorcha is smiling but she's also all business, setting about changing quickly, as I do my best to follow suit, wrestling inside my changing robe – which doesn't feel quite as big as it did before the swim. I must look awkward and ungainly as I hobble on the sand, trying to slip my feet into my thick socks but I try not to think about how I must look to the others. The chill is starting to seep into my bones now and I just want to be dressed and sitting with my mug of hot chocolate, allowing it to warm me from the inside out.

But even as I struggle, it dawns on me that I did it. I fought against my fears and I stepped out of my comfort zone, where it is safe and quiet, and did something that for all the cold and all the fear made me feel alive. As the cold makes itself known through my body, I can also feel the adrenaline, and the endorphins, rushing through me. It's a high like no other, and I embrace the feeling of it surging through my veins until I find myself unexpectedly breaking down into tears. Powerless to stop the emotions spilling out of me, I want the ground to open up and swallow me whole. This is not me being cool and collected and in control of my life. This is not me making a good impression in front of Sorcha Hannon.

I try to hide my tears, to brush them away before she sees them. I fight the urge to sniff or sob or both until it feels as if I'll suffocate from the effort. The sound of chattering and laughing reaches me and I glance to my side to see the rest of the swimmers walking out of the water and starting up the beach towards us. This is all I need. To have these people I barely know see me crying like a baby because I went into some cold water. What will they think of me? For fuck's sake! Maybe I am useless.

'Christina!' I hear Sorcha, her voice firm, and I look at her even though I know she will clearly see I'm crying, but what's the alternative? I can't exactly turn away and ignore her. I can't just leave. I've no way to get home.

'Oh you poor pet,' she soothes and she walks towards me. 'I cried after my first swim too. It's okay. A lot of us do. It's the release. It's healing.' She pulls me into a hug and I sink into it. God knows I want to be healed and I don't want to feel embarrassed at showing my vulnerability.

'Everything okay?' I hear another woman's voice, and Sorcha steps back, releasing me from her embrace.

'Yup,' Sorcha says. 'You know how it is, Joan. The obligatory first-time cry!'

'We all did it,' Joan replies and I turn to look at her, as she gives me a smile. 'There's no shame in it. What happens on the beach stays on the beach. Isn't that right, girls?' she says, loud enough so the others hear her and reply with a chorus of yeses and of courses.

'See?' Sorcha soothes. 'Now finish getting dressed and we'll get a cuppa and all will feel right with the world again.'

'I brought hot chocolate. There's enough for both of us,' I stutter, immediately feeling like Baby in *Dirty Dancing* when she tells cool Johnny Castle she carried a watermelon.

'My favourite!' Sorcha says. 'Happy days!' That brings a smile to my face and my embarrassment subsides as I put on my second sock and slip my feet into my cosy Uggs. We all dress, and I'm happy to be among the chatter of these women as I slip my hoodie on and pack up my wet swimming gear.

Looking out across the sea, it's clear that heavy grey clouds are getting darker, carrying a blurry mist in the distance. Rain is on its way.

'I don't think it's a day for having our tea on the beach,' Carla says.

'No,' Joan replies. 'That's going to come in heavy, and by the look of it, it's not taking its time either. I think we timed that swim nicely, girls! But we'd better get back as quickly as we can.'

There's a camaraderie among us as we gather our belongings to escape back to our cars before the rain hits. My tears have subsided with the flurry of activity and I think Sorcha was right. My crying fit was a release of sorts. One I didn't know I needed until it happened. Now that it has passed, what is left behind is a feeling of equilibrium. There's a calmness in me that there hasn't been in a long time and I'm savouring the feeling of heat returning to my body and of being among a group of new friends.

I find myself walking beside Joan. 'This has been just what I needed,' I tell her. 'I'm so glad Sorcha persuaded me to come along and give it a go.'

Joan gives me a tight smile, which I try not to read too much into. The first touches of light, misty rain are hitting and I imagine she, like all of us, just wants to get back to her car as soon as possible instead of dawdling and chattering on the beach. I certainly don't relish the thought of getting my lovely, warm and dry clothes saturated by the rain before the drive home.

'Sorcha's very good,' Joan says. 'And she does enjoy a pet project or two.'

A pet project? I wonder what Joan means by that. I don't have to wait long for her to keep speaking.

'She's always collecting waifs and strays. Likes to play the hero, you know,' she says, and there's something in the tone of her voice that makes me uncomfortable. Is she having a go at me? Or Sorcha? Or both of us? Or am I once again being paranoid? Joan and all the women have been so kind up until now, so surely she doesn't mean anything negative.

'Well, this waif or stray is grateful,' I say with a smile.

'I'm sure you are,' Joan says as we reach the top of the sand dunes close to where the cars are parked. 'Now, don't take this the wrong way,' she says, through a bright smile, 'but we'll be keeping a wee eye on you. Sorcha has been burned before. People like to take advantage of her generous nature. It has hurt her – more than she'd ever let anyone know. So I'm sure you understand that some of us like to keep a closer eye on those she seems to take under her wing.'

She has a smile on her face. Anyone looking at the two of us talking would see nothing to give them any cause for concern. There's this lovely woman in a brightly coloured beanie hat, her cheeks rosy and her smile wide, but I know I'm not wrong when I pick up a threat in her tone. They're keeping an eye on me. How much of an eye? How paranoid do I need to be? Is it a threat or a friendly warning? I know I should say something. I should absolutely say something – but I don't know what to say so I stand there like a stupid idiot while Joan doesn't drop her gaze, waiting for a response.

'Come on, you two!' Sorcha shouts and instinctively we break our gaze and look towards her. 'Let's get out of the rain!'

'Coming!' Joan shouts back brightly and continues on her way while I follow, trying to convince myself that she is doing what any good friend would do and is just watching out for her pal. But the whole exchange has made me uncomfortable. That I've been referred to as a waif or stray, and a pet project. That I must look like someone who would take advantage of a person's kindness.

* * *

Sorcha comments that I'm very quiet on the drive home. I tell her I'm just trying to process the experience, and the adrenaline is starting to wear off, leaving me feeling 'nicely chilled out'.

But I'm not nicely chilled out. I'm running Joan's words, and everything about her mannerisms and her body language, through my mind on a loop. I'm being watched. In case I take advantage of Sorcha. The warm welcome extended to me by the group so far is conditional.

I glance at the wingmirror to my left and see that a blue car – which I'm sure was among those in the car park at the beach – is behind us. Is it following us or just making its way home like we are? Just how paranoid do I need to be? I try to shake it off.

I know I have no intention of taking advantage of Sorcha's generous nature, but that doesn't matter. I am being assessed. I wonder just how closely. Is it just Joan or is there a core inner circle in the Soul Sisterhood who are currently assessing my risk factors as a genuine friend, or a weird fan girl?

I've been very careful to make myself as invisible as possible. I keep a very low profile online. Keep identifying details to a bare minimum. I've never been one for selfies – never liked having my picture taken. Maybe it's the case I've never seen the real me staring back out from the photo. I've only ever seen the socially acceptable version of myself – the one where I'm masking all my idiosyncrasies. As a result there are very few photos of me online.

But it is a truth universally acknowledged that if a Derry woman wants to find out every detail of your life, all she needs is half an hour at a computer, and Google to track you down. I'll have to be extra vigilant from now on. I can't afford to slip up and reveal too much about myself. Not while I'm under surveillance.

When I get home I have a long, hot shower to let the heat seep back into my bones – and then I start distracting myself from my doom cycle of thoughts with work. I do my best to focus on my to-do list for the remainder of the day. It's quite easy to lose myself in numbers and projections – once I switch that side of my brain on there isn't much room for anything else, except watching my phone light up every few minutes with another notification from the Soul Sisterhood.

While I'm dying to know what they're all talking about, I'm frightened too. What if they are talking about me? What if I've been declared public enemy number one? There was just something in the way Joan looked at me that made me feel transparent, almost.

I have managed to work myself up into a ball of anxiety by evening. I thought I would be able to do this but I'm wrong. Maybe

I should've left Sorcha and her fan club alone. I'm not sure what I thought I'd learn from her anyway. How to be happy? How to be successful? How to survive the loss of the man who broke both our hearts?

10

It wasn't love, I've come to realise. It was a madness. A slow, drawn-out descent from something that had felt so all-consuming into something sordid and degrading. I think I always knew from the moment it began that it would eventually blow my life to smithereens.

And yet, I'd been too intoxicated to walk away. He made me dizzy with longing. At first for his warm smiles. His appreciative sighs. His tender words – scattered compliments that made me feel worthy for once. The dinners. The flowers. The not rushing me to be intimate with him. The way he played out the role of a tortured husband, desperate for love but pained at the prospect of betraying his wife – who, of course, didn't understand him.

He took his time to build the tension between us to such a level that once we crossed that line – when he told me he had never felt like this before about anyone – I was caught in his thrall. I felt as if I had woken up – as if all my senses had been stripped raw in the most delicious of ways. I had never been desired like that before. No one had ever told me that I was beautiful and sexy before. Not with the same irresistible moans of desire that escaped his lips when I took him in my mouth. No one had run their hands over my curves and made me feel at home in my own body before. He had traced his lips over every inch of me and still wanted more. He craved me. Needed me. He, who had a model wife at home, longed for the solace of my bed and my body. He longed for how I could make him feel.

Intoxication soon turned to addiction. I needed him. I needed the dopamine hit of a message from him pinging onto my phone, or his name lighting up the screen when he called. I craved the feeling that pulsed through me when I heard his voice, deep and low, thick with longing on the other end of the line, or better still when we were able to find a few precious minutes or hours together.

A voice in my head – the one that is always right – warned me that it couldn't end well. I put my hands over my ears and closed my eyes and blocked out all the warning signs I saw and heard. A part of me always knew, instinctively, that this, like all addictions, would be destructive.

And it had been. Maybe I convinced myself it was something more. I was foolish to believe him.

But he'd pursued me relentlessly. Love-bombed me. That's what Una calls it. He didn't give me a choice – he consumed me. How could I resist when here was this beautiful, powerful, charming man telling me I was more beautiful inside and out than Sorcha Hannon ever had been? He'd asked me about my life, about my day, about my hopes and dreams and he'd listened to my answers. He'd told me he was grateful I trusted him enough to show him my vulnerable side. To tell him how I never quite fitted in.

He'd told me that I'd woken him up and reminded him of what life should be like. He'd pulled me into empty offices at work and cupped his hand over my mouth to silence my cries of pleasure as he pushed inside me. He gave me no reason, in those early months, to suspect he was telling me anything other than the truth.

So I believed him when he told me this was the first time he'd ever even considered cheating on his wife. I fell for every clichéd line. *Of course* I believed that his wife was too obsessed with her own career to care about the man who had stood by her all these years. That she didn't love him any more. That he doubted she ever really had.

She didn't make him feel the way I made him feel. I believed it because I wanted it to be true. I so desperately needed it to be true. I think he always knew it wasn't. I was just an easy target.

I'd resisted my feelings at first. I'm not one to go after other women's husbands – no matter the state of their marriage. In fact I'm not usually the kind of person who pursues any man. I'd become quite accustomed to being on my own. Life is easier that way.

But he persisted until he made me believe we were worth the risk.

It turns out we weren't.

Inevitably, he grew bored, or maybe it was the case that I grew boring. Or too complicated. I definitely became too complicated. I wasn't just a distraction of sex and whispered, lust-filled late-night chats any more and that was problematic for him even though he had done everything he could to make me believe that this was love.

He described what we'd had as a mistake – as if he hadn't deliberately taken my heart, and my body, and used them for the better part of a year. As if he hadn't told me he was mine and I was his.

I tried to show him that I was the person he'd thought I was. The person he wanted me to be. That I could be enough. Funny

enough. Pretty enough. Sexy enough... There was no reason why
any of that had to change.

He'd shouted his hatred at me – blasting bitter words and bitter
coffee-tainted breath into my face. 'Enough! It ends now! The
madness ends now! Leave me alone and get on with your life and
for God's sake, grow up! We had some fun, but it's over. It was
never going to be anything more. I never promised you anything
more,' he'd roared. 'You can't make it something it isn't or was
never meant to be!'

He'd left me on the floor of my living room, my eyes red raw
from crying. My head thumping and heart pounding. He had left
me with nothing – no dignity, no self-worth, no one to love. I was
broken by him in the truest sense of the word. Mortified to my very
core. Ashamed I'd been so stupid. How could I have been gullible
enough to have believed what he told me? How could I have been
so foolish that a man laying it on thick with his longing for me
would make me betray my morals?

I couldn't leave the house for weeks, terrified my shame and
my secrets were branded across my forehead. I certainly couldn't
risk bumping into him in the office, so more and more I called in
sick, or lied about appointments and deadlines that required my
attention elsewhere. Even now it's a delicate dance of trying to
avoid him as much as possible and hiding from him in the same
offices we used to sneak to when we just couldn't resist each other
any more.

My face blazes scarlet each time I think about it. My stomach
tightens and turns as if the shame of it is trying to turn me inside
out. I can't eat. I dread sleep but crave it at the same time. I've been
grieving for something that wasn't even real to begin with and the
worst of it is that I can't bring myself to tell anyone this full story –
not even Una or Shaunagh.

Shame is a heavy burden to carry and I can't put my burden

down. I've made myself the villain of the piece. I was the 'other woman' and as everyone knows the other woman never gets a redemptive story arc. All good and right-minded people would conclude that, because of my own actions, I deserve every shitty thing that has come my way.

11

Overnight I can't help but play the conversation with Joan over and over again in my head. I analyse and re-analyse what she said, how she said it, her tone, her facial expression, her body language. Could I be reading it all wrong? Is she just being a good friend to Sorcha?

Have I done something either at the beach, or at the coffee morning to offend her? Have I said something I shouldn't have in the group chat? Is there any way she could know about Ronan and me?

My head is sore from thinking too much and I'm not even sure I'm remembering all the details correctly any more. That happens, doesn't it? When your brain is trying to make sense of something. It plays tricks on you and the memories reshape themselves to fit the new narratives and none of them provide me with a solid, irrefutable answer.

Meanwhile my phone has been pinging with notifications from the group chat all night. Jokes being shared. Plans being made. There's talk of beach picnics and a weekend wellness retreat. Sorcha has teamed up with a spiritual guru to do a guided meditation on a live Instagram session. There has been a genuine buzz of excitement and support and I've been too afraid to join in with any of it in case I let my guard down too much. Living under surveillance is not fun.

Aoife and Carla both sent me private messages to congratulate me on my first swim. I haven't replied. I was foolish to think this could be a way to make new, genuine friendships. Not when I have to hide the real me.

No matter how I try, I can't dismiss what Joan said. Regardless of her tone or the look on her face, surely staying involved with the group would mean me taking much too big of a chance of her digging up something I'd prefer stayed buried.

I'm making a cup of extra-strong coffee after my fairly sleepless nights when my phone lights up with a message from Sorcha herself.

> Hey Christina, hope you're okay? You haven't posted on the group and Carla told me she'd messaged you and got no response. I just wanted to check that we didn't scare you off yesterday and that you're not still feeling embarrassed about crying. Honestly, we've all done it and that's why we're here. The whole ethos of the Sisterhood is to support each other in a non-judgemental way, so please let me know you're okay or if there is anything I can do to reassure you that we're all here for each other. Much love, S x

That message is all it takes to make me decide that I won't walk away based solely on Joan's little chat. I'll just be smarter. I'll be more careful. I'll remind myself of all the steps I took to make sure that it would be at best difficult for snoopers to track me down. I may be an overthinker but that also means I'm an over-planner. This was not some on-the-spur-of-the-moment decision to join the Sisterhood. I'd considered it carefully, planned it for weeks. I'd done my best to make sure I'd covered as many of my tracks as possible.

I wait for an hour, to make sure I don't look too needy, and then I message Sorcha back. I thank her for her message and tell her I was just overwhelmed with work and, yes, feeling a little embarrassed at my crying on the beach too. I tell her I'll take her at her word that the Sisterhood is a safe and supportive place and I ask when she's going to the beach next. It's a blatant lie when I say I can't wait to get in the water again. Just remembering the bite of the cold is enough to make my body tense up, but I am looking forward to the numbing sensation it eventually brings, and the dopamine hit that comes after.

She tells me she's going again tomorrow and that I'm more than welcome to join her – as long as I bring some more of my delicious hot chocolate. With a smiley-face emoji she tells me she is delighted that I'm okay. Of course I agree to go – knowing I'll push my work to the side for another morning just for the chance to be among people. When I read later that Joan won't be joining us in the morning, I'm extra glad I've agreed to go.

Sorcha gives me the biggest of hugs when I get into her car to go to the beach the next day. 'I can't tell you how delighted I am that you've come today,' she says. 'I really think you will benefit from this. I see something in you I recognise,' she adds and my stomach clenches. If only she knew just how much we have shared... She'd most certainly not be pulling me in for a big embrace.

'I'm glad too,' I tell her. 'I think I might really benefit from this too – even if I do find it all a bit scary.'

'Which part?' she asks and I can't help but laugh.

'All of it,' I tell her. 'The cold water, the social aspect. I've become a bit of a hermit these last few years so I'm not used to dealing with big groups of people and trying to remember every-one's name and story and I worry I'll make a fool of myself.'

'So what if you do?' she says. 'We all do from time to time. And this group is about swerving all judgement so you'll be fine.'

Of course, I think of Joan's face and wonder just how much judgement I'm really swerving, but it's clear that she and Sorcha are close and I sense it would be foolish to bad-mouth her on any level.

When we reach the beach, the sun is bright in the cloudless sky. There's more than a hint of summer in the air and the sea is calm – the waves merely ripples towards the shore.

'This,' Sorcha says, 'really is the life! What a gorgeous day!' She beams that trademark wide smile of hers and grabs me by the hand, pulling me along to where the small group of Sisterhood swimmers are waiting for us. They let up a cheer when they see us approach, which of course I know is for Sorcha, but still it feels nice. Just as it feels nice when Carla pulls me into a big hug. 'Look at you joining us again! Didn't I tell you it's addictive? It's good to see you, Christina!' And it really does sound as if she means it.

When I walk into the water, still nervous, it is Carla who holds my hand until I feel brave enough to continue walking on my own.

12

JULY

Over the next few weeks I find myself addicted to the dopamine hit of a notification telling me there's a new comment, or picture, or video uploaded to the Soul Sisterhood page. Between that and the very lively WhatsApp group chat, my phone lights up every couple of minutes and though I keep reminding myself I'm not obliged to read every new message as soon as it pops onto my screen I find myself reaching for my phone anyway.

I start to look forward to my wild water swims, making sure to go two or three times a week. I'd go more but I don't want to appear too keen. I have to dial down my enthusiasm so that I don't draw too much attention to myself but it's hard when I really feel as if I might have found my tribe. Maybe that sounds very clichéd and maybe I'm falling under the Insta mantra spell but it's true. And it's so long since I felt that sense of belonging to something that it's hard not to gorge on it.

'You seem lighter,' Una says when I see her towards the end of July for one of our occasional check-in appointments. 'I mean, you look... I don't know... happier? There's a sort of glow around you,' she says with a smile, which I can't help but echo back to her from my spot across the room in her cosy therapy space.

'I am happier,' I tell her. 'I'm starting to feel a part of something really good. And the sea swimming – it's transformative.'

Una laughs. 'I'll take your word for that. I'm not a fan of open waters. If some seaweed, never mind a fish, brushed my leg I'd have a conniption. But I'm delighted it's helping you.'

'It really is,' I say and take a sip from the glass of water Una has left for me on the little side table beside the armchair I always sit in. This is the first time I've not been counting down the days until I see Una for an appointment – where I've not been counting down the hours until I have someone I can have a good conversation with.

'And making friends? That side of it? How has that been? I know that's something you've said you struggle with,' Una asks.

'I think I'm building friendships, but it's hard to let my guard down,' I admit, and that much is true. 'I find myself holding back a little, you know?'

'And why's that?' Una asks.

'Because I know I can be a bit much for people,' I say, my face colouring with shame at the memory of all the times I've been told I'm too loud, or too quiet, or too emotional, or too giddy. 'And then again I know I'm not enough for others,' I say, the memory of Ronan and how he told me he was leaving flooding my brain. 'I'm afraid of being rejected, again, I suppose. I'm afraid of believing these women could become my friends and then have them disappear out of my life.'

'And this is because of your previous experiences?' she asks, and I nod because while I've kept the full truth about Ronan's marital status from her she knows more than anyone how much I fell for him and how desperately I wanted the life he had promised.

'Mmmmm,' Una sighs and crosses her legs. She watches me for a moment, over the rim of her glasses, and pushes a stray dirty blonde strand of hair behind her ear. I know I have to sit with this silence for a bit. To give her time to think and time for me to process what I've said myself.

'Well, that's understandable,' she says eventually. 'But you must remember that these women are not your ex. Or any of the friends who have fallen to the wayside as their lives became more complicated. And you're not the person you were when you were with any of them. You're a new, resilient you who is picking herself up from the floor and healing her hurt. This is different and you deserve to be loved for the person you are.'

Of course that makes me cry, but even as I drive home later, I think that for once my tears were happy ones. They were healing tears, just like those I shed the first day I walked into the water. And healing tears are good tears.

I start to believe Una that this time won't be like the others. This time might actually work out, so I promise that I will open up, just a little bit more. I will trust in myself – I will believe that I am worthy of love and friendship. I will push down the fears that I'm starting to believe were unfounded.

Apart from that first day on the beach, Joan has been perfectly cordial. Friendly even, on occasion. She hasn't whispered anything else in my ear or given me the evil eye. I don't think we'll ever be best pals, but that doesn't really bother me. Not everyone is going to be my friend – the world just doesn't work that way. I'm still cautious that I'm being watched, but the more I feel myself establish relationships – like the good, solid friendships I'm building with both Sorcha and Carla – the less paranoid I feel. Our chats on the way to and from the beach feel so effortless and fun. We laugh and it feels so good just to laugh.

Yes, of course, I have to watch that I don't give too much away. I don't want anyone to connect me with Ronan, not even a little. I especially don't want Sorcha to make that connection.

So, they know me by my full name, Christina, and not as Tina, which is what just about everyone else knows me as.

The only surname they associate with me is my mother's maiden name. When they have asked where I work, I have replied with honesty that I work from home. I do embellish the truth a little and tell them I'm a freelance project manager. In my experience no one really knows what that involves anyway so it's easy to fudge around the topic with talk of budgets and deadlines. Thankfully no one has asked me to manage any projects for them.

I stick to my line that when it comes to my personal life, there has never been anyone who has felt like 'the one'. It was Carla who called me out on that one as we drove home one evening from a full-moon swim, wrapped in our dryrobes, our bodies slowly warming up, our endorphins released and the promise of a good night's sleep assured.

'Really though? You're like thirty-five. And there's never been anyone serious? What about your last relationship? The one who broke your heart? Surely he must've had "the one" written all over him?'

'Okay,' I'd said. 'First of all, I'm thirty-seven. Almost thirty-eight but I'll take the compliment. And second of all… maybe at one stage, for a very short window of time, I thought we'd end up being each other's happy ever afters, but life isn't a fairy tale, or if it is, I'm just an ugly sister.' I'd forced a laugh out, even though laughing was the last thing I felt like doing.

'Well, I hear you when it comes to life not being a fairy tale,' Carla had said. 'If it was, I wouldn't be a divorcee who's had her fill of dating apps, but I don't want to hear you say you're an ugly sister ever again.' Her voice had grown serious and there'd been an immediate change in the atmosphere in the car. 'Whoever he was, he wasn't the one for you. But there will be someone. Because you are far from ugly and you deserve to be happy. We all deserve to be happy.'

And I wanted to believe her. I still want to believe her. I do deserve to be happy. Yes, I've made mistakes in my life but I didn't make them with the intention of hurting people. And Sorcha has even admitted that the breakdown of her marriage has ultimately been a good thing. Her profile has sky-rocketed, she has set up the Soul Sisterhood and she is in demand as a motivational speaker. I wouldn't go so far as to say I did her a favour but... well, it's not exactly done her a lot of harm either. She's moving on and doing great things.

It's not callous or selfish of me to want that for myself, is it?

13

AUGUST

In mid-August it is announced that the Soul Sisterhood will be
having their first annual Summer Beach Festival at the end of the
month to mark the end of a wonderful summer of friendship and
self-care. Sorcha is going all out and has proposed a barbecue on
the beach, followed by music, a moonlight swim and perhaps a few
drinks. She's inviting as many of us as possible to camp on the
beach overnight so we can all watch the sunrise together and greet
the changing of the seasons with sun salutations and positive affir-
mations.

The thought of spending the night under canvas on a Donegal
beach leaves me cold, as does the thought of nipping off into the
sand dunes for a pee in the wee small hours. I'm imagining sand
getting into my clothes, the temperature dipping to unpleasant
levels and the horribly claustrophobic feelings that can come just
from climbing into a sleeping bag.

But at the same time, there is something so appealing about
lighting a bonfire, sitting around it with friends and then walking
into the water together. It's cleansing in every sense of the word. It
could, I think, really signify a rebirthing of sorts for me. I can't

remember the last time I spent a night away from home, and certainly not with friends. Yes, Shaunagh and I keep promising to do a weekend away together but she's so busy with the baby and I'm so set in my ways, it just hasn't happened. But if I can do this, then maybe I can expand my horizons and find some inner courage.

So I reply enthusiastically to the group chat saying it sounds amazing and offering to help with organising things. I'm sure there's a lot to be done. Will we need some sort of permit from Donegal County Council? How will we arrange the catering? Do we have to take certain safety measures? If there is one thing I can do well, it's admin and I'll be honest, I'd get a buzz from being more active in the group. I'd feel as if I was giving something back.

Sorcha replies almost immediately with a giant smiley-faced emoji.

> Christina! You are a legend! Thank you so much.
> All offers of help welcome! What would we do
> without you?

I am beaming with pride and a sense of belonging at last when I message back that I'm only too happy to help and just to give me my orders and I'll get to work. The next thing I see I'm added to another WhatsApp group – 'Sisterhood End of Summer Bash', which appears to have only five members. There's Fiona of the incredible brownies fame, Aoife of the pink hair, Carla, Joan and Sorcha. And of course, now there's me bringing the new total to six. I feel as if I've been welcomed into the inner sanctum of the Sisterhood and I know it's a little pathetic that it makes me feel as good as it does, but I feel like dancing around my living room.

I jump right in with suggestions and ideas, and immediately start collating information on a spreadsheet as Joan and Sorcha assign tasks to each of us. It's been so long since I've felt this fired up about something that my mind is racing with ideas and I start making a list.

When Sorcha tells the original Sisterhood group later in the day that she has the A team working on making it a night to remember, I feel as if I've just been given a gold star by the teacher, and I know that makes me sound like a complete loser but it's the truth.

Later that evening I'm cooking dinner and singing along to a new Spotify playlist I've started to compile with the big beach bash in mind when my phone rings. It's listed as a private number and even though I hate answering calls from private numbers I know I can't ignore it. It might be work-related, or it might be a call back from one of the catering companies I contacted looking for a quote. So I stop Spotify, accept the call and say 'hello' in as cheerful a voice as I can muster.

'Hello, Tina,' a low, gruff-sounding voice replies – I think. It's quite hard to hear what was said. The line isn't particularly clear – almost as if the speaker is driving, or walking in heavy traffic. Did they call me Tina?

'Hello,' I repeat. 'Who's calling?'

There's more muffled noise, and the sound of the engines or the machinery or interference or whatever the hell it is gets even louder – I hold the phone away from my ear, wincing at the sudden increase in volume.

'Hello?' I say again, and okay, by now feeling a little uneasy. 'HEL-LO?' I repeat, louder this time, getting ready to hang up.

'You're making a fool of yourself,' the voice, deeper now, tells me. Or at least I think that's what he or she says. The background noise is making it impossible to hear clearly.

'I'm sorry?' I say, now acutely aware there is a shake in my voice. Did they just say I'm making a fool of myself? 'I can't quite hear you. It's very noisy there,' I say doing my best to speak slowly and clearly, sure I must've misheard. 'Can you say that again?'

Even as I speak I'm aware of the dread that is growing inside me as I feel rejection waiting just around the corner once again. I should've expected this. A part of me did, I think.

My instincts scream at me to just hang up, that I know that whoever this is, they are not a friend or ally; but still, like the masochist I have become, I ask them if they can go somewhere quieter perhaps so I can hear what they're saying. A mumbled response follows, even less clear than before. Now it sounds as if it's being distorted deliberately, somehow.

'I'm sorry,' I say, anxiety now winding its way around my lungs, making it hard for me to breathe properly. 'I can't hear what you're saying. It must be a bad line. I'm going to ha—'

I don't have the chance to finish my sentence when all background noise suddenly and abruptly stops. I hear footsteps and heavy breathing, though I'm holding my own breath in an attempt to hear the caller more clearly.

'I... I'm going to... hang up now...' I start again but there's a cough. A loud rattling clearing of a throat.

And there's a voice, still low, definitely distorted as if someone is speaking through one of those annoying plastic toy microphones you buy for children that add an echo to their words. 'I said, you're making a fool of yourself,' the person on the other end of the phone says. 'You're not wanted.'

'Who is this?' I blurt, a moment too late.

The caller has already gone and I am left to stare at the phone screen.

14

SORCHA

I'm not surprised that Christina has decided to insert herself right bang in the middle of the planning of the end-of-summer party. She's a perfect example of a 'pick me' girl – always eager to please. Perhaps a little too eager. Bordering on desperate. From the first day she arrived at our coffee morning I could see her desperation to fit in and get involved.

It's endearing in a way. It shows me that the Soul Sisterhood is doing exactly what I hoped it would and is providing a place for women to make connections. Real-world connections – not just social media acquaintanceships.

It's quite nice, I think, as I scroll through the group chat, to see people grow in confidence and develop their own sense of owner-ship of the group. It makes my life easier because there's less for me to do and, God knows, I'm busy enough between trying to keep up with an ever-changing influencer landscape, keep monetising what I'm doing in a way that helps provide for my family and secure my future, and raise two daughters who can be a handful at times. That's especially true of my eldest, Ivy, who is standing at the door to my home office talking incessantly about Olivia

Rodrigo as if she's the second coming. 'And she's touring and, Mum, can we get tickets because I swear she is like my favourite ever singer and it would make my life so happy.'

'Sweetheart, I'm trying to work,' I say, trying to keep my voice light. 'I'll have a look at it later.'

'Reading WhatsApp messages isn't work,' she says with a roll of her eyes. She's twelve going on sixteen with an attitude that tests my patience on good days. 'You don't understand. She's just the best and—'

'It is work, Ivy,' I say, cutting her off. 'We've had this discussion before. A thousand times. This is my job. This is what pays the bills. If I don't do this then we can't pay for the roof over our heads never mind concerts and trips.' It's not exactly true – I've managed to squirrel away a large portion of my recent earnings to give us a sense of stability that we lost when I became a single parent.

Of course, Ivy rolls her eyes again, this time with extra flair, as I mention boring things like bills and responsibilities. 'But the summer holidays are nearly over and you're always working! At least when we go and stay with Dad he spends time with us and takes us places. You're always worrying about all your sad internet followers instead of worrying about me and Esme and doing stuff with us. You always just tell me to come back later because you're *busy*.'

Her voice has developed that particularly annoying whiny tone of a teenager that has the same effect on my nervous system as nails being dragged down a blackboard. This attack on my patience is switched up a gear by her launching into the latest version of her patented 'why Daddy is a more fun parent than you could ever be' speech.

I have vowed to not be the kind of mother who bad-mouths the absent father in front of her children, but my God there are days when I find it hard to hold my tongue. It's been easy for Ronan to play the doting daddy when he spends two days a fortnight with his beautiful daughters, taking them on days out and shopping trips and filling them with ice cream and pizza before dropping them back with the wicked witch of Derry to do all the hardcore discipline and the daily drudgery side of parenting. Even with an army of followers, this influencer still has to fight with her twelve-year-old to brush her teeth, pick her washing up off the floor and go to sleep at a reasonable hour. All these demands are, in Ivy's eyes, tantamount to child abuse and she is not beyond invoking the name of her father to try and guilt me into going easy on her.

And the thing is, I do go easy on her. Ivy and Esme are loved. They are spoiled more than I ever was. We do spend time together and I do treat them. I'm not able to treat them for the entirety of the time they are under the same roof as me – nor do I want to. Can you imagine how unbearable they would be?

My phone pings and I glance at it, resulting in an immediate and loud 'huff' of indignation from my oldest child.

'See!' she says. 'You care more about *them* than you do about us!' She turns on her heel and I hear her mutter and rage as she walks down the hall then stomps up the stairs. She is going to call her beloved daddy and no doubt rant to him about what a witch I am, and he will soothe her and promise her the sun, moon and stars. The agreement that we do not bad-mouth each other in front of the children is allegedly mutual but as with just about everything else when it comes to Ronan, I'm not sure I trust him to keep up his side of the bargain.

Of course, there was a time when I did, and when I would've followed him to the ends of the earth. There was a time when he could have told me the sky was purple with orange dots and I'd have believed him – and that's only a slight exaggeration.

But that was before it all went wrong.

Feeling a headache start to build behind my eyes, I try to focus on the incoming messages about the end-of-summer bash. What started as something fairly informal and fun is growing by the second. I'm grateful to those offering to help as I know I've a week of Zoom meetings and collaboration pitches to get through. But as Olivia Rodrigo starts to sing her angst-ridden hits at full volume, my temper threatens to break.

It didn't have to be like this. This is not the vision of motherhood I had painted for myself when Ronan and I first decided to start our family. We were supposed to face these challenges together. But he had planted landmines through our relationship – the biggest of them having recently resurfaced.

I read the messages in front of me again. 'I've started to create a Spotify playlist,' Christina wrote an hour ago. 'I'll ask everyone for suggestions. Should we stick to summer songs?' She has added a row of dancing-figure emojis, and grinning smiley faces.

I wonder, does she ever think about the consequences of her actions – about our broken family and the two girls left being jostled between two different homes. She's got balls, I'll give her that. Slipping into the support group of the woman whose marriage she was responsible for imploding isn't a move I saw coming, but I can be unpredictable too.

15

CHRISTINA

I'm still reeling from the nasty call when I speak to Shaunagh on the phone an hour later. I tell her about it but of course I play down how much it has shaken me. I want to see what way she reacts to it. She's always telling me I am too quick to jump to the worst possible conclusion and this time I really need her to tell me that's the case here.

'It'll just be some teenager acting the absolute dickhead,' she says as I hear baby Thomas start to fuss in the background. 'You've said everyone is nice to you in the group, and sure hasn't Sorcha brought you onto the organising committee? Don't let it annoy your head,' she says and I'm almost about to tell her about Joan's quiet word on the beach that first day when Thomas's cries rattle up a notch.

'Oh shit,' Shaunagh says. 'He's just poo-namied all up his back. Look. Tina, I have to go. I'm sorry. But in my opinion just ignore it, and keep being you! Love you!' With that, she's gone and I'm left desperately wanting to believe she's right but not being able to shake the feeling deep in my heart that she isn't.

Dejected, I message our little committee of organisers and lie

that a new project has just come on board unexpectedly in work
with a mega-tight deadline and as a result I'll not be able to help
out after all. Worse than that, I tell them, I will be tied up with it
the weekend of the big beach bash and I won't even be able to
make the main event. I tell them I'm gutted – and that much is true
– and that I'll send them the files I've been working on including a
list of the businesses I've called for quotes and even my short-lived
Spotify playlist. I apologise and try to sound nonchalant as I watch
them one by one express their disappointment but also their
understanding.

I can't get rid of the notion the call might not be the work of
'teenage dickheads' as Shaunagh put it. That one of these women
now expressing their disappointment may well be behind it. But
these are grown women. Professional women, even. Carla's a ward
sister, Joan's a manager, Fiona's a teacher and Aoife owns a
boutique in town. They are all vocal in the main group about being
welcoming and kind. I've seen them take care of new members.
Even Joan's warning shot on the beach could be construed as
someone merely watching over her friend. Can I really believe she
would resort to bullying behaviour? I can't believe it of any of
them.

I tear myself apart looking for reasons why someone has taken
against me so strongly. I read over every interaction I've had in the
group chat and try to see if I've said the wrong thing, or been unin-
tentionally offensive. I replay every conversation I've had face to
face with group members to search my memory for something –
anything – that gives me a clue about my wrongdoing. Was I just
too eager? Too much? Did I overstep? I'm not sure which would be
the worst-case scenario – that someone would know about Ronan,
or that I'm just intrinsically unlikeable. Or maybe, it's a combina-
tion of both.

Whatever the reason behind the malicious calls, I leave our mini WhatsApp group and cry until my head hurts.

Deciding to skip swimming for a few days, I throw myself into my work. God only knows I've been letting a few things slip as I've gone to the beach on office hours more than I should.

I'm not that surprised to find it's easy to slip back into a pattern of living that simply revolves around work. I work long past my allotted hours, both at home and on the two days a week I'm in the office. I keep myself to myself and when I do get upset that I'm not being flooded with 'Are you okay?' messages from my Sisterhood 'friends', I remember that I've told everyone I'm flat out working on a new project. I don't tell Shaunagh that I've crawled back into my comfort zone. I don't want her to judge me as weak for not ignoring the stupid phone call.

I post occasionally in the group chat, hoping that when enough water has gone under the bridge I can maybe return, but in a way that doesn't ruffle any feathers. But while I post rarely, I can't help but read every word because I so desperately want to feel a part of something and also so I can search for clues as to who my mystery caller might have been. If it was someone from the group who called me – and let's face it, it could've been anyone from the group – then I refuse to publicly acknowledge that their words got to me. They're bound to have connected the phone call with my disappearing act, but I won't give them the satisfaction of seeing me lose my cool over it.

I do this in the hope that whoever it was will leave me alone now. I've done what they wanted and pulled back. So when my phone rings again two weeks later, and on the morning of the big beach bash, and the number is once again listed as private, I feel my heart sink. I've come to dread the ringing of my phone and today more than ever I am on edge. I should be posting excited messages and pictures and talking about where I bought my tent –

and instead I'm in my flat crying over everything that's happened during these last three years and wondering if I will ever escape the pain of it.

Just like before, I can't ignore the call, so I answer it. When I lift the phone to my ear I'm relieved that there is no crazy background noise like last time. My relief is short-lived when the same, almost robotic, deep voice speaks. 'Have you missed me, Tina Try-Hard?'

My blood runs cold.

'Don't even think of showing your face tonight. You're not wanted. You're not one of us. You're just a nasty bitch.'

The call ends before I can speak, not that I have any idea of what to say. What do you say to that? How do you pull yourself back from that?

Tears slide down my face again, stinging skin that is already scourged from all the crying I've been doing. When my phone rings again, just seconds later, I scream at it to 'just fuck off!' and am about to lob it across the room when I see that it is Sorcha's name that is illuminated on the screen.

I answer without thinking.

'Hey, Christina!' she says in a cheery voice. 'I just wanted to check in on you. We've really missed you and I thought you might be feeling a bit sore about tonight.'

'I'm... I'm fine,' I stutter. 'Busy.' I'm pretty sure my voice sounds thick with emotion, which I'm hoping she doesn't pick up on.

'Are you sure?' she asks. 'You sound a bit odd.'

I sniff and mumble a quick, 'I'm sure.' I don't trust myself to say any more because I know if I do I will dissolve into tears. It's ridiculous how much this is hurting me. I've been a part of the group for just over two months and yet this separation feels like a huge loss. I'm not sure I can ever go back after this latest phone call.

There's a pause before she speaks again. 'I was just calling because I wondered if you'd maybe change your mind? Are you further along with work than you expected maybe? Or have your plans changed?' She sounds hopeful and I desperately wish I could say that I can go. I wish I was like Shaunagh and just put two fingers up to whatever absolute bitch has been calling me, but I just don't have the strength left in me to do it.

'Sorry,' I say. 'I'm flat out.'

The conversation is stilted, awkward. It's not the usual back and forth that Sorcha and I have enjoyed in the past. I know there's a very real chance that I'm coming across as rude but at this moment in time I don't feel I've a choice – not now I've been very expressly told to stay away.

'Oh... right, okay,' Sorcha mutters. 'Well, that's a shame. But maybe we'll see you soon?'

'Maybe,' I reply and as my voice breaks I end the call. I can't even risk saying goodbye because I know I won't be able to hide my emotions.

'Has she changed her mind?' Aoife asks as she stacks the boxes of cheap plastic leis I bought for the party ready to transfer them to her car. My kitchen has been taken over by all things Big Bash-related and I'll be glad to see it all go.

'Nope,' I tell her. 'Says she's up to her eyes in work and can't get away.'

'I'm not sure that's a bad thing,' Joan sniffs, between blows into an inflatable beach ball. I glare at her. Now is not the time to have this conversation.

'No?' Aoife asks, one eyebrow raised. 'Why's that?'

Joan opens her mouth to speak so I jump in as quickly as I can with: 'Joan thinks Christina can be a bit full on, that's all.' I nod in Joan's direction, hoping she will take the 'that's all' as a definitive instruction to keep her mouth shut. I'm fairly open about my marriage break-up but I don't want the world and his wife to know the intimate details, or the extent of his infidelity, or that Christina was directly involved. I've never been a 'name and shame' kind of a person – I prefer to take care of problems in a more discreet manner. Like every human on the planet, I have a vindictive side. I just prefer that as few people as possible know about it. I wouldn't want to get cancelled, after all.

'Ach sure, we can all be a bit full on.' Aoife smiles. 'I don't think there's any harm in her.'

Joan splutters at this and I glare at her again.

'Sorry,' Joan says with a croak in her voice. 'These beach balls were not designed to be blown up by people with lungs as old as mine.'

'Wise up, Joan.' Aoife laughs. 'You're in better shape than the rest of us all put together.'

After I help Aoife load her car with the first batch of party supplies, I return to the kitchen where Joan has made what can only be a conciliatory cup of coffee for me. 'I'm sorry,' she says, but the sentiment doesn't quite show in her eyes.

'No, you're not,' I say. 'I know you don't like her, Joan, and God knows we have a good reason to not like her but I don't want it to be the subject of gossip. You know what it's like – it will be all over social media before I've time to bless myself and then I'll just become Sorcha whose husband had an affair, rather than Sorcha who has made something of herself.'

Joan puts her hands up in a mock-surrender pose. 'Okay. I get it. I'm sorry. I just hate to see her getting away with what she did, Sorcha. And that's what's happening here. It's not right.'

'She's not getting away with anything,' I say and take a sip of my coffee. She can trust me on that one.

CHRISTINA

September

September brings both an unseasonal heatwave and a raft of memories I wish I could simply erase from my mind. There is something about the evenings drawing in and the slow slip of the seasons that reminds me of my time with Ronan. When it was good and we were lost in each other.

Two years ago, I'd not long returned to the office on my new two days a week schedule, when Ronan had knocked on the door of the finance office and walked towards my desk with an exaggerated pleading look on his face. 'Tina,' he'd said. 'I'm totally, completely confused by these figures and I've a meeting this afternoon that I absolutely don't want to make a fool of myself at. Could you go through them with me?'

He'd looked so comically pathetic that I'd laughed and told him of course I would. He'd pulled a chair over beside me while I scrawled through his files, and I was instantly aware of the warmth emanating from his body, the heady scent of his cologne and the sound of his breathing. Ronan Hannon is a handsome man.

Always groomed to perfection but with just the smallest hint of ruggedness about him. And he is funny. Witty. He made me laugh, just as he made me blush when he complimented me. First he would tell me I was a lifesaver. Then 'a genius', followed by 'sincerely. All this is nonsense to me, but you just seem to know what you're looking at and make it all make sense.'

He'd drop by my desk more often. First to ask for more advice, but this soon segued into asking me if I fancied a coffee – which he would invite me to drink with him in his office while we chatted about whatever was on our minds. What TV shows we watched. What books we read. What our weekend plans were. It might be hard to believe but we rarely talked about Sorcha or the girls. Not at that stage. It was all surface-level stuff. Then he started sending me funny, occasionally flirtatious memes and messages. Even though I knew better, I started doing the same, convincing myself it was okay because they were *only* jokes. We were just being funny. I started to get a little buzz when a message arrived from him, and a bigger buzz when his head popped around the finance office door. I did my best to keep things looking strictly professional in front of the others in the office but I knew I was, at times, behaving like a giddy schoolgirl. It took all my effort to hide my happiness, and to remember that when push came to shove, Ronan was just a work colleague.

But then he needed help on a day I was working from home, and so he offered to treat me to lunch so we could look over his latest project. It was, he said, 'the least he could do' so I agreed because it was *only* a lunch with a work colleague and we were meeting to discuss work. This became a regular thing, once or twice a week. He told me my company was much better than sitting alone in his office with a soggy sandwich and YouTube for entertainment.

After a while our discussions, perhaps inevitably, moved on to non-work-related topics. But I figured it was still okay, because we were *just* friends.

He started opening up about his marriage – about Sorcha's influencer role, about the pressures of raising children. There was a seven-year gap between Ivy and Esme. It was never meant to be that long but they'd tried for years before Sorcha fell pregnant the second time and then, he said, he'd felt it was as if he ceased to exist. He loved his girls – adored the very bones of them. But they were hard work. He asked me if I thought that made him sound cruel – of course I shook my head and told him no, it made him sound human.

That was the first time he reached across the table and touched my hand. It was just for a moment but that was enough to feel something ignite between us. We both felt it. As clichéd as it might sound, our eyes met and we knew then that this was not *only* a professional relationship or only a friendship.

We fought it for a time. I stayed away from Ronan – was always busy when he arrived in our office or sent a message. He kept things strictly professional but it was like once the genie was out of the bottle it was impossible to put it back in.

Our first kiss came after a long day of meetings – an audit by HQ. It had been stressful and we were all tired. A drink was called for in the pub and, even though I am not a fan of large social gatherings, I didn't want to look like the odd one out by saying no. One by one our colleagues started drifting off until, perhaps inevitably, only Ronan and I were left.

Alcohol having made us more relaxed, more likely to drop our barriers, I agreed when Ronan offered to walk me home. It was a brisk September evening. The leaves were starting to fall, and the moon was bright in the sky and he told me he'd missed me. Missed us. When he took my hand in his, I didn't pull it away, which is what I should have done but it felt so good. I felt cared for. When we reached my apartment block, we had stared at each for what felt like forever but was probably only seconds.

'You make me want to break all my own rules,' he'd said, his gaze fixed on me and something bubbled and fizzed deep inside me, in the very centre of my being. I had not been kissed in a long time. I don't think I'd ever really been kissed by someone who felt utterly compelled to do so. His hand was on the side of my face, his thumb brushed my lips and I knew then that I was gone. We would break our rules for each other because we had no choice. When his lips finally met mine I knew I would do anything for this man – and I believed he would do anything for me.

It's hard not to lose myself to those memories, especially now that I feel so very alone again. I haven't returned to the Soul Sisterhood. I have driven to the beach, with all my gear, and sat on the sand staring at the waves. I've tried desperately to build the courage to walk into the water alone, but my fear of the sea always holds me back. It's easier when you have someone whose hand you can hold. Someone who can remind you to breathe when the bite of cold water constricts your lungs.

I've considered messaging Sorcha, or Carla maybe, and asking them to join me outside of the big group swims, but isn't that more likely to raise questions and draw attention my way? I already worry if my every step is being monitored. Sitting on the beach, watching a group of swimmers laugh and joke as they get dressed after their dip, I freeze when I notice one of them is looking my way. It's only for a split second, but when she turns to her friends and says something I can't hear, a peal of laughter follows and I wither a bit inside.

I do my best not to look too often at the group chat. I can't quite bring myself to leave it yet but I am getting better. It was an obsession at first. I needed to know what everyone was doing. I needed to feel a part of it but then, slowly or not so slowly perhaps, it has started to feel like a noose around my neck. It's a reminder of what could've been and a reminder that someone in the group doesn't like me and isn't afraid to let me know it.

I don't like feeling on edge and yet it seems to be where I spend most of my time these days – even with the distance I've kept from everyone. The feeling that an unknown person has it in for me. I wonder how much they know about me and what is feeding their dislike of me so much. Is it the case that I really am too much? That I came on too strong? Or is it that I haven't been as careful as I thought and someone has worked out my connection with Ronan?

When I post my occasional updates, I worry about who is reading them and what they're reading into them. When my phone rings and it's from a private number, I tense – anticipating a crackling, distorted voice on the other end of the line.

I'm feeling particularly sorry for myself on the last Saturday of the month, having watched the pictures load from that morning's sea swim, when there is a buzz at my door. It must, I think, be someone hitting the wrong button by mistake because no one ever comes to my flat save for the occasional Amazon delivery man but I know I've not ordered anything.

I ignore it, and continue lying on the sofa, torturing myself with memories and jealousy at the pictures I'm seeing.

It buzzes again. Twice. I want to pull the device from the wall to silence it, but that would require getting up and walking across the room to reach it. So, again, I ignore it. Until it buzzes three times in a row and at the same time my phone lights up with a message. It's from Sorcha.

> I know you're in there, Christina. I'm not leaving so you might as well let me in.

Immediately I feel sick, sure that someone *has* figured it all out and she knows the truth about who I really am. My heart is in my mouth as I do what I'm told because regardless of whatever she might be here to say, she deserves the chance to say it. Even if I'm scared she will walk in my door and slap me around the face for sleeping with her husband, I know I'll deserve it. Maybe it might even make me feel better. It will be a justice of sorts, as if I haven't already faced my own justice.

She seems to take forever to make it up the stairs and to my door, during which time I do my best to make myself look semi-presentable while fighting the urge to throw up as anxiety throttles me.

Tears are already pricking at my eyes when I open the door to her, not sure of what's coming. I can barely bring myself to look up at her.

'This,' she says, her voice loud and authoritative, 'is an intervention.' She pushes past me and into my flat, casting her eyes around it before walking to the windows to open them. I hadn't realised just how stale the air has become in here.

'You need to give that a little wiggle,' I say weakly as she struggles with the dodgy sash window that I really should get fixed. Of course, she manages to open it and then she turns back to look at me.

'Put the kettle on,' she says. 'We need to talk.'

My hands are shaking as I do what she says.

'I need to know why,' she says, and my stomach twists in on itself and my mouth dries. I don't know what I can say. How can I make this better? No amount of apologising will make it right. As I try and find the words she speaks again.

'You seemed to be so invested and involved with the group and I could see it was really doing you a lot of good. Then you pulled out of the beach party, and you've almost disappeared altogether. Tell me what's going on,' she says and I can hardly believe that this is what she is asking me and that she's not here to interrogate me about the affair I had with her husband.

'I've... just been busy,' I say and it sounds pathetic, especially given that she has walked in on me clearly in full-on sloth mode.

'I don't believe you,' she says. 'It's more than that. I'm not going to have watched you do so well and grow in confidence just to back off again. There has to be more to this.'

'It's... it's nothing. Honest,' I lie again, even less convincingly than the first time.

'Christina,' she says. 'Come and sit down. Tell me. Has something happened to put you off the group? Is there anything we can help you with?'

She looks so sincere in her concern that I want to tell her, but I'm not sure I should. How will she take the news that one of her friends has been making nasty, bullying phone calls?

'What is it?' she says and takes my hand in hers as the memory of Ronan taking my hand that first time plays in my mind again. I think of how I need to get over him and what happened and find something positive in my life. The only thing that had been working was being a part of the Sisterhood.

'I got some strange phone calls,' I say, and feel heat rise in my face at the memory.

'What do you mean?' she asks, her face flooded with concern.

'I was told to stay away, basically. That I was a try-hard and a bitch and I wasn't to show my face again.'

Sorcha's face is a picture of shock and disbelief. 'Someone from the group, from the Sisterhood, called you? Do you have a number? Did they give a name? I mean... I doubt they did, but did you maybe recognise their voice?'

'It came through as an unknown number. Both times. And their voice was distorted in some way. And no, there was no name.'

'Their voice was distorted?' she asks, incredulous. 'And when was this?'

'About six weeks ago?' I blush. 'Just after I joined the committee for the beach party. They called again the day of the beach party. Just to make sure I stayed away.'

I decide not to mention Joan's 'friendly warning' on the beach – Sorcha looks shocked enough.

'And that's why you didn't come that weekend? You weren't working at all?' she asks, shaking her head in disgust or anger or I don't know what. 'Why didn't you say anything?'

I nod. 'I was just a newcomer. I didn't want to start any trouble.'

'You didn't start this,' she says. 'But I'm going to finish it.' I watch as she reaches in her bag and pulls out her phone, her perfectly manicured fingers tapping at the screen, her face set with steely determination. With a flourish she taps the phone one more time and sits back.

'Right, that should sort it. And you're coming back. I'm not taking no for an answer. Do you hear? And you can be as involved as you want to be. No one has the right to tell you what you can and can't do and if anyone has a problem with that they can come directly to me. I'm going to pick you up in the morning...'

I try to interrupt, to say I'm not sure how I feel about that but she raises a finger to silence me. 'I won't hear any excuses or arguments. We're going swimming in the morning and whoever is behind those pathetic phone calls can suck it up. Now... go and get me that cup of tea.'

Dumbfounded, I just nod and get up to do as I'm told as Sorcha stands up. 'And if you could direct me to your bathroom that would be great, because I am absolutely bursting for a wee.'

I show her where the bathroom is and go back to my tea duties, aware my phone is absolutely lighting up with messages. I lift it and see that Sorcha has posted to the chat. And she is angry.

I've become aware of bullying behaviour among some members of this group. Let me make it very clear – there is NO ROOM for bullies in this group and there never will be. We are grown women and we are here to raise each other up and hold each other up. Anyone caught bullying will be banned from attending any other events and will be blocked from any group-related social media. This is not in the spirit of the Sisterhood and I am disgusted that a member of the group has been made to feel victimised. I'm drawing a line under it now.

I brush tears away from my face and drop two teabags into two mugs. Relief floods my body.

* * *

Curled up on the sofa later that day with another cup of tea, I scroll through my phone. Sorcha's angry message seems to have had a positive effect. There are a flood of messages on the group chat expressing shock and dismay that someone has been misbehaving. Of course, there have been calls to 'name and shame' the offending bully, but since we don't actually know who it is, that's not likely to happen.

I'm reading the notifications, still not having been brave enough to post anything myself, while I get ready for Sorcha to pick me up for our return to the beach. Thankfully there's only a small group swimming this morning but among them will be Joan and Carla. Of course, I can't rule them out yet as my mystery caller and I may never be able to, but Sorcha says they are good people. 'The best,' she told me, revealing they've been friends long before the Soul Sisterhood came along and that neither of them has a bad bone in their body. 'Stick with us,' she says. 'We'll keep you right.'

I have to believe her, I suppose, or I'd never go back. And I do want to go back. Once I'm ready I make sure to mark myself as 'Do Not Disturb' on Teams and when my phone pings with a message letting me know Sorcha is outside, I feel a flutter of butterflies in my stomach. I'm not sure if it's excitement or fear. Perhaps it's both.

Sorcha smiles brightly when I reach the car. 'Right,' she says. 'Let's put all this nastiness behind us and get back in the water. And I want you to tell me if you get any more calls. Straight away. Okay?'

'Okay,' I tell her while pulling my seatbelt across my body and clicking it in place.

'Good,' she says, with a smile – and with that we head back to the sea where I hope to wash away the horrible feeling I've been carrying about in my chest this last six weeks.

18

CHRISTINA

October

I try to keep some level of distance from the Sisterhood. I don't want to get anyone's back up despite the support of Sorcha and all the people who have been in touch to offer encouragement. I don't want to provoke anyone into making any more nasty calls. I've been made to feel welcome at the swims. I was encouraged by Sorcha to go to one of the group coffee mornings and I did, bringing a plate of home-baked oat cookies with me. I'm not much of a baker, but Shaunagh sent me the recipe, telling me it was 'basically foolproof'. I wasn't sure she'd really taken on board my level of incompetence in the kitchen when I first saw it, but to my surprise it was relatively easy to follow and the finished product tasted good. Okay, they were a little misshapen, but they seemed to go down well.

I found myself starting to relax a little into the group again. Everyone was friendly, even Joan, who offered to share her world-famous scone recipe with me. I'd laughed and told her I knew my limits and it was best to leave scones in her hands.

The group chat is as busy as it ever was. It has become a part of my evening routine to switch off from work, change into my PJs and scroll through the chat enjoying the banter or commenting on Sorcha's latest uploads. Her follower figures are continuing to climb at an exponential rate and she's told me in confidence she's been asked to write a self-help book for women looking to form meaningful friendships and build their own self confidence. I'm delighted for her, of course. But I did have to turn her down when she asked me if she could feature me as one of her case studies. No, I absolutely have to keep a low profile and this is what I tell her. That I'm still a little on edge after the phone calls and I really don't want to bring any attention to myself. She'd been fairly cool about it.

Tonight though, the chat in the WhatsApp group has segued from Sorcha's book to the forthcoming inaugural meeting of the Soul Sisterhood book club, which has been scheduled for the following night. I've stayed clear of all book club discussion because while I've always wanted to be a member of a book club, I'm still determined to maintain some distance from the group and that involves not jumping at every new venture.

Joan asks for a roll call of who is coming along as she is planning to bake and wants to be sure she makes enough for everyone. There's a flurry of replies as people confirm they're going, including Carla and, of course, Sorcha. It's all go apart from one small hiccup. The venue she had booked to host the club has had a leak and needed to close. She tells the group not to worry though – so much effort has gone into planning this meeting that she has decided to host it in her own home rather than let people down.

A nip of what I think is jealousy pulls at me. I've never been to Sorcha's house and I'd love to go. I'd love to see where she lives – where Ronan lived. I'd love to look for clues about their life together, maybe meet their girls. Before I know it I'm offering my services to help out given the short notice and change of venue while lying and saying I've started reading the book-club pick – which of course I immediately download onto my Kindle. While the taunt of being a 'try-hard' runs through my mind again and again, I do my best to push it away. This is too good an opportunity to miss and I know Sorcha is on my side if anyone starts acting up. Sorcha replies with a row of smiley-face emojis, telling me I'm a star, and I flush with pleasure.

Sorcha's reply seems to give the green light to other members – Joan included – to reply.

Joan has typed:

> Will be great to see you. And don't forget to bring some of your now famous oat cookies… and a bottle of wine too! What's a book club without wine?

And she adds a flurry of wine-themed emojis. The response from the other girls leaves me under no illusion that this might actually be more of a wine club than a book club but whatever the reason, it will give me a chance to get a good nosy in Sorcha's home.

I reply:

> Yay! I'll bring a bottle!

And a shiver of excitement runs up my spine as Carla types back:

> Bring two!!!!!!

19

SORCHA

Christina, or Tina, or whatever the hell she is called, was the straw that broke the camel's back for Ronan and me. His longest-running affair. 'Someone from the office.' It was the biggest cliché in the book. Well, that and the fact he denied it had been going on for months. 'It was just the once,' he'd insisted, unaware I'd already searched through our credit card statements and found evidence of romantic dinners, weekend breaks when he told me he was away with work, and expensive gifts that never came my way. Emma Thompson in *Love Actually* had nothing on me.

By that stage I had become the main breadwinner in our house, having been able to monetise my social media content remarkably successfully. It didn't seem to bother Ronan that his wife was partially funding his extramarital shenanigans or that one day I might cop on to the fact given the very poor effort he made at covering his tracks.

We tried marriage counselling again after that one, but I think I knew from the very first session it wasn't going to work. We had drifted too far in the intervening years since our first hopeful hours spent with the counsellor to be able to swim back to each other.

Perhaps more importantly, I no longer *wanted* to swim back to him. He was no longer the loving, devoted man he had once been. He was selfish and cruel. He was incredibly jealous of my rising profile and did his best to belittle it, and me, as often as possible. The only thing that made me want to fight for our marriage was our two girls. I knew Ivy would be heartbroken if her daddy left. Esme was younger and not as attached to him as her big sister, but she still loved him. The thought of not wanting to hurt them is what gave me the strength to keep hurting myself. But there comes a time, doesn't there, when you just can't do it any more.

I was going online to my Instagram followers and painting a picture of a perfect home life when the truth was, we were all living a lie. I realised I didn't want to do that any more, so on a day when he was in the office, I packed him a suitcase and I changed the locks to our house, and the key code to the electric gates. I shifted my money from our joint account and changed all our house-related direct debits so that they would be taken from my personal account in the future. Then I booked him a hotel, sent his case to his hotel room and a hand delivered note to his office to outline exactly what I had done and what way we would move forward.

The fall-out wasn't pretty. Despite everything, I did still love him – I just couldn't trust him and once that is gone everything else is sure to follow. I cried and I grieved. I held our girls as they cried. I dealt with Ivy's angry meltdowns and the times she lashed out. I took it all in my stride because that's what a mother does.

And I talked about it online, realising that a lot of women felt the same or had similar experiences, and the Soul Sisterhood grew. I became stronger. I became more able to withstand Ronan and his angry reactions.

I just never expected to see Christina join our Facebook page and insert herself into our lives. I knew who she was, of course. I'd googled her when he'd told me about his latest dalliance. The fact that she had changed her name slightly didn't hide her identity from me. I doubt she'd make a good master criminal. Her face was branded in my memory: the other woman, the homewrecker. She had been elevated to the very top of my shit list and I'm not sure what it would take to knock her off that position.

I suppose I was curious at first when she joined the Sisterhood. I'd have thought I was the last person she'd want to be near – regardless of what time had passed since her affair with Ronan had ended. She was either incredibly ballsy, or incredibly stupid. I didn't quite know which.

I could've blocked her and kicked her out of the group as soon as she joined, but I needed to try and understand her. I needed to try and understand what it was about her that Ronan had found too irresistible. What it was about her that made him throw away everything he had with us? Did she even care that my eldest daughter had cried so hard the day her daddy moved out that she made herself sick? What kind of a woman goes after someone else's husband? And then has the brass neck to join that woman's sisterhood? Once I understood her, I figured I would know the best way to get my revenge because what she had done could not go unpunished. She hurt me, and that was bad enough, but she also hurt my children and there was no way I was letting her get away with that.

I can't lie – I'm fascinated by her and there had been something quite delicious about watching her squirm over those nasty phone calls. I know Joan had a word with her too, even though I had asked her not to. I didn't want to scare her off quite so quickly, but I didn't want to let her off scot-free either. Don't they say to keep your friends close and your enemies closer?

I definitely wanted to know more about Christina. I still do. Having her come over tomorrow is just perfect. Maybe that will be the day I tell her I know exactly who she is and what she is capable of. And maybe it will also be the day she finds out just what I am capable of.

20

CHRISTINA

Sorcha's house is as stunning in real life as it is on her Instagram, if not more so. Of course it is. Her driveway isn't quite long enough to be classed as tree-lined but there's a respectable distance between the road and her house, which is partially hidden from view by several mature trees in her garden, scattering their leaves like confetti onto her perfectly manicured lawn. Their twirling dance is illuminated in the soft glow of her ground-level lanterns. It almost looks as if it has been choreographed. Wind chimes hung from the tall oak tree near her gateway tinkle melodically.

Sorcha's house is off the Limavady Road in the Waterside, close to the Foyle Bridge. It's one of three similar houses built along the river about five years ago that were marketed at the time as the most exclusive homes in the city. Viewing was by invitation only and the rumour mill went into overdrive that they were purchased by some of the big celebrities to hail from the north-west of Ireland. There was much excitement when the rumour circulated that one of the homes had been purchased by a rock star and his TV megastar girlfriend, and that another had been purchased by a pop princess.

Needless to say those rumours turned out to be false. Ronan told me the other two houses are owned by a dentist and a property developer.

Earlier today Sorcha had posted a reel on her Instagram of how she was getting ready for book club, and I very quickly realised this wasn't going to be a low-key night. We aren't going to be sitting around drinking tea, sharing a packet of chocolate digestives and discussing the book. This is going to be an everything-ramped-up-for-the-'gram kind of a night. There's a charcuterie board to die for that probably cost the same as an average person's weekly food shop. There's shortbread biscuits (home-made, of course). Hand-crafted chocolates from a local chocolatier, complete with the cover image of the book of choice: *The Burning* by Jane Casey.

There's even a specially created themed cocktail. 'Kerrigan's Cosmo' is named after the book's protagonist. Of course there will be a non-alcoholic option available, just as there are vegan snacks for those who wish to steer clear of the deli meats and cheeses. Every detail has been planned to perfection. My Tupperware box of misshapen cookies isn't likely to make Sorcha's Insta grid.

I feel a little inadequate arriving with it, and my bottle of Marks and Spencer Prosecco.

By the time I reach the sage green door of Sorcha's beautiful double-fronted house, my adrenaline levels are already in overdrive. My heart desperately wants to catch a trace of Ronan here, because even though he smashed my heart to smithereens, I miss what we had so fiercely.

I don't like that he has this effect on me. I want him to not matter. I want this to be solely about my continued journey to draw strength from the only other woman who could really know what it is like to feel the pain of losing Ronan Hannon – even if I can never discuss him with her.

But the battered part of my heart that still misses him is almost giddy with the thought of being in his space – even if it isn't his space any more.

It's Carla who opens the door to welcome me in. 'Sorcha's in the kitchen with the others,' she explains. 'Just go on through.' She is already looking over my shoulder to see who else is coming up the driveway.

I don't tell her that I don't know where the kitchen is. Instead I just try and follow the noise of excited voices chattering. The walls in this hallway are painted a bright white and there are black and white portrait images hanging from the walls in tasteful matching black frames. I see images of two girls who I recognise immediately as Ivy and Esme. They are angelically beautiful. Wide eyes and button noses, rose-petal lips and soft dark curls. They are the perfect combination of their mother and father and they are pictured staring at each other, Esme displaying a wide smile that just adds to her innocent beauty. Ivy's face is more serious, but no less beautiful. She just happens to be in that in-between stage where she would rather eat glass than have a family portrait taken and yet not yet confidently indignant enough to defy her parents' wishes. These girls are picture-perfect – as if they have just stepped out of the pages of a magazine shoot.

I see a beautifully styled Sorcha grinning at the camera with the two girls wrapped around her. Her hair is full and glossy, her bare arms toned, her smile bright white. I feel a pang of disgust at my own appearance.

Then I see him, in the third picture. Standing with his wife and his girls. I hate that my body reacts to him still. That my heartbeat quickens and my stomach clenches. This man destroyed me and still I react to him – maybe there really is too fine a line between love and hate. He is looking at her as if she is the most precious, beautiful thing in the world and I wonder how I was ever stupid enough to think I'd a chance. How naive have I been? My heart aches when I see how he is looking at her in that picture, because there is no mistaking that there is love in his eyes. He never looked at me like that. There was always something he held back.

I only realise there are tears pricking at my eyes when I hear Carla's voice again. 'Come on, slow poke!' she says. 'You're causing a traffic jam.'

I startle, aware that I'm staring at a picture of Sorcha and her family like it's the fucking *Mona Lisa*. 'I... I don't know where the kitchen is,' I offer pathetically, turning my head away for fear the tears that have gathered will start to fall. I sniff and clear my throat. 'And I was just admiring the pictures of the girls. Such beautiful children,' I say.

'Wee stunners,' Carla says. 'And such good girls too. Take after their mummy. Come on, the kitchen is through here...' I let her lead the way, with two other women following behind us. I recognise their faces as group members but I don't know their names. Not yet. They are lost in their own conversation and it would be rude of me to join in so I just follow Carla, until the noise of chatter gets louder, and we walk down the hallway and into the large open-plan kitchen/ diner/ family room that I immediately recognise from Sorcha's videos. The ambience is more wine and cheese party than book club, though I do notice several copies of the book being taken out of bags, leafed through or placed on the table.

'Christina!' I hear an excited voice, and I turn to see Sorcha beaming at me. She, of course, looks gorgeous in some sort of pale pink cashmere co-ord loungewear get-up that screams of relaxed nights at home with the girls, and speaking of girls, I wonder if Ivy and Esme are here or still with their daddy. Will I get to meet them? Is there a chance he'd be dropping them back and our eyes might meet? My stomach swirls at the thought.

Sorcha pulls me into the tightest of hugs and I get a lungful of her no doubt very expensive perfume. 'I'm so glad you came you along,' she says into my ear as we hug.

'I'm delighted you're all okay with it. Especially since I've not finished reading the book. Just show me where the kettle is and I'll start on the teas,' I say, handing her the flowers, which she sniffs appreciatively.

'These are gorgeous,' she says. 'Let me just get a vase. And don't you even think about making tea. Get yourself a glass of fizz or one of my signature cocktails. There's more than enough for everyone!'

She leaves me standing while she opens a cupboard and takes out a clear crystal vase. Within seconds she's arranging my £15 bouquet from M&S as if floristry is her passion in life. I cringe thinking of the times I've filled my measuring jug with water and balanced still-cellophane-wrapped flowers in it.

'Here,' another voice from behind me says and I turn. It's Joan and her smile is broad and bright. Handing me a glass of Prosecco, she takes the bottle I'm still carrying from me. 'I'll just pop this one in the fridge,' she says. 'It always tastes better chilled, don't you think?'

She is oozing the warmth and friendliness I first saw from her at the coffee morning and it's enough to make me wonder if maybe I *was* just being paranoid about her tone at the beach.

'Make sure to grab one of those gorgeous chocolates,' she says, her back to me. 'They are ah-mazing!'

'I will,' I say, and look at the impressive spread Sorcha has put on. The chocolates do look 'ah-mazing' as Joan says and so who am I to argue with her suggestion to try one.

By the time we all sit down, gathered around the wood-burning stove in what Sorcha calls the 'den', I feel a little buzzed – no doubt from the combination of alcohol and sugar I've just consumed. Though I've only had one glass of Prosecco and a few sips of a second, my head is definitely a bit light. Maybe it's the heat from the stove? But then again, no one else looks red in the face or as if they have broken into a sweat. Meanwhile I'm all too conscious of the beads of sweat running from my hairline down my neck and under the collar of my definitely not cashmere jumper.

The conversation moves on around me and while I try to keep up, the fact that I've not read the book, and that I'm feeling a little dizzy is proving to be very distracting. Maybe if I just splash a little cool water on my face or run my wrists under the cold-water tap I might feel better. I could grab a glass of water and stick to drinking it from now on. While the others chat excitedly about the twists and turns of the book, I excuse myself and ask Sorcha discreetly where the loo is.

'Just through the door, down the hall and second on the right,' she says, waving her hand in the vague direction of the other end of the kitchen. I go to mutter a thank you but she has already turned her attention back to the discussion.

The cooler air hits as soon as I leave the kitchen and I stop for a moment to breathe it in. I don't feel right at all, but I'd be hard pushed to explain it in words. At this particular moment, I think I'd be hard pushed to find any words at all. The bright white hallway dances in front of my eyes, and occasionally the images of Ronan from the walls seem to surge towards me. This feels wrong. *I* feel wrong.

I'm grateful when I reach the small downstairs loo, and stumble my way towards the window to push it wide open so that the even colder air can wash over me. Sliding to the floor, lest I faint and fall, I haul my jumper over my head and then just in my jeans and bra, sweat still pooling between my breasts, I wait for the breeze to start bringing me back to myself.

Only it doesn't work that way, and I realise I'm about to throw up.

Christina doesn't look good, I think as I try to focus in on the chat around me. She was very pale and when she put her hand on my knee and asked where the bathroom was, it was definitely clammy.

It must be strange for her being here in the house I used to share with Ronan. Unless she's been here before. The thought makes me feel a little nauseous myself. I don't think even Ronan with his extreme arrogance would be bold enough to bring a lover into our family home, or God forbid, into our bed.

No, I tell myself, she wouldn't be asking me where the loo was if she had been here before. Surely, she would just swan round the place like the queen of the castle, but I hadn't got that vibe from her, and I don't think she's socially competent enough to fake it.

She seems genuinely nervous, which is understandable given that she is in the heart of the home she wrecked. Perhaps I should've left things as they were and not staged my own intervention to bring her back into the fold but I'm not ready to give up on her just yet. I've not done everything I wanted to do.

Joan, of course, thinks I'm off my head. I've had to warn her to be on her very best behaviour tonight, which she is doing, perhaps with a little too much gusto. There's a wickedness to her that I both fear and admire. I wouldn't want to go head-to-head with her, but her heart is generally in the right place. Sometimes she needs to be reminded of that.

I know schadenfreude is frowned upon a little, but is it wrong of me that I'm getting a little pleasure from Christina's discomfort? Does it make me a bad person that seeing her overheated in her jumper, her face an unflattering shade of red, gives me a shiver of satisfaction? No, I think that's the very least I've earned.

22

CHRISTINA

Scrambling as quick as I can over to the toilet, all I can think is that I could not live with the shame if I were to throw up all over myself, or all over Sorcha's designer bathroom. As soon as I reach the loo, the glass of Prosecco I'd enjoyed, and the chocolate I'd eaten, and whatever else happens to be in my stomach, spill in violent waves out until my now empty stomach is left with just spasms of pain to push through. I just about manage to find the strength to hold my head up and rest it against the cool porcelain of the cistern. My breath ragged, I try to centre myself. This isn't right. This is more than just a glass of Prosecco disagreeing with me. I'm not this much of a lightweight when it comes to alcohol and this feels much, much more than just 'tipsy'. Even though I've been sick, the room is still juddering and distorting in front of my eyes.

My breath is still coming in shudders when there's a loud knock on the bathroom door and someone tries the handle. I have never been more grateful to have managed to lock the door before I hit the deck. The last thing I need is anyone walking in on me in a heap over the loo, bra on show, my chin wet with drool and my hair hanging in damp shapeless clumps.

'Christina?' a muffled voice calls. Is there an echo? It feels like there's an echo. Like the strange voice on the phone maybe? 'Are you okay in there? You've been a while,' the voice calls again, this time clearer. Sharper. I blink and try to focus my eyes but they just won't do as I want.

Using all my energy, I pull myself to sitting. 'Yes, I'm fine,' I mumble, though my tongue feels thick in my throat and my voice sounds funny. I flush the loo. 'I'll be out in a moment,' I attempt to call out. Hauling myself up to standing, I find that the room is, much to my annoyance, still refusing to stop spinning and I struggle to keep my eyes open.

With clumsy and uncoordinated hands I reach for the taps and run the cold water, splashing it liberally on my face. 'Just washing my hands,' I call out. It takes all my effort to find my jumper and pull it back on, over my wet face and the straggling ends of my hair. I know my skin is damp with sweat and I know the itch of this jumper will make the combined sensation a sensory nightmare, but it's not like I have a choice. I can't saunter out of the bathroom half naked.

When I catch a glimpse of myself in the mirror, I see a train wreck. The foundation I carefully applied before leaving the house is now streaked and running into the make-up-stained collar of my jumper. Mascara runs in black spidery lines down my cheeks. To top it off sections of my hair are matted to my head with sweat. I don't think there's any way to rescue this situation – but that doesn't stop me looking around the bathroom in case a miracle solution suddenly makes itself known. Unsurprisingly there is no make-up kit, or hairbrush, or even a bottle of perfume to spray on myself to make sure there's no lingering smell of vomit.

All I really want to do though is lie down and sleep. My eyes are heavy and the room still feels as if it could just fold in on top of me at any moment. Seasickness claws at me as the walls look as if they are rolling and waving back and forth, and I'm forced to close my eyes to try and find my centre again. Defeated, I grab the hand towel to dry myself off, aware that I'm leaving what looks like a death mask on Sorcha's no doubt expensive white tufted Egyptian cotton. Still shaking, and not just from my new-found mortification, I open the door to find Carla waiting outside, her face a picture of concern.

'Oh my God, Christina, you look dreadful. Are you okay?' she asks. 'You've been out here twenty minutes. We were starting to worry about you!'

No. It's not been twenty minutes. I can't believe that. Five maybe. Ten at most. Definitely not twenty. I shake my head because I seem to have lost the ability to form coherent sentences and Carla takes me by the hand and guides me to sit on a beautifully upholstered silver and black chaise longue at the end of the hall.

'You're an awful colour,' she soothes and she kneels in front of me, her tender approach reminding me of when my mother used to look after me when I was sick.

'I... I don't feel good,' I manage.

'You poor thing,' she says, and raises her palm to my forehead to check my temperature. 'You're very clammy. Let me get you some water.'

Before I can object and just beg her to magic me home to my own bed, she has left and I hold my head in my hands as if that will be enough to stop the sensation that I am somewhere between this world and somewhere else. Once again, I'm acutely aware of Ronan staring down at me from the walls – a self-satisfied smile on his face.

When she returns, she brings an audience. I'm thankful she's only brought two people with her, but mortified that of course Sorcha is one of them, with Joan being the other. Carla kneels in front of me again and holds a glass of water to my lips so I take a few sips. I'm incredibly grateful that she keeps a hold of the glass because I'm not sure I'd be able to stop it from slipping from my fingers just yet.

'What happened?' Sorcha asks, crouching down. I blink up at her, see her brow is crinkled in concern.

'I'm not sure,' I say. 'I was fine... and then I wasn't. I'm so sorry.'

'Too much Prosecco?' Joan asks and if I wasn't feeling so horrid I'd throw her a withering glare.

'I only had one glass. A few sips from a second,' I say.

She raises her eyebrows in what looks like disbelief, and I want to remind her it was she who gave me the glass in the first place. 'And no cocktails?' she asks and I can't help but feel judgement in her voice. Is she insinuating I'm drunk? Because I'm absolutely not drunk.

'No. Just the one glass of Prosecco. I must have eaten something funny. I'm so sorry. I'll call a taxi and go home. I probably just need a sleep. I really want a sleep.'

The three women look at each other and then at me. It feels as if they're all in on something that I'm not privy to. Paranoia, never far away in the first place, creeps up my spine.

'I don't think you should go home alone,' Sorcha says. I start to shake my head and am about to tell her I'll be fine because the truth is, all I want to do now is get home and away from this humiliation. It doesn't matter that I could cry at the thought of moving from where I'm sitting – I just need the sanctuary of my own space.

'I don't think she should go home alone,' Sorcha says again as if I'm not even in the room.

'I'll take her,' Carla says, then turns to me. 'I'll get you settled and see how you feel once you're in your own space. Besides, we might find it hard to get a taxi driver brave enough to agree to take a woman who looks like she's had a skinful home in the first place.' I want to scream that I've not had a skinful but I know there's truth in what she is saying. That no taxi driver in their right mind will want a woman who looks like an extra from *The Walking Dead* in the back of their car.

Carla continues, 'I've not been drinking, so I'm safe to drive. I'm probably about the only one in the group who has been on the mocktails.' She smiles. 'Had a heavy weekend and still suffering for it. The joy of being in your forties.'

Her face is filled with kindness and concern and maybe it's just because I'm sick, and feeling broken with embarrassment, but it's enough to start me crying.

Sorcha sits down beside me and takes my hand, and I manage to stutter out an, 'I'm so sorry.'

'You've nothing to be sorry for. Or embarrassed about. You poor thing,' Sorcha soothes.

'I'll go fetch your bag and coat,' Joan says. 'You can do an Irish goodbye and just head on without a fuss. I know when I'm sick the last thing I want is to be the centre of attention.'

I nod gratefully, and the very movement kicks off the worst of headaches.

'Bring a bottle of still water from the fridge too,' Sorcha calls after Joan, then turns to me. 'You can take that with you and just have some sips on the way home if you feel rotten. Then straight to bed. I'll check on you in the morning.'

'Thanks,' I say, as Carla leaves to get her own bag and coat.

'Carla will take care of you,' Sorcha tells me. 'She's a good soul. And sure you couldn't ask for better than a nurse so to be honest there's no one better to make sure you're settled.'

'I hate that I've ruined her night,' I say.

'Oh my God, love. You've not ruined anything. Sure we love a bit of drama!' Sorcha says with a reassuring smile.

Or at least it should be reassuring but instead I'm overwhelmed with the fear that my embarrassing episode will end up as fodder for Sorcha's social media content. She must see the alarm on my face and she gives my hand another squeeze. 'I'm only teasing,' she says. 'The golden rule of the Sisterhood is what happens in the Sisterhood stays in the Sisterhood, remember?'

23

CHRISTINA

I'm not sure I truly understood what feeling as if your head is in a vice means until I wake up with the worst headache of my life. The very act of even opening my eyes hurts and makes a sound that causes me to wince. As I blink again, I swear there is a screeching, sweeping sound again akin to someone running their nails down a blackboard. I scrunch my eyes tighter, not sure I ever want to open them again.

I peel my tongue from the top of my mouth, which is Sahara-level dry. My lips feel welded to my teeth. My limbs ache as I try to stretch, and my stomach feels like I've done a hundred sit-ups. Something happened last night. I know that. I'm just trying to get my brain to stay quiet long enough to remember what it was. All I have are fragmented memories, which make little to no sense, and putting them all together feels like an impossible task.

Sorcha was there. Or I was with Sorcha. At her house, yes, that's right, I went to her house. And then I was sick? A memory comes at me of being in her downstairs loo and wishing for an early death. Oh God. I'm not sure what hurts the most now, my aching stomach muscles – which I can now at least attribute to the purging I did in Sorcha's bathroom – or my ego at the thought of making a complete show of myself in front of the book club members.

Gingerly I try to open my eyes again, just to make sure I actually made it home to my own bed, suddenly aware I'm still wearing my jeans and socks, but not my jumper. A damp film of sweat clings to me. This feels like a horrible hangover, but I don't remember having very much to drink. Did I overdo it and blank further drinks from my memory? It seems unlikely. I'm not a heavy drinker at the best of times and I can count on the fingers of one hand the times I've been drunk in my life. On none of those occasions have I ever been so far gone that holes have appeared in my memory. I do my best to grab on to what I do remember. There was a glass of Prosecco. Joan gave it to me, didn't she? Did I have a second glass? I think I might have.

I try to sit up, desperate now for water, or caffeine, or toast or something I haven't yet identified, only to find the change in position sends a whole new wave of pain to my temples. Okay, so my head, which already feels as if it's in a vice now also feels as if someone is pressing down on it with a concrete block. The pressure is excruciating and I cry out. It comes in electrifying pulses in my temples, strong enough to nauseate me. My strained eyes land on a large glass of water on my nightstand. I don't remember bringing that to bed with me, but at this moment in time I'm heartily glad of it even if it is tepid and I feel the need to be sick as soon as it slides down my parched throat and hits my stomach.

Pain tears through me once more as I retch unproductively over the toilet, my skin now soaked in a cold sweat that makes me shiver violently as soon as the retching subsides. The force of retching has multiplied the shockwaves in my head. All of this gets worse as I rest with my back against the side of the bath as more memories from last night start to resurface and slot into place. I have a memory of Joan, and Carla and Sorcha sitting with me. Of the walls in Sorcha's hall feeling as if they had come to life. Ronan's face. Was he there? Surely not. I feel seasick again at the memory of how they seemed to wave in and out of focus. But everything else remains a mystery.

Obviously, I know I got home. Someone must've helped me because I'm pretty sure I didn't get a taxi. I can't imagine I would have been fit to get in a taxi and I can't see Sorcha letting me travel in one alone if I was in such a state. That I can't remember exactly how I got here unsettles me.

When I feel able, I haul myself to standing and look at what can only be described as a nightmare drawn large across my face. Bloodshot eyes stare back from the mirror, their red extra vivid against the corpse-like pallor of my skin. My hair is a mass of frizz and curls pointing in every conceivable direction. A hazy memory of attempting to brush my teeth last night comes back to me, and by the looks of my almost bare face I at least made an effort to wash off my make-up.

With a make-up-free face, the dark circles under my eyes seem more pronounced than ever, accentuated now by a smattering of small red dots, which don't look unlike freckles. Petechiae. Little burst blood vessels brought on by the force of copious vomiting. I'll need concealer, and lots of it, if I'm to leave the flat today – but given how heavy my legs feel, I don't think of leaving the flat as anywhere near a priority.

I splash my face with cold water, and eye the shower. I know I should force myself to wash off the sweat and sickness but I don't trust myself to stand up under running water for long enough. I just about make it back to my bed when my phone lights up with an incoming message.

Hi Christina. It's Carla. I wanted to check in on you. Please let me know you're still alive? C x

Carla! Yes, it was Carla who helped me home and who got the water, and pulled the curtains. I message her back to let her know I am indeed alive, but feel like I have the worst hangover of my entire life. Remembering my manners, I thank her for getting me home safe and sound and for checking in on me. The truth is I can't remember the last time someone actually checked in on me when I've been unwell.

My eyelids start to droop, the effort of getting up, washing my face and sending a text message having rendered me exhausted once again. I should fight it. I should go and put on a pot of coffee even though the thought of putting anything into my body makes me feel nauseous. I know I've things to do. Right now, my brain is so fuzzy I'm not sure what those things are but there are things...

The room starts to feel as if it is swimming around me again, and I know I need to lie down. It's not a choice. It's going to happen. Maybe I should just try one more sip of water... Turning my head to my nightstand, I see the glass still there but there's something beside it. Something that shouldn't be there. Something I put away just days before. That I buried under the cards and letters and old photos in my drawer. With the most private of all my things. I don't remember taking it back out, but then again I was so out of it, anything was possible.

That thought floods me with dread. God knows what I might have said and done while I was in that state. Shit. I could've said anything – revealed everything. Did I take the picture out last night when Carla was here? Jesus! Did I show it to her? Did I tell her about it? About him? A memory of her being in this room nips at my head. Was she standing by my bed? It's almost as if I can see her, as if I was at the door and she was already here. That doesn't make sense. I try to grab that memory and hold tight to it. Had she been looking for something? I can't remember... My stupid fuzzy head. She couldn't have been looking for this picture though, could she? She'd have no reason to... unless I had told her about it.

She's Sorcha's friend. There's no way she would keep knowledge of Ronan's extramarital carrying-on from her. There's no innocent explanation for having a photo with him in my fecking bedside drawer. Could I really have been stupid enough to take this photo out of its hiding place while she was here?

I feel like banging my stupid, fuzzy head off the wall.

Maybe it was simply the case that Carla put the water on my table, and that's where my fuzzy memory comes from. Maybe – hopefully – I simply took the picture out after she was gone to cry over it like the sad case I am? I want that to be true but I just can't remember and I can't escape the possibility that I might have just fessed up to this virtual stranger.

Dread sits heavy in the pit of my stomach, despite my every attempt to push it away, telling myself my mind is making me a paranoid wreck after the horrors of last night. Rationally, I know Carla had no reason to snoop through my bedside table and I had no reason to tell her about Ronan. But if I did, for whatever stupid addled reason my brain came up with, it doesn't bear thinking about.

Once again the after-effects of last night kick in and I find myself giving in to the need to sleep. Lying down, the pain in my head eased by the softness of my pillow, I decide to close my eyes for just five minutes but find myself in another restless dream where everyone is staring and pointing and judging. 'You've really fucking done it now,' they say and I feel the world I've rebuilt, again, over the last few weeks, start to crumble away from me.

24

I don't feel much better when I wake. My shattered memory around Carla and the picture of Ronan has me on edge. The best case, I tell myself, is that the picture on top of my bedside table is a result of my own rifling through it in a bid to try and convince myself, in my intoxicated state, that what happened between Ronan and me had been real.

But there is no way of knowing for definite what happened last night and the more time passes, the more I think my memory will remain lost to me.

It's not like I can message Carla and ask her if she happened to see 'that picture of Ronan Hannon on my nightstand'. Not without generating more questions than answers.

Sipping gingerly at a glass of blackcurrant cordial in a bid to try and rehydrate, I log into Teams and do my very best to concentrate on the work I should've been doing all day. It's not easy. Even with around twelve hours of sleep, my body still feels leaden. My stomach is still gurgling in such a fashion that I know it would be deeply unwise to attempt to eat anything. I wonder if I'm the only person from last night to be feeling as if they were hit by a truck. Could there have been something wrong with the food? I check the group chat to see if anyone else is sick but there's no mention of it – instead there's just all the usual banter. It was a great night, by all accounts. The chat is hopping with in-jokes and selfies.

It does strike me as a little weird that the only person to check in on me this morning is Carla, but then again Sorcha is very busy and people make constant demands on her time. There's nothing to tell me she hasn't been in touch because Carla's told her I was sleeping with her now ex-husband. I check the group chat again, and she hasn't posted there today either – which is very reassuring.

And as for Joan not checking in? Well, Joan is Joan. I'd be more shocked if she had.

I swallow two paracetamol and hope that my empty stomach will keep hold of them as I try again to focus on my work.

Cricking my neck, I try to ease the tension my body is holding. I take a deep breath and stare at my computer screen again. There is now a long line of emails that require my attention, several of them marked urgent.

So I set my Teams to 'Do Not Disturb' and start to methodically work through them – even if it feels like I'm taking two steps forward and fifteen steps back.

I have to check and recheck every piece of work to be sure I've not made any errors. I've already caught enough mistakes to send me into a minor panic, because in my job the only acceptable number of errors is zero. One misplaced digit can affect an entire project. Once I've dealt with the most urgent emails, I switch off my Wi-Fi altogether so that I can concentrate on number crunching without the temptation of just having a two-minute look at Facebook that turns into a full-on tumble into some rabbit hole, or a look at Sorcha's Instagram to see any updates she might post about the previous evening. I promise myself if I get my head down and keep working, then I will absolutely allow myself guilt-free internet time this evening.

Deciding to be brave, I make myself a cup of tea, stronger than usual, to try and infuse some much-needed caffeine into my body. I open the window closest to my desk and am hit by a blast of cool autumnal air, which is both deliciously refreshing given my mental state, but also bloody freezing. Still, if it keeps me awake and alert it will be worth it.

I'm so rattled by my poor levels of concentration that I switch off notifications of incoming data to my phone. I need to be able to work without interruption, so I force myself to stay at my desk until it is dark once again and my eyes are straining to look at the screen in front of me. Still I don't get up and switch on the light. By now I'm afraid if I move at all, I will knock myself off my stride.

I don't even allow myself to get a fresh cup of tea when mine has long since passed a drinkable state. I only stop when my bladder threatens to stage a coup and no amount of moving about on my seat can stop my urge to have a wee.

Besides, the paracetamol has worn off and my body is screaming at me that I need more pain relief, and I also need to eat something.

The flat is now beyond chilly and well into out-and-out cold, so after I've made friends with my bladder again, I switch on some lamps, stick the heating on for a quick boost of warmth and grab my cream-coloured cardigan from on top of my bed and wrap myself up in it.

I hunt in the fridge in case something has magically appeared since lunchtime that is appealing, but unsurprisingly, its contents are still fairly uninspiring. I settle for poached eggs on toast. It's a pretty sad dinner, but it fills a hole and passes some time.

By this stage, I'm itching to unmute all my notifications and see what's happening in the outside world. I'm hoping that Sorcha will also have messaged me by now to see how I am and that will allow me to bury my paranoia once and for all.

What I'm not expecting when I switch my Wi-Fi back on is the sudden influx of new emails from work. Most don't look urgent, thankfully, except for the few from my boss. My boss who is pissed off because it's 'unacceptable to switch my calendar to Do Not Disturb for prolonged periods of time' – something he has noticed I'm doing more and more. It's also 'unacceptable to leave myself unreachable during a working day' he writes. Even though there was nothing stopping him from picking up the phone and calling me, I think wryly.

My boss is *really* pissed off that I 'don't even seem to be reading *his* emails' – and of course he knows, because of read receipts, which he insists on using at every opportunity. My heart sinks. It sinks right to the very depth of my soul. How am I supposed to explain this?

Do I tell him I was out last night and got so sick I could barely move my head this morning, but no, it wasn't a hangover? Or that I'm so distracted by new friends I had to turn off my internet while I worked? Have I regressed to a thirteen-year-old version of myself who needed someone to switch off the Wi-Fi to get me to buckle down?

My heart is now racing with an added flush of anxiety, and I know one of two things. There is no way on earth I am calling him to explain. Not tonight, anyway. If I have to deal with someone actually berating me verbally after the last twenty-four hours I will break down. It will give him the worst possible impression of me and I'm not sure his impression of me is that great anyway. Sean is a friend of Ronan's and I've always wondered if he knows about our out-of-hours activities.

Think, I urge myself. Hands shaking, I start to tap a reply. Of course apologising is my first priority, so I draft a big 'I'm sorry' even though it sickens me. I try my best to play it cool and not over-apologise. If I adopt an 'it's no big deal' attitude then hopefully he will echo that back to me. I've seen my male colleagues do it a hundred times – and have always been in awe of their ability to brush off even the biggest of fuck-ups as nothing to get stressed about.

I type:

> Sorry, Sean! I wanted to go through all the figures with a fine-tooth comb to make sure they were on track and there were no surprises lurking for the client. You'll be aware there were amendments made to some of the costings yesterday, as per the email you were CC'ed in on. I didn't mean to go radio silent for so long though, so that's on me. I forgot to switch my Wi-Fi back on, as I was just so engrossed in the work. The good news is, everything adds up and I've checked and triple-checked all the figures. I'm confident that the client will be happy with our ongoing work on his behalf. I'm in the office tomorrow so let me know the best time to pop in to see you and I can talk you through everything. I'll even bring you a coffee as a peace offering!

I hit send and offer up a silent prayer that it's enough. The thought of seeing him face to face tomorrow doesn't fill me with joy but I can't escape it. I just need to bring my A game and prove to him that I'm doing a great job.

The problem is, however, that I've lied about having finished running through the figures so I've just managed to set myself up for a long night of work. Sighing, I realise I've no one to blame but myself. So much for my planned night of relaxing and catching up on the online gossip.

I stretch and pull my laptop onto my knee, knowing that my back cannot take any more sitting on the painfully uncomfortable kitchen chair that I know I should replace with something ergonomic and unlikely to leave me wincing with pain.

Four hours later, as midnight approaches, all I want to do is sleep. Surely if I grab a few hours I can get up early and finish it off before I'm supposed to be at the office. After powering down my computer and switching off the lights, I climb into bed and as I'm reaching down to plug my phone in to charge, I realise I haven't had so much as a single notification from the Soul Sisterhood group all night. Not even after I switched my Wi-Fi back on. That seems very odd, given that at most times of the day or night there is some form of conversation or craic on the go. Of course I know I should leave it and just go to sleep, but the nosy part of me – the paranoid part of me – is suddenly beset by the need to know what's happening.

I open the link to the Facebook page for local members of the Sisterhood but get a notification that the page has not been found. That can't be right. I must've mistyped – God knows I've made enough mistakes today; it would be no surprise if this was another one. So I try again, but again the group cannot be found.

I don't like this.

I open WhatsApp to find the group chat, but there are only a smattering of notifications since teatime, which seems very odd. Yes, I've only been a member of the group a very short time but even in the last week I've learned that it's not unusual to see more than a hundred notifications on any given evening. That was even the case last night, despite the fact so many group members were at the book club meeting. So this is definitely, undeniably odd. The little hairs on the back of my neck prickle with what I can only assume is a sense of foreboding.

Nerves now completely in tatters, I click into the chat to see if something has happened or if there's a reasonable explanation for the silence. As soon as I see the words at the bottom of the screen, I immediately feel the urge to throw up and it's not because of whatever has been raging through my system. There in italics, for the world and me, of course, to see is:

You have been removed from the group chat.

25

It's too late to phone anyone – not without looking like a madwoman – and possibly like a guilty madwoman. Anyone else would probably think there has been a glitch in the matrix somewhere and while they might be annoyed they can't access their favourite group chat of choice, they'd let it go and vow to try again in the morning.

God knows, I'm tired enough that I should do exactly that but my brain just keeps turning it over and over and over. The Facebook page has disappeared. The group chat is inaccessible. What I want to do is message Sorcha to ask her if everything is okay, although maybe it would be better to message Carla. After all, she has been in touch with me today to see how I am. But it's midnight now and as well as it quite clearly being an unacceptable time to call anyone in anything other than an emergency, I know Carla had been working a long shift and would have no doubt been exhausted by the time she got home. The last thing that would endear me to her would be sending panicked messages in the middle of the night. And besides, what would I say? I can't exactly start with: 'Hey, just wondering if you saw that picture of Sorcha's husband in my bedroom and if you've told Sorcha about it and if that's the reason I can't access the Facebook page and have been removed from the group chat? Because I swear, he doesn't mean anything to me. It was a hideous mistake...'

I look at my phone screen again. *You have been removed from the group* screams up at me, in tiny little italic letters. There was no discussion before my removal to give any clue about what has prompted my swift exit. I dread to think if there has any been any chat after. Has the group been alive with a systematic tearing apart of my character all night? Has there been much discussion about why I would have a picture of Sorcha's husband in my bedroom of all places? Do they all know that I made the biggest mistake of my life and ended up being the kind of woman I always vowed I'd never be? The kind of woman who plays with people's hearts and destroys marriages. The kind of woman my father left my mother for and forever broke her heart and mine.

I have been so incredibly, deeply stupid. No feelings were worth this. They were not worth losing the essence of who I was, or who I could be.

But what can I do about it? I can't turn back time. I can't make people understand. There's no adequate justification for my behaviour in all the world. Nonetheless, I need to know what I'm facing now. I need to know how strong the hate is. Only, it's not like I can call Sorcha or show up at her front door and ask her if I've done something wrong. Would that even be the right approach? Should I fake ignorance or just come clean and beg for forgiveness?

It's extremely sobering to reach a point in a crisis where you realise that you have very much made your own bed and are absolutely to blame for how uncomfortable it is.

There isn't a hope in hell I'm going to get any sleep now, I realise, as I can feel the full force an adrenaline surge take hold.

And I really do need to get some sleep before I go into the office, especially given Sean's email earlier.

My body's fizzing with a nervous energy that has to be expended before it causes the pressure in my brain to implode. So I force myself out of bed, grabbing my socks and Uggs from the floor, and pull them on. I don't bother changing out of the worn-out old grey joggers and slightly misshapen T-shirt I wore to bed. I just pull on my long-padded coat – the one I'm sure makes me look three times bigger than I am but which I know will keep me warm – and my beanie hat. Grabbing my keys and my phone, I leave my flat having decided that a walk might be the best course of action.

I feel a profound disconnect from the world around me and, just maybe, grounding myself in the cold and the rain, with the feel of hard tarmac beneath by feet, might help. It might quiet the buzzing in my head like a persistent wasp wondering where to sting to inflict maximum pain. The loud blare of a car horn makes me jump and I look to my right, blinded by the glare of headlights and the downpour of fat, cold rain. I raise my hand in apology and, my eyes cast downwards once again, I hurry across the road feeling the driver's stare on my back.

This static-like energy pushes me on. I can feel it surge through my blood, my muscles, my bones. It's anxiety but it's also grief of what I have lost, because I can't help but fear I've lost the life I hoped would heal me. 'Don't catastrophise,' I whisper to myself, as I power on, head down, through the now dead quiet centre towards the Peace Bridge – a footbridge that wends its way across the River Foyle and joins the two sides of a still-divided Derry together.

I have my AirPods in my pocket so I pop them in my ears and try to concentrate on my audiobook but my brain is just too noisy and there isn't a chance it's going to let me take in a word the narrator speaks, so I stuff them back into my pocket and increase my walking pace. The clock on the Guildhall chimes once to tell me the time, its deep tones reverberating off the water of the river and the natural amphitheatre that rises from either side of it. The wind picks up and buffets my face as I walk over the bridge and while it's a solid construction, the little bit of sway that occurs when it's particularly windy or particularly busy, just adds to my sense of everything being off balance.

I'm not even thinking about where I'm walking; I just keep going, my head down, playing over every conversation I've had with Sorcha and Carla and Joan in my head. The smiles, the warmth, the warnings... I knew I should've been more careful with them all. I've done what I always do and rushed in head and heart first. I made myself noticeable. I stood out as the stupid woman who stabbed herself in the eye with her mascara wand. Who needed someone to hold her hand when she walked into the sea. Who *is* a fucking try-hard who went OTT with her sea swimming get-up and her hot chocolates for two. Who threw up at fucking book club and staggered around the place like I was off my head on drugs and then who didn't just go home on her own, in a taxi and go to bed. No, she was so desperate for friends she took a lift from someone and let them into her flat and into her space and into her head.

I realise what I should've realised long ago – and what the universe has been trying to tell me over and over and over again since the start of the summer. There's no way this was ever going to work, and I've just landed myself in an even bigger mess than I ever thought possible.

Sorcha might be coping beautifully with her marriage break-up – but her life was and is nothing like mine. She had people who would protect her – who weren't just friends, but who were loyal fans and no doubt they'd been able to sniff out that there was something not right about me from the start.

I thought I'd been careful. But of course I'd fucked up because that's what I do. That's been my signature move my entire life.

The muscles in my calves are burning as I walk faster and faster, pushing against the breeze and the rain that has now started to fall. My Uggs are damp. They aren't meant for heavy rain. Soon, no doubt, my socks and feet will be soaked through as well but I'm at least two miles from home now. I've no choice but to walk on, before realising where my feet have taken me. They could only ever really take me here, I think as I look down from the peak of the hill I stand on now, to the valley of the river – its blackness carving its way through the city save for the lights on the Foyle Bridge.

I'm back to where I was last night. At Sorcha's house. I don't really remember walking off the main Limavady Road towards her house, but that is where I am – on the outside of her beautifully lit garden with its dancing leaves and the gently tinkling wind-chimes on the oak tree.

I'm divided from her, and her perfect world, by a natural stone wall topped with silver railings. A solid sliding gate, of oak and steel, is closed. I didn't even notice last night that she had electric gates. They must've been left open to allow us all to arrive.

There's a keypad. A call button. For a moment I think about pressing it, but obviously I must have some sense of self-preservation after all. I look up at the house, and it's in darkness save for the floodlit exterior.

My breath catches and a feeling I can only describe as a punch to my stomach bends me double. A noise – somewhere between a moan and a cry – escapes my lips.

I had not been expecting to see Ronan's car parked alongside Sorcha's.

26

There's no good reason why Ronan's car should be outside his former home at this time of night. That the house is in darkness, and its residents most likely asleep, would suggest he's staying overnight. This is not just a case of him dropping the girls off or picking them up to go somewhere. Not at night. In a storm. He couldn't be there with Sorcha, could he? No, that would make no sense. Hadn't she spoken about how they were over and done with when I was in her car on the way to the beach? Someone would've noticed before now and social media would be ablaze with talk of any reunion. I'd have seen something – unless that something was in the Soul Sisterhood group, or on their WhatsApp chat.

Hands shaking, I pull my phone from my pocket and unlock the rain-splattered screen. Maybe I'm not blocked. Maybe it was a temporary glitch, I kid myself as my trembling fingers stab at the screen, hoping things are different to how I left them. Please. If there's a harmless explanation for all this then believe me I am open to it. I am here and listening.

But of course nothing has changed. I've still been booted from the WhatsApp chat. The Facebook group is still missing –

although now I've come to suspect that it's only missing to people who have been banned from it. And I still don't have anyone I can call or any way to deal with this tsunami of anxiety that is clawing at me. Okay, so it shouldn't matter if Ronan is back in his own home with his wife and children. It's not like there was ever a chance he would come back to me. That particular bridge went up in flames a long time ago and I know, or at least I think, there is nothing on this earth that would make him welcome back under my roof again. But this still hurts like an absolute bastard.

Shoving my phone deep into my pocket, I look up at the house again, searching the dark windows for any sign of movement, which I know is ridiculous. Anyone with a sensible head on their shoulders is long since asleep. Even the traffic on the roads has slowed to just the occasional car every few minutes – their headlights dazzling my eyes through the prisms of rain now pelting down without mercy.

I need to go home, I realise, and though my feet are indeed now saturated and squelch uncomfortably with each step, they are the only things that will get me back to my safe space. Instead of continuing on the loop of my walk, back to the city side over the Foyle Bridge and along the other side of the river, I turn and retrace my steps, speeding up when a car slows down to a crawl beside me. When it continues to travel alongside me, my heart thuds and I resist the urge to break into a run. I dare not even glance over towards it. I don't want them to know I'm rattled. I hear the mechanic whirr of their window being lowered, and I half expect to hear the same, gruff voice that I heard down the phone speak to me. 'Are you okay, love?' a female voice asks. 'It's a bad night to be walking.'

Joan's words come back to me again. 'We're watching you.' Are they watching me now? I raise my hand in a wave without so much as looking towards the car. 'I'm fine. Thank you,' I say in a shaky voice.

There's a pause but the car crawls on, matching my speed. I want to scream at them to leave me alone.

'It's a bad idea for a woman to be out walking on her own at night. Anything could happen,' the woman says, and my throat constricts. Is that a threat?

'I'm fine. Thank you,' I say louder and sharper this time, fear increasing my volume, grateful to have reached the pedestrian turn off to Ebrington. The car can't follow me there. I only breathe a sigh of relief when I hear it speed up.

Ebrington Square, so often alive with concerts and other events, is now empty and silent – and as I walk back over the Peace Bridge towards home I'm thankful not to come across anyone else. My heartbeat only rises again when I'm back walking along the quay, beside the traffic, nervous that the same car will find me.

I know it sounds irrational, and overly dramatic – but that's me all over, so Ronan would say. A drama queen. One who loves to make mountains out of molehills. Who takes life too seriously. And maybe he's right. But I'm also someone who used to believe that people were ultimately good and decent until she met someone who proved to her that not only was that absolutely not the case, but she wasn't even good and decent herself.

By the time I get home I am so soaked through I feel as if I've started to disintegrate under the sheer volume of water running down my skin. Robotically, I peel my wet clothes off but let them fall where I stand. My skin is icy cold, so pale I can see the blue of my veins tracing their way under my skin. I am frozen but there is no dopamine hit from the cold with this. There is no release of endorphins or feeling of achievement for having braved the cold water. There's just me, and my disappointing, flabby body standing in my own bathroom and trying to find the impetus to switch the shower on and stand under it.

* * *

When the alarm on my phone sounds, I swear. I've had four hours' sleep. I'm expected in the office in just over two hours, which gives me less time than I'd like to give the figures I worked on last night a once-over. Part of me – a big part of me – is past caring if they are right or wrong, but I must have a sliver of self-preservation still somewhere in my soul, because I force myself get up anyway.

My muscles are aching, no doubt a result of the long walk in the wee hours and the battering they took from the bitter cold rain. Not even a warm shower when I got home was enough to ward off the aches of muscles that really need to be exercised more frequently than they currently are. But at least warming myself up meant I didn't have to fight a fierce case of hypothermia on top of everything else.

Of course, I committed the cardinal sin of going to sleep with my hair wet but thankfully my hair is neither long nor thick and usually has a kind of unkempt, intentionally messy vibe to it anyway. Its straggly appearance this morning doesn't look too far from the norm.

I push down all the negative thoughts of last night, closing my eyes each time a memory comes at me as if that will stop the intrusive thoughts in their tracks. The blaze of shame on my face when I realised I'd been kicked out of the group. The walking for miles in the rain and finding myself outside Sorcha's house. I didn't intend to walk there... did I? And Ronan's car... And mystery phone calls and Joan's warning that first day on the beach, and then the blare of the car horn, all reminding me how useless I am. They all come at me again and again, as does the driver's warning last night. 'Anything could happen.'

I put the radio on, loudly, hoping that will distract me as I slip into a long black knitted dress, and my knee-high boots. I create the illusion of a shapely waist with the help of a wide belt and a deep inhalation. I apply Clarins Beauty Flash Balm liberally to try and hide the train wreck my tired face has become.

Then it's time for a spray of perfume and slick of lip balm. Glancing in the mirror, I see the approximation of a well put together professional woman, as long as you don't look too closely and see the cracks under the surface, that is.

I'll review my figures when I get to the office – it might look good for me to be seen in work early. But if I'm going anywhere early, I'll need more than one coffee to jolt me into full consciousness. Without thinking, I down one lukewarm cup before making up another in my travel mug.

My phone has been ominously silent since I got up. The screen hasn't lit up with any notifications. There has been no warming feeling that comes with being part of something good and dynamic and positive any more. I know it was only a short time, but the Sisterhood had made me feel less alone.

And now it's back to how it was until I was stupid or brave enough – or maybe both – to think it could be any different. I should've left well enough alone instead of getting too close to Sorcha. I'd been drawn in like a moth to a flame and, predictably, I've had my wings singed.

I force myself to take a long breath in, to hold it for three, and then release it slowly. I'm not religious, but I recite the Serenity Prayer in my head, encouraging myself to accept what was not in my power to change.

All I can do now is focus on work, especially if I want to keep my job. And I do want to keep my job – but more than that, I *need* to keep my job.

* * *

The thing I love about numbers is that they make sense. There is a right answer and a wrong answer. It's black and white. There is no fuzzy grey area open to interpretation. Things cost what they cost. Everything is openly transactional in my working world. There is no reading between the lines. There are just cold, hard numbers.

In theory, anyone should be able to throw a few numbers together but it's more than that. It's like a puzzle sometimes and it's my job to find the quickest, easiest way to put a project's costings together – preferably in a way that benefits both our clients and our own profit margins.

I get that most people don't understand how numbers can be exciting to me, and that's okay. I don't need people to understand. I just need to be able to sit at my desk and do my work. Most of the time I only need to communicate with the higher-ups through email and the occasional phone call. On increasingly rare occasions I attend meetings but most of my interactions with my colleagues are quick hellos as we pass in the corridor, or bump into each other at the coffee machine. It's not unusual for me to spend a day in the office and speak only a handful of words to anyone.

With the mood I'm in today that will suit me just fine. That said, I know Sean wants to see me today face to face so I can chat him through my figures. Obviously, he is more senior than I am and has been in this game long enough to know his way around a spreadsheet. That makes me uneasy. It always feels as if he's trying to catch me out, or maybe that says more about my own sense of self-worth.

My desk in the office feels alien to me these days, I think, as I take a seat and switch the computer on. Ever since I started working more from home, this space doesn't feel quite like mine in the same way it used to. I've arrived some days to find evidence that someone else has been using it in my absence. Maybe there's some scribbled-on sheets of paper, or my chair is set lower than I usually have it. On one occasion there was a half-drunk coffee cup growing a new form of life waiting for me. On another, a teenager on work experience had very helpfully left me a notepad covered in love notes to Harry Styles, doodles and the occasional depiction of a cock and balls.

These little invasions of my personal space, even without the depiction of genitals, make me feel uncomfortable at the best of times and today is not the best of times – so it's no wonder I tense when I spot an orange sticky note in the middle of my screen.

Come see me as soon as you get in!

I know immediately who it's from. He doesn't have to sign it. I'd recognise Ronan Hannon's handwriting anywhere.

27

I stare at the note, and at the familiar curl and swoop of Ronan's handwriting and my insides immediately turn to ice. I have not seen Ronan in person since the day he walked out of my flat two years ago. We have, on occasions, exchanged strictly work-related emails but that has been the sum total of our contact. In every other regard it has been as if he simply disappeared off the face of the earth. There have been no WhatsApp messages or voice notes. No occasional FaceTime chats in the wee small hours.

There have been no more incidents of 'accidentally' bumping into each other in the staff kitchen, or of him arriving at work at the same time as me just so we could sneak a couple of minutes together on the walk through the car park and into the office building. He always held the door open for me and I know that's not the biggest gesture in the world, but for me it meant something. It made me feel as if I was being cared for – which is ironic given how it ended.

I sit down before my legs give out from under me. I do not want to see Ronan. Not here. Not anywhere if I'm being honest, but especially not here and not today. The timing can't be by chance. The world doesn't work that way.

I can't help but worry that it might be something to do with the picture.

My mind has already played out the scenario in my head that Carla rushed with the news to Sorcha – and she in turn demanded Ronan come over and explain himself. That that's the reason he was at her house last night, in the small hours and in the darkness. Maybe they had talked, and cried, and he had confessed how everything had gone so wrong for him and they ended up making love on her perfect kitchen island.

The thought of them curled up together in the darkness after, his hand draped on her hip, his chest against her back, the way it used to rest against mine, as they sleep, makes me want to cry.

My heart is beating so fast it feels like it is vibrating – there's no way to get out of this though. Shit! Running from this will only make me look more guilty, not to mention it will likely lose me my job. I can feel a cool sweat break out at the back of my neck and I curse myself for wearing a knitted dress, which will no doubt start to itch like the bejaysus soon. Even though I can't see it, I can already imagine a red mottled rash appearing on my neck and décolletage as my nervous sweat mixes with the scratchy wool fibres. Grabbing a tissue, I dab the back of my neck, my nose and forehead, all to try and hide the sheen my nerves have laid bare across my face. This could be nothing, I assure myself. This *could* be just work-related. Surely Ronan wouldn't want to risk causing any kind of a scene here or doing anything that could in any way tarnish his Mister Nice Guy persona.

And yet, when the phone on my desk rings, it startles me so much that I swear loudly, and hope that no one has heard me.

'Good morning,' I say as I answer the call with shaking hands.

'Did you get my note?' It's Ronan's voice. Just the sound of it sends me back in time to when I craved hearing it. But this is very different. His tone is cold. There's no hello. No 'Hi'. No 'How are you?' Just that one question.

'Ronan,' I reply and wait for him to speak again.

'Did you get my note?' he repeats.

'Yes,' I tell him. 'I've just arrived in. I'll be up in a moment.'

'Good,' he says and hangs up.

I walk on shaking legs to his office, every cell in my body screaming at me to stop or turn back. Although I hate myself for it, I can't help but wonder what I will look like to him. Will I look a mess? Sucking my tummy in and pushing my shoulders back even though I crave making myself as small as possible, I stand outside his office door and will myself to just knock and get it over and done with.

A cough sounds from behind the door – the sound of him clearing his throat. Bracing myself for whatever he will accuse me of, I knock gently before turning the handle and opening the door to walk into a room where I will be alone with the man who destroyed me, for the first time in almost two years.

'You wanted me to come and see you?' I say, forcing my voice to be steady and strong. I don't want him to know how rattled I am. Carefully I plot each step, aware that I'm feeling increasingly light-headed, no doubt down to my inability to keep my breathing as slow as I should.

He doesn't even look up. He keeps his eyes on his computer screen while he tells me to 'take a seat'. Like a good little employee, I do what I am told and wait for him to turn his attention to me. But he keeps his focus on his screen and starts to type. He's enjoying having this power over me.

When I open my mouth to ask what he wants, he silences me before I have even uttered my first word. A raised hand – universal sign language for stop – is waved in front of my face before he resumes his typing.

It may only be a minute or two that passes, but it feels like much longer and with every second I feel my muscles tense more.

Eventually, he stops typing and turns his head to look at me. Try as I might to harness all the rage and hurt he has made me feel, I can't help but feel a surge of pointless hope at his eyes on mine. I hope for some warmth, maybe, but there's none.

He looks tired. Older. He needs a shave, I note, but he's not scruffy as such. The scent of his favourite cologne hangs in the air, and something deep inside me contracts with the memories it brings. Heat rises on my face.

'Right,' he says and I think this is it. He'll tell me he knows. But he doesn't. Instead, he says, 'Sean won't be in today. He's not well. I know he wanted to talk over the latest projections with you, but you're going to have to run through them with me instead.'

'Oh... okay,' I say, relief flooding through me that it's only work he wants to discuss. 'I'll have to email them across to you but if I just nip back to my desk, I can do that now.' I bite down the annoyance that he didn't just put this info into an email in the first place, or ask me to send the figures over when he left the note. It would have saved me the minor heart attack over why I was being summonsed to see him.

'That would be helpful,' he says. 'Send them over and give me a half hour to look over them before you come back. Grab yourself a coffee or something. It's the day for it.'

'You tired?' I ask, and it's out before I can stop myself. I don't want to slip into ordinary chit-chat but a combination of nerves at being in the same space as this man, and the muscle memory of the easy, comfortable way we used to chat with each other has just taken over. I tell myself it's not because I can't get the image of his car parked outside their house out of my mind.

He drops his gaze to the table. 'As it happens, yes. Sorcha's not well. I was up half the night helping out with the girls.'

'Is she okay?' I blurt and he looks up, his expression unreadable. I'm not sure of the etiquette when it comes to asking about an ex-lover's ex-wife – especially when I might be part of the reason for their marriage break-up in the first instance.

'Well no, she's not okay. I've just told you, she's sick.' His voice is terse. My body remembers that about him too, and I tense. He pinches the bridge of his nose and lets out a long sigh as if he has the weight of the world on his shoulders and it is he, and not Sorcha, who is unwell.

'She's in hospital as it happens. Severe dehydration. She fell very ill during the night before last. Ivy found her passed out in the bathroom and couldn't wake her.'

There's a shake to his voice, but I can barely breathe. I want to jump in with a hundred questions. Had she been vomiting too? Surely, if she was severely dehydrated that's more than a slight possibility. My immediate urge, which I have to swallow, is to say: 'I wonder if it's the same thing I had.' But saying that would be admitting that I'd been in her – their – house, and that I've made friends with his wife. From what I can tell here and now, he doesn't seem to know that.

'That must have been terrifying for Ivy,' I manage to say.

'She was smart enough to call an ambulance,' he replies. 'Then she called me. Esme was awake by then so Ivy had to keep her calm.' When he looks at me there is a hint of softness in his eyes – a hint of the man I had thought he was.

'Ronan, maybe it's you who should be off today. It sounds like you have more than enough on your plate,' I say.

He shakes his head, switching immediately back into business mode. 'Not at all. My mother is with the girls. Sorcha's mum will be staying with her once they let her out of hospital. I'm just the ex-

husband,' he says, his voice dripping with bitterness as he looks
me directly in the eye. There it is, I think. The man he really is.
'Now, can you go and get me those figures?'

I stand up. 'I'll do that now,' I tell him, eager to get out of the
room and away from him so I can properly process what he has
just told me. But I can't resist asking him something first. 'Do they
know what caused it?'

He blinks at me as if he can't work out what I'm talking about.
It takes a moment for him to connect my question with Sorcha,
and not with work.

Shaking his head, he rubs the bridge of his nose again. 'Not for
sure,' he says, as if he's annoyed that I've asked the question. 'But
it's possible, they think, that she may have taken some sort of
illegal substance, though she says she hasn't and never would.
Unless one of her so-called new "friends" did it. It leaves me
wondering what kind of company she's keeping.' He sniffs. Part of
me wants to tell him it was a book club meeting and hardly Sodom
and Gomorrah, but was there some sneaky drug taking going on? I
really can't see Sorcha being the type, especially not with the girls
in the house. Could someone really have slipped her something
without her knowing? Does that mean someone could have
slipped me something too?

I think of the phone calls I'd received. No, there haven't been
any more since my return to the Sisterhood but that doesn't mean
there isn't still someone out there with a grudge.

I have the urge to say something – to ask for more information,
but anything I say could only incriminate me. Would it give him
some sense of satisfaction to be able to paint me as a stalker? He
does like lying about the women in his life, after all. I'm not
stalking him. I'm not even stalking Sorcha. I've just been trying to
build a life for myself that is more than what he left me with.

I manage to mutter, 'That's awful. Oh my God, I'm so sorry,' before I leave his office and hurry back to my desk to email my work across to him. I'm not surprised to find my hands are shaking as I try and type his email address into my computer. Would anyone really drug Sorcha? And if so, why? Isn't she universally adored? I wonder if anyone else has been sick, or are Sorcha and I the only two 'victims'? Could it have been the same person behind the anonymous phone calls? Or whoever it was that has blocked and deleted me from any Sisterhood chat?

Once I have attached my work to an email and sent it to Ronan, I open up a private web browser and started searching for information on spiking drinks. I know it happens, of course. Even if I'm beyond the age of going out and being in any danger of anyone targeting me, or so I'd thought. But this was a group of women, at a book club meeting. It was probably just something off in the mini quiches, or a bottle of Prosecco that had soured and our palates weren't refined enough to detect it. I very much doubt that would be the case for Sorcha though. She has the look of someone who knows their way around a bottle of fizz.

Should I see it as a good thing – in a sick kind of way – that Sorcha was targeted too? That means it couldn't have been personal. Not when the Queen Bee was targeted as well. Nothing about this makes sense to me.

before I leave his office and hurry back to my desk to email my

28

For the remainder of my day in the office, I keep my head down and do my work. When Ronan asks, I run through my figures with him in a manner that is strictly professional, and I'm grateful he doesn't find fault in them.

When his phone rings and he answers with: 'Sorcha, are they letting you home?' I don't give in to my temptation to stay and listen, but instead stand up and leave, giving a small wave to indicate I'm done speaking with him and I'm giving him his privacy.

When I'm back at my desk I send a message to Carla – the one person to contact me since the book club incident. I'm hoping this means she, at least, is still speaking to me and she might be able to give me more information about why I appear to have been booted from the Sisterhood groups.

The best course of action, I decide, is to play it completely dumb.

Hey Carla, hope all is well. Strange thing – the Sisterhood group seems to have disappeared from Facebook and someone seems to have bumped me out of the group chat??? Have you any idea what's going on? Xxx

The three kisses are very deliberate, as are the three question marks. Keep it friendly. Make it sound as if there is no other possible explanation for this than some sort of glitch in the matrix. I press send and hope for a swift response, but I suppose I'm not overly surprised when none comes. I tell myself she must be at work, and it probably isn't the case that I'm on her shit-list too. Surely if I was, she wouldn't have got in touch yesterday.

At least, I think, as I tidy up at the end of the day and prepare to go home, the powers of online communication mean I can tell she hasn't blocked me, that she has indeed received my message and she just hasn't read it yet. If she's on a day shift, I suppose it's possible she hasn't had time to give her phone any attention.

I scan Instagram to see if the other women I friended in the group have been active, or if they have blocked me too. Everything seems to be as normal, if a little quiet. There is no mention of a hospital stay on Sorcha's page, which strikes me as a little odd. I think I expected to see a video of her looking pale and wan and milking the drama for all it's worth – which is probably a little unkind of me, but putting her life on social media for the world to see is her job. It wouldn't be surprising to see her share even the less glam side of life.

I start typing a message asking how she is, when I remember that I'm not supposed to know she's been sick and I only do because Ronan told me. Maybe it's her I should be asking about the disappearing Facebook group and unceremonious booting out of the group chat? I decide to wait until seven, and if Carla hasn't responded, I will do just that.

It's cold when I get home, much colder than it has been, and I
don't think it's just down to another drop in temperature. This feels
different. As soon as I open the door into my flat I feel it. It's the
kind of cold that quickly gets into your very bones. There's a fierce
draught blowing through the place but I know I didn't open any
windows this morning. And I distinctly remember setting the
heating to come on an hour before I was due home. I've been
dreaming of walking into my cosy little sanctuary and making
something comforting and carb-heavy for dinner.

But I know I'm not imagining the cold, or the draught. The
scent of autumn – of fresh air, and rainy nights, the vague hint of
smoking chimneys – hangs in the air. I shiver, knowing it's not only
the unusual cold that is setting my senses on high alert. The
energy here feels different. I flick on the lights in the hall and walk
towards the door of my open-plan living room and kitchen. As
soon as I open it, the noise of the traffic on the street outside fills
my ears. Even in the darkness I can see that all the windows are
open – as far as they can go. They're sash windows, not the kind
that could blow open if I'd been careless enough not to fasten
them properly. This requires effort. Strength. I know my door was
closed and locked when I arrived home so this can't be a break-in,
but I don't understand what it actually could be.

I flick the switch on the overhead lights and see that the open
windows are the least of my problems. The room is in disarray.
Sofa cushions are upturned, boxes of work-related paperwork
poured onto the floor. The kitchen cupboard doors hang open,
packets of sugar and pasta having vomited their contents onto the
work surfaces and floor. Tears prick at my eyes and I feel my breath
come in shaky gasps. Although I don't want to, I force myself to
walk through to my bedroom, knowing before I see it that this
room will have been ransacked too.

The curtains are billowing in the wind, drenched from the rain that has blown through the open windows. All my drawers are turned out onto the floor – a mess of clothes trampled on and twisted. My bedding has been hauled off the bed and discarded on the floor; my mattress hangs half on and half off the bed. My night-stand is lying on its side, spilling its contents all over the floor. It looks as if someone has rifled through them, looking for money perhaps? Cards, letters and photos have been torn to pieces. That's when I feel bile rise in my throat. Please, not that. Don't let them have torn apart what little I had left to remind me it had been real – that he had been real.

Without thinking I find myself on my knees scrabbling through the detritus that has scattered across the floor. I just want to see that stupid, blurry image. They could have torn apart or stolen almost everything else in this flat but please don't let them take that away from me. Thick, warm tears land on my hands as I scoop notebooks and envelopes together and flick through pages, hoping to find it undamaged.

I want to cry and scream, but I can't so much as speak as I try to take in the devastation all around me. When I finally put my hand to the picture, my heart almost implodes with relief and a loud sob escapes my lips. Thank God, they didn't tear this to pieces. I will never let it out of my sight again. Some memories are much too precious.

My relief is, however, short-lived as the reality of what I still have to face sinks in. All those hours I spent cleaning. All those days and weeks and months I spent making this place feel like a safe space. Someone has been in here. Someone has gained access, in some way I can't understand. Did they have a key?

Why would anyone do this? Do I phone the police? Do I tidy up? I want to tidy up. I want to pull the windows closed but what if there are fingerprints on the window frames and I disturb them? But it's so cold. I wander in a daze through to the second bedroom, where I so painstakingly organised the shoeboxes and rails of clothes I've yet to wear to find everything scattered, among torn boxes and discarded hangers. The bathroom is no better, with every shampoo and gel, every bottle of conditioner and expensive body lotion emptied in the bath and toilet and all over the floor. I don't even know where to start.

An ordinary person would pick up the phone and reach out to a partner, or a friend or a family member. They'd be assured that whoever they spoke to would be right round with a shoulder to cry on and the promise of a cup of sweet tea. I could call Shaunagh, but I can already hear the disappointment and exasperation in her voice. The air of 'what now, Tina?' that exists between us. She doesn't mean anything by it, but she's tired and the baby is often crying, and she doesn't have time for my drama. I'm not sure this counts as emergency enough to call Una – who would probably ignore my call anyway given that I've been ghosting her these last two months. I don't have anyone else I can count on – at least not anyone who wouldn't ask awkward questions, which I am not prepared to answer, and not able to answer without admitting the worst of my secrets.

I'm still shaking and shivering as I walk back into the living room, right a sofa cushion and sit down. The noise of the wind and rain blowing in through the window seems deafening but it's nothing compared with the sound of my own heart thudding and my blood surging through my veins. My face blazes red with shame, and my skin prickles with fear. Just how much am I expected to take?

I look around my flat again, trying to work out what might have been taken but nothing jumps out at me as missing. My TV is still where it always is. My laptop is still at my desk. I go to my bedroom again to see that my jewellery, for all that it is worth, is still there. My expensive hair straighteners haven't been touched and I know they'd be worth a few quid on the black market – enough to fund a quick fix for the enterprising thief anyway.

Even my new Nike trainers, still in the box, are more or less where I left them. Scattered on the floor now, of course, but still there. Whoever was here didn't come to steal. I can't imagine they were here to look for anything either. Apart from Ronan Hannon, there are no skeletons in my closet and there is little to no evidence of him in mine.

Whoever was here came to send me a message, to scare me. While I know I should call the police, I'm not sure it would help. What effort will they put into a case where there is no sign of forced entry, and where all that is left is a mess? And when they ask me if anyone might have it in for me in any way, what could I tell them that would be of any use? That I slept with my senior at work? That my friends on Facebook don't want me to be part of their gang any more? That I'd had a couple of phone calls telling me I'm a bitch who no one likes? Did I really think a group of women who love to hold coffee mornings, and swim in the sea and hold book club meetings are responsible for trashing my apartment? I can only imagine the laughter that would cause down at the station.

The urge to laugh washes over me. Hysteria, no doubt. Because I have clearly fucked up on a monumental level and have made things worse, more awkward and more painful than they were before. Typical Tina – a specialist in ballsing up her life. I've put myself in the firing line once again. As the cool folk on Twitter – or whatever it's supposed to be called these days, would say, I've fucked around and found out.

The noise of the wind and rain, and the traffic outside, becomes too loud and too overwhelming and, knowing I'm not going to humiliate myself by calling the police, I close the windows – slamming them shut one by one until the noise dies down and all I can hear is the slow drip-dripping of what is left of the contents of a bottle of shampoo into the bath, its swirling pearlescence mixing with the vivid green of Radox bubble bath and a mountain of decanted bath salts that I've had for years and never used.

I should start tidying up straight away but where do you start when everything is upside down? An image of my mother imitating Maria in *The Sound of Music* arrives unbidden in my mind, urging me to start at the beginning because it's a good place to start.

I nod and brush the tears from my eyes, the scratchy wool fibres of my dress scouring my cheeks. I'll get changed, I think, and hunt through the discarded clothes from my chest of drawers on the floor until I find a pair of tracksuit bottoms and a T-shirt. I will wash the rest of my clothes, although it will take forever, because the thought of someone having had their hands all over them makes me feel sick to my stomach. I want to wash everything. My skin crawls when I think of someone so completely immersed in my room, in my bed, in my bath. I want to run but I won't.

Mostly because I have nowhere to go.

I put a wash in the machine before starting to put things right in my living area. It will be a late night, I reflect, as I fill a basin with hot water and probably too much disinfectant, but I want every trace and every skin cell of this person gone.

I can feel the need to take action grow in me, as if my body can't stand to stay still for a moment longer. It needs to move. I need to disperse the adrenaline, so I grab a cloth and plunge my hand into the too hot water, not even registering the pain at first but persisting anyway, and I start to scrub every surface.

I am damp with sweat and tears when my phone rings. I figure it must be Carla finally getting in touch, but it's not. The name flashing on my screen is Sorcha's.

29

'Hello?' My voice is thin and reedy as I answer the phone. I'd watched it ring a few times before I picked it up, unsure if I would even lift it. Today has been trying enough and the thought of having someone else give it to me all guns blazing is almost more than I can bear. But that's the key word in that sentence, isn't it? 'Almost'.

'Christina!' Sorcha exclaims and I try to gauge her mood from that one word. 'I've been dying to talk to you. Actually, for a while I thought I was actually dying...' She laughs – it's a brief, brittle sound. 'The thing is, I've been really unwell. Like, in hospital unwell.'

'Oh my goodness,' I say, forcing fake surprise into my voice. 'Are you okay? What happened?'

'Well, here's the thing,' she begins. 'I think it was the same as what you had. At my house?' I don't know why it's a question. It's not like I've had multiple episodes of being sick as a dog and hardly able to stand on my own two feet.

'Really? Seriously?' I ask, surveying the mountain of work I still need to get through in this flat to make it look habitable again. 'But you said you were in hospital?'

'Yes. I got home this afternoon. I was very dehydrated and couldn't keep anything down. Poor Ivy found me out of it on the bathroom floor and had to call an ambulance.' Sorcha's voice is far from her usual confident self. She speaks quietly but the emotion is heavy in her voice all the same. It's the same fear I recognise from my own voice.

'Oh God, I'm so sorry. That must've been awful for you all,' I say.

There's a sniff. 'Yes. Yes, it was. I couldn't keep my eyes open – I felt like I was in another world. Does that sound like how you felt?'

I nod even though she can't see me. 'Yes,' I say after a beat. 'Although obviously I didn't have to go to hospital. I think I slept it off, mostly. It must've been a bug or something. Was anyone else sick?' I ask, knowing of course what Ronan has already told me.

There's a pause again before Sorcha answers. 'No. Everyone else was fine. As far as I know. But look, this is really embarrassing and I don't even know how to say this but...'

I'm listening as my eyes focus on a now empty bottle of Prosecco on the floor, its contents spilled across the carpet and saturating it and some scatter cushions I've yet to pick up. Ronan bought that bottle. In happier times, of course.

'The hospital can't be sure, but they said there's a possibility that maybe my drink had been spiked and...'

I know I should react immediately and with shock so I force myself to gasp, feeling like the hammiest actor in the world. 'Oh my God, Sorcha! Who would do that? Surely not!'

'Well, that's what I told them,' she says. 'I said it was just me and the girls from the Sisterhood talking about books and I don't think anyone from that group would have any reason to spike my drink, or yours for that matter.'

My skin prickles.

'So can they not do a blood test, or a urine test or something like that?' I ask although I already know the answer.

'They've ordered blood tests but said some of those types of drugs don't stay in your system long enough to get a reliable result so I might never really know,' she says. 'Look, Christina, I don't know what's going on. It seems insane to even suggest someone would spike a drink at a book club but on the off chance the hospital are right, I'm so sorry you got caught up in whatever madness is going on. I can't wrap my head around it.'

I look at my messy flat, think of the phantom calls, the times I think I might have been followed, my own illness and I realise she doesn't know the half of it.

'I'm sure they were wrong and it was just a bug,' I tell her. 'But, look, this is a little awkward, but I noticed the Sisterhood group has disappeared from Facebook and someone has removed me from the group chat, and I just wondered...'

I'm nervous saying those words, aware I sound needy and desperate but also aware that if there is any chance at all that Sorcha knows about Ronan and me, this is her chance to challenge me.

'What?' she gasps. 'Someone removed you from the group? Who? Let me know and I'll sort it out.'

'I don't know who. It was just a phone number,' I say. 'There was no name attached to it.'

'Send it to me. I'll look into this. It might be tomorrow, because I'm wiped, but I *will* get to the bottom of this. Jesus, Christina. I'm sorry. God knows what you think of us! Getting sick at our book club, this mad talk of drink spiking and now someone booting you from the group!'

'And the group page disappearing from Facebook?' I add.

'Shit,' she says. 'Of course you won't have seen the message in the chat. I temporarily deactivated the page after the doctors told me they suspected my drink had been spiked. I took the fear of God and panicked. I did send a message out… and I posted on my page. Oh, Christina, what must you think of me? Of us? I'm so sorry. It was a total knee-jerk reaction on my part. But the more I've thought of it, the more I want to get my head straight and find out what really happened before I reactivate it. I'm just feeling a bit vulnerable right now. God, this is a mess.'

I almost laugh and bite down the urge to tell her I could show her what a real mess was if she wants to call over to where I'm currently sitting. 'I think you've had more than enough on your plate,' I say instead. 'Maybe we should just write it off as one of those weeks? You know, the absolute bastard kind?'

There's her laugh again, but this time it sounds more genuine than before. Maybe I'm imagining it but I think I'm starting to relax. The tension in my muscles is certainly easing a little now that I know I haven't been unceremoniously banned from the Facebook group. I have not been booted from the WhatsApp group at Sorcha's behest. And most of all, it's really quite clear that she hasn't fallen out with me and nor is she currently making an effigy of me to burn.

'I think I'd like that,' she says. 'I could definitely do with getting down to the water and clearing my head with a swim, but I still feel a little wobbly. I'm not sure I could face it. Or face everyone asking questions.'

It's unusual to hear Sorcha sound anything but confident and it throws me a little. 'People will understand,' I tell her. 'If you don't go, or if you tell them you feel overwhelmed. They'll support you.'

'People will gossip,' she says. 'We might be the "Be kind" generation but in my experience that kindness never extends too far. Especially not if there is some juicy gossip involved. The rumour mill will already be in overdrive at my deactivating the group. I can't wait to hear what the gossips are saying about me being in hospital.'

'They might not know,' I offer, and Sorcha scoffs.

'Of course they'll know, Christina. There is nothing that happens in this city that doesn't start people sharing any one of five different version of events within minutes.' I wonder just how true that is. Are there five versions of what happened between Ronan and me currently doing the rounds? Or maybe more?

There's a pause on the other end of the line, followed by a sigh. 'I suppose I'll maybe look at it tomorrow,' she says. 'Tonight I'm exhausted, and I need to reassure Esme and Ivy that their mum is okay and not about to croak it in the night.' I can hear the weariness in her voice. I feel for her, just as I feel the tiredness that seems to have seeped into every bone in my body as I look around the mess I have yet to tidy up.

'How about I come over tomorrow?' I find myself saying, even while everything in my brain is screaming at me to stop and to disengage from Sorcha and everything to do with her before this goes any further and either of us end up more fucked up than we already are. 'We can compare our symptoms, or even just chat if you want. You won't have to explain anything to me. I understand exactly what you've been through these past few days. I mean, I know I'm not anyone important...'

'Stop that now!' Sorcha says. 'Of course you're someone important. And I really appreciate your offer. That would be lovely, actually. I think I could do with some company. My mother is here now, but she's champing at the bit to get back to her own house. And the girls are great, of course, but there's only so much Squishmallow talk or Olivia Rodrigo music a person can take. And, you know, it would just be nice to have someone to talk to – but only if you really don't mind and you really don't have anything else you should be doing.'

'Have we not established that I very rarely have things I should be doing?' I say with a laugh that feels as hollow as it sounds. 'It's a Saturday, which is a work-free day, so honestly, I can come round. How about at two? Would that work for you?'

I want her to say yes but despite all she has just told me, it's hard for me to believe she will. I wait for the inevitable excuse. When it comes to the nitty-gritty – and to actually making plans – they always back out.

'Two is perfect,' she says. 'And I'll make us some lunch, if I haven't put you off eating or drinking anything in my house ever again.'

I can't help but smile. 'I think I'll chance it,' I tell her. 'But don't go to any trouble.'

'It's no trouble at all,' she says, before we say our goodbyes and she ends the call.

30

SORCHA

Christina sounded a little shaken and unsure of herself, I think, pulling the duvet up over my lap and sinking into the softness of my mattress. I suppose she has a lot on her mind. It's been quite the eventful week for her. She was probably settling back into her comfort zone after the end-of-summer-bash furore, and now things are taking a more sinister turn again.

When she had been sick on Wednesday night I assumed she might just have had too much to drink. Maybe a little pre-gaming before she had come over. She has never quite lost that slightly nervous vibe about her. I'd assumed she was just trying to steady her nerves and it badly backfired. It was only when I started feeling ill myself later that I even considered something else was at play. I'd never have guessed at our drinks being spiked though. That part doesn't make sense to me.

'Mummy! Can I sleep in beside you tonight? I'm scared!' Esme breathlessly asks as she appears at my door in my pyjamas and slippers, clutching her favourite teddy bear. My youngest child is the queen of the petted lip and puppy dog eyes. It's impossible to resist her on a good day, let alone when we are both feeling emotionally and physically vulnerable.

'Of course, darling,' I tell her, patting the bed beside me to signal she is more than welcome to run over and jump up for a snuggle. She has barely left my side since I got home from hospital.

'Is Daddy coming back tonight too?' Esme asks, blinking up at me with her pale blue eyes wide and her expression earnest.

'No, sweetheart. Daddy was just here while I was in hospital. He's gone home to his own house again now.'

She looks at me and I can almost see the cogs whirring in her head as she plans her next sentence. 'Will you go to hospital again or be here with me and Ivy every night-time now?'

'I'll be home, angel,' I tell her and kiss the top of her head. She nods and smiles and my heart fills with love for her.

'Good,' she says. 'Because Daddy bes grumpy sometimes.' I don't correct her wrong choice of word. I just give a little nod and keep my mouth shut. It will do no good for me to quip that I'm not surprised to hear that, or that Daddy 'bes' grumpy with me a lot too.

'I'm going to do my very best not to get sick again so I never have to leave you,' I say.

'Daddy is not grumpy,' a voice from the hall chimes and in walks my eldest child – who just so happens to be Ronan Hannon's number-one fan. If you looked up *Daddy's Girl* in the dictionary there would be a photo of Ivy Hannon, probably with her dad who is also, she tells me, her BFF. 'He's just working hard, and he was worried about Mummy.'

There's a defiance in our twelve-year-old, but also a sadness. Not seeing her beloved daddy every day is hard on her.

I gesture for her to come and join us in my bed and she doesn't argue. She walks straight over and jumps in beside me so I now have both my girls with me. I already know that means I'll sleep better tonight than last night. Then again, a night in a hospital ward, hooked up to a beeping drip was never going to be particularly restful in the first place.

'You know your daddy loves you very much, don't you?' I ask and both girls nod – with Ivy nodding a little more enthusiastically than her sister. 'And he'd never do anything to hurt you?' They nod again and I kiss both their heads. Ivy pulls away a little before deciding I must have earned her affection after all and cuddling back into me. 'But we don't all live together any more, and he has his own house, and his own life that he needs to get back to. He'll see you both next week and you know you can always FaceTime him whenever you want.'

''Cept not at night-time cos he might be out on a smoochy date or something,' Esme says with a smile before her eyes widen and her hand flies to her mouth. Ivy sits forward and glares at her.

'Sorry, Mummy, I wasn't s'pposed to say that,' she says, her bottom lip trembling properly now.

'It's okay,' I assure her. 'Daddy's allowed to go on smoochy dates,' I say even though I feel a part of my heart crack just a little. I shouldn't care. It's been two years and he was hardly faithful before then, but still the thought of him being 'smoochy' with someone else has the power to make me sad.

At one time I believed him when he said he'd never hurt me. I believed him because he showed me, time and time again, that it was true. Ronan Hannon was, for a time, the perfect man. At least, he was the perfect man for me. He was, and still is, handsome and sexy and able to charm the birds from the trees. But he was so much more when we first met. He was kind, and loving and he showered me with affection – the like of which I'd never experienced before. Flowers, self-penned poems that were awful but showed he'd made an effort, chocolates, dinners together, strolls along the beach. I felt like I was living in a Mills & Boon novel. He made it impossible for me not to fall in love with him and he told me, constantly, that he was in love with me too. That I was beautiful and smart, and together we'd have the kind of happy ever after most people only dreamed of.

I was young and naive, and I believed him. So, I married him and within a year I was pregnant with Ivy. Still then he never let me down. He was the perfect doting father.

I'm not sure when it started to change, but it did. Maybe I was too caught up in being a mother to notice him pulling away at first. Ivy demanded almost all of my attention and in a way, despite his incredible love for her, he resented that I put his daughter above him in my list of priorities. Ivy was just three when he cheated for the first time. Or at least that was the first time I found out about it. We went to marriage counselling, cried thick, hot tears and talked until it felt like we made sense again. For a while, at least.

The wheels came off again when I was pregnant with Esme. We'd had a tough time conceiving and I'd had two miscarriages. I was not going to take any chances and I thought Ronan would understand that. The Ronan I first fell in love with would've wrapped me up in cotton wool and cared for me like I was the most precious thing in the world to him.

The Ronan I lived with later seemed to check out of what was left of our marriage. And he sought his comfort elsewhere, including, I remember with a start, with the woman I just invited over for lunch tomorrow.

31

CHRISTINA

I've jammed a chair under my front door just in case the unknown intruder comes back. I can't help but wonder again if I should've called the police but if I had I imagine I'd just be sitting here, waiting for the scenes of crime officers to leave fingerprint powder everywhere, while a po-faced overtired and overworked police officer tells me they'll do their best but the chances of catching anyone are slim and I should console myself with the thought that nothing appears to be missing.

I imagine the same po-faced officer looking at me with a mixture of pity and curiosity, wondering if I've been desperate enough to wilfully waste his time. 'And you really haven't given anyone else a key to this place? Because there are definitely no signs of a forced entry. Are you sure you closed your door properly this morning?'

I'm pretty sure I did. It's an old wooden door and needs a good pull to slam it shut. I do that every morning. But when I think about it in great detail, I start to doubt myself. I suppose it was possible I was distracted by my own exhaustion after only half a night of sleep and the drama of seeing Ronan's car outside his house. That might have been enough to give some opportunistic messer the chance to rifle through my things only to decide there was nothing among them that they considered worth stealing. It's possible someone left the door to the apartment block ajar and someone wandered in. It has happened before.

I should ask my neighbours if they saw anything or let anyone unusual into the building, but they'd only start asking their own questions and I don't want to pore over the details of my life with anyone else.

I rack my brains, trying to think of any possible way in which someone might have a key to my flat. Would the management committee have a spare I don't know about? They're only responsible for communal areas as I'm an owner-occupier. They'd have no right and no need to gain access to my home. Not that there would be any logical explanation for them wrecking it either.

There were no cleaners with keys. Shaunagh had one when she still lived here, but I'm pretty sure she returned it before she moved. The only other person who'd ever had access to a key was Ronan, but hadn't I been working in the office alongside him all day? He'd hardly nipped out for a quick half hour to wreck the place while I thought he was in the loo. It wasn't a solid lead for the police to go on, so all things considered I'm pretty sure I made the right decision to not call the police and instead use my energy putting things right. I can hear the washing machine spinning as I climb into my bed, which I've made up with fresh sheets and blankets from the back of the cupboard, which seems to have been left untouched. I am desperate for sleep. God knows my body is tired enough for it. I just hope my brain is ready to switch off all the non-stop internal chatter.

I push away everything negative and focus on what I know for sure. I know that tomorrow I'm going to spend time with a new friend. I know that feelings are not the same thing as facts, and I know my fears are not my realities. I don't have to give anyone the power to upset me or control me. Una would be proud of me for thinking this way.

To my surprise I manage to sleep well and when I wake in the morning there is both a message from Carla waiting for me on my phone and an invite link to rejoin the WhatsApp group chat. I opt to read Carla's message first off, which is full of apologies for not coming back to me sooner but explaining her work had been busier than ever and her shifts had left her so exhausted all she had the energy to do between them was sleep. *I haven't had time to bless myself*, she wrote, before explaining what Sorcha has already told me about the Facebook page being deactivated. She says there was lots of 'weird activity' on the group and they'd had a few trolls join et cetera et cetera...

And, of course, she asks how I am and says she can't believe Sorcha was so ill as well.

She wrote:

> I know there's a rumour about drinks being spiked but honestly, I think that's some overzealous junior doctor on a mission. There's a lot of spiking happening in the bars at the moment – never heard of it in a book club before! *laughing-face emoji*. If you want my official nurse's opinion it was some 24-hour gastrointestinal bug. They are spreading like wildfire at the moment. We've had so many staff call in sick, V unpleasant! But I know that's not as headline grabbing as spiking drinks.

A gastro bug is certainly a plausible explanation, and certainly more savoury than thinking there is someone out there wilfully causing harm to me and Sorcha. But don't such bugs usually spread like wildfire? As much as I'd prefer that to be the explanation, it doesn't ring entirely true.

Looking around my trashed flat and thinking of how much work I still have to do to pull it all back together, I don't think I should completely rule out the possibility that someone does have it in for me. But it's good to just keep it in mind rather than focus on it as the only possible explanation. Every new piece of info that suggests this can only be unrelated and coincidental is a good thing, I think.

I reply with a smiling-face emoji, telling Carla I hope she's right about the gastro bug before thanking her once again for taking care of me on Wednesday night.

She replies:

> No problem! And please don't forget to rejoin the group chat. Although with the Facebook page down, it's busier than ever. I haven't been able to keep up with it at all.

Carla ends her messages by saying she hopes she will see me during the week, maybe down at one of the swims.

With a renewed spring in my step, I get up and start again on putting my flat back in order. Despite the fact it will cost me a fortune, I also arrange for a locksmith to call out and change the locks. If there is an extra key to this place knocking about out there somewhere, I'll make sure it's no longer usable. I also order one of those security camera doorbells for directly outside my flat so at least I know that if I get any more surprise visitors I'll be able to see them arrive, and keep the evidence.

32

At two in the afternoon, I have pulled up to Sorcha's gate and pressed the buzzer to alert her to the fact I've arrived. Beside me, on my passenger seat, are a bunch of flowers I bought in M&S along with two giant chocolate chip cookies for the girls. Although I've no real reason to suspect Ronan to be there, I still find myself breathing a ginormous sigh of relief to see that there is no sign of his car in the drive. I'd have simply had to turn around, go home, and make some excuse for my absence had it been any different. There is no way I want to bring that particular shit-show down on my head by having all of us in the one room together.

Sorcha's voice over the speaker jolts me from my thoughts and she tells me to come on up to the house, as the large gate starts to slide open. The house is no less impressive in the daytime, and I can see that the front entrance has been decorated for autumn, with a selection of pumpkins, mini scarecrows and a door wreath decorated with leaves in every shade of orange, red and yellow. It's exceptionally tasteful – and perfectly Sorcha. Even when she's recovering from a hospital stay she can still whip together some new touches to her home to make for perfect Insta-worthy content.

I'm just taking in the small pumpkin-shaped LED lights wrapped around the potted bay tree on her porch when the front door springs open and a little girl, with an angelic smile, peeps her head out. I instantly recognise her as Esme and my heart contracts. She is a perfect combination of all the best bits of her parents. She has Sorcha's pale skin and bone structure and her daddy's wide, stormy blue eyes and dark hair with just a hint of a curl. It's clipped back from her face with sparkly rainbow-patterned clips, which match the bright colours of her knitted dress and leggings. Seeing her in person, I am flooded by a wave of emotions. She truly is a beautiful child, more beautiful than her pictures could ever portray. More beautiful than I remember.

'Hello!' she says with not a hint of shyness. 'My mummy said I could come and get you and bring you to her in the kitchen. Are those flowers for my mummy? She loves flowers, 'specially roses and lilies.' Esme reaches out to me and I half expect her to take the flowers from my hand to inspect them for her mother, but she doesn't – she takes my hand instead and for a moment I can hardly breathe. The feeling of her small hand in mine, and the trust she must have to let me wrap my fingers around her own – it's enough to threaten to crack something open inside of me. This is all I ever wanted. This is what I should have.

'It's this way,' Esme says as she starts to walk, pulling me after her down the hall and past the gallery of pictures I had stared at while the room was spinning around me and I was trying not to be violently ill for the umpteenth time on Wednesday night.

Esme glances back and sees me look up at the wall so she comes to an immediate and abrupt stop before smiling broadly and pointing with her free hand. 'That is my mummy, my daddy, my Ivy and me,' she says proudly and the way she has referred to her bigger sister as 'my Ivy' does nothing to quiet the storm of emotions raging through me.

'I have a little something for you and Ivy,' I crouch a little and tell her, and she rewards me with an unexpectedly solemn expression.

'That's very kind, thank you very much,' she says, in a sing-song voice that shows these words have clearly been learned by rote and rehearsed often. This kid is everything and I want to tell her just how very precious she is, but I don't. I don't want to be the weird lady. 'My mummy says it's bad manners to ask about presents or prizes but I can't wait to find out what you got us.'

'It's just a little treat – one I really loved when I was a little girl,' I say, hoping I don't have her hopes too high. I hope she isn't one of those kids who will respond with instant dissatisfaction to find out it's only a couple of cookies.

'I like all treats,' she says earnestly, before she drops her voice to a stage whisper. 'I think we should hurry in to my mummy before she wonders if we got lost,' she says with such a serious expression that I feel my heart swell even further. Will I ever have an Esme of my own to love and share secrets with? Who I can buy rainbow clips for, and brightly coloured leggings and whose hair I can brush until it shines.

'I think we better had,' I whisper back as we reach the end of the hall and she leads me back into the gorgeous open-plan kitchen and living area, where Sorcha is sitting on a stool at her kitchen island, cradling a coffee mug and dressed in soft cream joggers, a matching hoodie and what look like brand-new Ugg boots. She's wearing just a hint of make-up – or at least it looks like just a hint of make-up. It may well be layers upon layers of a no make-up, make-up look. Her lips are slicked with gloss, her cheekbones brushed with a little highlighter. She has her hair tied up in a perfectly groomed ponytail. There are no flyaway hairs, or rogue greys. In fact, she looks as if she could be on the front cover of a lifestyle magazine. She'd be perfect in an 'At Home with Influencer

Sorcha Hannon' feature, with her French manicure and her deli-
cate gold jewellery. I feel dumpy and frumpy in comparison, even
though I'm wearing my nicest (read most expensive) mom jeans
and a classic Breton long-sleeved T-shirt. I can only imagine how
flyaway my hair is right now.

'Excuse the state of me,' Sorcha says, with a serious expression
that matches Esme's perfectly. Of course there is no 'state' of her –
she looks serene and beautiful. 'I still haven't come back round to
myself since the other night. I probably shouldn't be drinking
coffee but I swear if I don't get some caffeine into my system I won't
be responsible for my own actions,' she adds.

'Mummy, your friend brought you some flowers and a
surprise for me and my Ivy!' Esme says enthusiastically, letting go
of my hand and looking up at me, her eyes wide with
expectation.

'Can you give those to your mummy from me?' I say, handing
her the flowers and she nods, clearly delighted to have been given
such an important task.

'Christina, you didn't need to go to any trouble,' Sorcha says, as
she hops off her stool, takes the flowers from Esme and sniffs them.
'They smell gorgeous, and thank you so much but there was no
need.'

'I know there was no need, but I wanted to get them all the
same,' I say. 'After all, if anyone knows what you've been through
this week, it's me! Sort of.'

Sorcha gives my hand a little squeeze and if I'm not mistaken,
she looks a little overwhelmed with emotion. 'I'm so sorry about
all of this,' she says. 'For you getting sick here, and the mix-ups
with the group and all. We are usually so much more organised.'

I want to give her a hug. I want to reassure her that it's all okay.
That I am a friend and there is nothing to apologise for with me.
But I'm aware of an increasingly impatient Esme looking at us

both, doing her very best not to snatch the paper bag she must now see from my hand.

'Honestly,' I say. 'There's no need for apologies. I, erm, brought these cookies for the girls if you're okay with them having them?'

Sorcha smiles and Esme practically fizzes with excitement. 'I love cookies!' she says.

'She does indeed,' Sorcha says. 'And Ivy does too. Why don't you call your sister, and you two can take some milk and these lovely cookies to the playroom to enjoy? As long as you remember not to make—'

'—a mess!' Esme sing-songs and nods. 'I really promise, Mummy!' With that she is running from the room and I hear her sweet little voice transform into a loud holler as she calls her sister.

I can't help but laugh. 'She's a dote, Sorcha,' I say. 'You are so very lucky.'

'I really am,' she says. 'Those girls are my life, you know. Even when they're being madams. Everything I do is for them.'

She stares at the doorway for a moment, and then with a jolt she turns and walks to the sink. 'I'd better get these beautiful flowers in some water,' she says, reaching into one of her kitchen cupboards and pulling out a vase. 'And then I'll get you a coffee, or a tea? Or a cold drink? A glass of wine even?' she asks. 'I've made a quiche for lunch, if that's okay. It will be ready in about twenty minutes. So what can I get you to drink?'

'A glass of water would be perfect,' I say.

'Still or sparkling?' she asks and I tell her that ordinary tap water will suit me just fine. Of course she tuts and takes a glass from a cupboard and fills it with water from the built-in filter at the front of her fridge, before dropping in a few ice cubes. 'Slice of lemon?' she asks, as she opens her perfectly curated fridge and I see she, of course, has a Mason jar filled with ready-prepared lemon slices on her top shelf. Her fridge is an influencer's wet dream of jars and labelled glass storage boxes. Each is filled with a rainbow of colour and a full selection of fresh produce and healthy snacks. There's nothing on show that would cure a hangover or sate a PMS-induced craving for salt and sugar.

'No thank you,' I tell her. I'm not a fan of lemon slices in water. *There's no need for all that vegetation,* my granda used to say. I smile at the memory of him.

Sorcha must have clocked that I've been ogling her fridge, as she grins as she hands me my glass. 'Don't believe everything you see,' she says, with a nod behind her. 'Remember I told you, it's all smoke and mirrors. There's a fridge in the garage filled to bursting with Diet Coke for me, and Fruit Shoots for the girls. Not to mention their favourite yoghurts, a couple of multipacks of Dairylea Dunkers and enough chocolate and wine for a damn good night in. Insta would not approve.'

'Do you not get fed up with wondering what Insta will approve of?' I blurt. 'You live your life so everyone can see it – and look, these last few days is proof enough being an online influencer isn't all it's cracked up to be. If you did have your drink spiked, in your own home, by one of your followers? Doesn't that just prove it's not worth it? I mean, I admire your confidence. I love that you are so open, but do you ever worry about putting so much of yourself out there? And having so many followers hanging on your every word?'

She takes another sip from her coffee cup. 'I don't consider the people who come to book club to be my followers. I'm not Jesus Christ,' she says with a short, sharp laugh. 'I don't need or want disciples. I didn't set out for this to become what it has. I was just an ordinary mum talking to the world about the highs and lows of being a woman in this day and age and if people relate to that and it makes them feel less alone then that's not a bad thing.'

'Of course not,' I stammer. 'I'm not suggesting it is. I'm just wondering how you keep your sanity amid it all. You deactivated the page – so I know it must get to you sometimes.'

Sorcha bristles and I wonder if she's annoyed that I'm delving into her more vulnerable side, but surely I'm not the only person to ask her these questions.

'As I said, I'm not Jesus. I'm not a saint or even close to it. Of course there are days I wonder if I'm doing it for the right reasons, or if it is worth the hassle. Especially when Ronan moved out. That was brutal. But I don't think I'd have gotten through it if it wasn't for the support of my online community and especially from the women who are in the Sisterhood. They held me up when I could barely stand on my own two feet. I'd never consider those women *just* followers. They're my friends.'

It makes for quite an impassioned speech – and something about it, be it her tone or the clipped way in which she speaks, makes me think this is not the first time she has said these exact words. They sound over-rehearsed, delivered in the same voice she uses when she is making content for her channels.

'So do you really think any of them would spike your drink, or mine for that matter?' I ask.

She shrugs. 'I'm really not sure but I'm sure the doctor must've had his reasons for saying it. Still, I'd prefer to think they had it all wrong. That maybe they just saw the symptoms, a woman with a public profile and came up with a mad explanation. It must've made for some juicy gossip in A&E. I'm just so sorry you were caught up in it – whatever the explanation.'

I shake my head. 'No need to apologise. It's hardly your fault.'

Sorcha shrugs. 'Oh, I meant to ask you something. I'm going to record a video about keeping your drinks safe when you're out and about. The doctors thought I'd be the perfect person to get the message out there and I wondered if maybe you would join me in it? I've an idea to approach this company who sell little covers to slip over the top of your glass to stop people dropping anything dodgy in it. We'll be running into the Christmas party season soon and... well, it might be an idea to strike while the iron is hot. I know we don't know if it actually happened to us, but just in case?'

My throat tightens. There is no way I'm going to record a video with Sorcha. I'd be asking for trouble. Ronan would lose his shit – spectacularly – and if Sorcha finds out who I really am, she will more than likely lose hers too.

I'm trying to find the words to turn down her invitation when Esme runs back into the room, her taller but equally beautiful sister sloping behind her with her nose stuck in her phone. She looks up briefly to take me in. Ivy definitely has more of her father's looks about her than her sister – I'd recognise that slightly disapproving stare anywhere. Her brow creases in exactly the same way Ronan's does as she looks from me to her mum and back again. It's more than a little disconcerting just how alike they are in both their appearance and I guess their temperament too. Ivy Hannon may only be twelve years old but her body language screams of the attitude of a spoiled twenty-year-old princess who has never been told no at any time in her life.

I take in her skinny blue jeans and her crop top, which shows off a strip of pale skin around her middle. She has AirPods in her ears and is clutching her phone as if she would die if she was parted from it. I notice her nails are painted a very pale blue – which matches the colour of her eyes perfectly. I wonder if she painted them herself or if they are the product of an appointment with a manicurist. I imagine they are the latter. I can see that even at twelve her hair has been professionally highlighted – this is one high-maintenance young lady.

'Can I have a Coke, Mother?' she asks in the pseudo-American accent all teenagers seem to have these days thanks to TikTok and YouTube and whatever other apps the younger generation use.

Sorcha rolls her eyes. 'No, Ivy. You can have a glass of milk, or water if that doesn't suit. As well you know.'

'Milk is for babies.' She sniffs, throwing her mother a withering glance. There's the slightest hint of a foot stomp.

'Milk is good for your teeth and your bones, because of the cal-see-mum,' Esme mispronounces, which only serves to enrage Ivy.

'It's cal-see-um,' her sister says slowly, her voice dripping with disdain. 'God, Esme, you're such a suck-up,' she says, before filling her glass with sparkling water, taking out not one but two lemon slices and dropping them into the glass and stomping out of the room.

'Don't take that upstairs!' Sorcha calls. 'Go to the playroom! There's no food allowed in your bedrooms!'

There's an inaudible muttering of complaint before I hear a door slam. Sorcha looks at me, a faint blush on her cheeks. 'She's almost thirteen. I think it's fair to say the hormones have well and truly kicked in. Plus, she's always been a daddy's girl, and that is even more the case now. She didn't take well to the break-up. Of course, she sees the whole messy affair as entirely my fault. I'm the wicked witch of the west for asking him to leave.'

'That must be hard,' I say, aware that my own cheeks are flushed thanks to the talk of messy affairs. This is not a comfortable topic of conversation.

'You've no idea.' Sorcha sighs, and places her coffee cup down on the granite-topped kitchen island. 'I don't want to speak ill of him in front of them. He's still their dad after all. I don't want to be one of those women who poisons the children against their dad just because our relationship broke down.'

I just nod, not trusting myself to speak.

'But that said, the teenage attitude? I was not prepared for that,' she says. 'Not yet, anyway. Naively, I'd hoped I'd get another few months out of her being my sweet little girl before she turned into

the Antichrist in a training bra. I didn't hit puberty until closer to
fourteen. But children are growing up faster and faster these days.
Christina, if you ever have children of your own, enjoy every
second with them because one minute you have this tiny little
newborn in your arms and you're in a blind panic, scared you'll
break them – and the next they are screaming at you because you
won't let them get their belly button pierced for their thirteenth
birthday! I've lost count of how many times that one has told me
she hates me this week alone.'

She grimaces and then smiles and jumps up from the island to
put her coffee cup in the sink. 'You know,' she says, with her back
to me as she rinses the cup out, 'you're lucky to still have your
freedom and not have to deal with soon-to-be teenagers. Don't
have children, Christina. It's all a ploy to keep women in their
place. And teenagers are in on it, I swear. If our drinks were spiked,
it wouldn't surprise me if it was Ivy who did it.'

She laughs, but I don't. I don't feel lucky. I don't cherish my
'freedom'. The one thing I wanted more than anything in this
world – even more than I wanted Ronan – was a child of my own.
But he took that from me too.

33

Sorcha's words hit me like a punch to the gut. I've heard them, or a variation on them, many times before. 'At least you get to enjoy your weekends!', 'At least you get to holiday without a child begging you to play with them in the pool!', 'At least you don't have to try and manage a hangover and a toddler at the same time.'

I don't reply to her. There is no safe way to poke that particular bruise. Instead I change the subject.

'So, are you all set to relaunch the group Facebook page?' I ask, as she sets her upturned coffee cup on the drainer and takes a large glass bowl of prepared salad from the fridge.

'I am, because I think I probably should but at the same time it's a lot of work maintaining and moderating it. I know I've not been well these last few days but it's been quite lovely not having to worry about it,' she says and pops a cherry tomato in her mouth.

'Do none of the girls help out with it? Joan or Carla or any of them?' I ask.

Sorcha nods and raises her finger to gesture that she'll be able to talk in a moment once she has stopped eating. 'They offer,' she says, 'and I did let them for a bit, but I think I'm too much of a control freak. I like to keep an eye on what's happening. Especially as people associate the group so strongly with me. It's my reputation at the end of the day.'

'But you trust the girls, don't you?' I ask and Sorcha opens her mouth to answer but just as she does her Alexa announces that her timer is up.

'That'll be the quiche ready.' She smiles. 'Hang on.'

'What can I do to help?' I ask.

'Nothing! You're my guest, and remember – I'm a control freak! I have everything covered.' We're interrupted by the ringing of a doorbell, which I quickly realise is actually not a doorbell but someone buzzing at the gate. For the briefest of moments my heart quickens as I think it might be Ronan, but then Sorcha looks at her Alexa device and I see a pixelated image of a woman staring directly into the camera from behind the steering wheel of her car. 'That's strange,' she says, her Botoxed brow doing its best to crinkle. 'It's Joan. I wasn't expecting her.'

My heart sinks. Bloody Joan the bodyguard – she's the last person I want to see just now. I'm still tired and stressed from the break-in, and now I'm going to have to deal with Joan's judgey face too.

'Hang on, I'll let you in,' Sorcha says towards the camera before tapping the screen twice. The gate starts to open painfully slowly.

'I meant to leave that open earlier. It's more trouble than it's worth to open and close during the day, especially when we have visitors so often. I wonder what she wants,' Sorcha says and I smile what I know is a small, reed-thin smile. Had Joan known I was going to be here? Could she just not stay away in case I staked some claim on her precious bestie?

'God knows,' I say through gritted teeth.

There's a clatter of feet until a very excited Esme pops her head back around the door. 'Did I hear the buzzer? Will I go and open the door?' Esme says, breathless with excitement.

'Thank you, sweetheart,' Sorcha says. 'That would be really helpful. It's just Auntie Joan.'

'Auntie' Joan, I think, as something curdles in my stomach.

Esme nods and smiles. 'Okay, Mummy! You didn't tell me Auntie Joan was coming!' she says before taking off at speed again towards the front door. I can't help but smile.

'Now, that's a good thing about having children,' Sorcha says. 'If you're lucky, you get one like Esme who thinks it's the most exciting thing in the entire world to answer a door and escort visitors through to the kitchen. I think it might just be a ploy to get treats, but hey, it saves me doing it,' Sorcha says.

'She's a sweetheart,' I reply, knowing that I need to change this topic of conversation again because I really, really don't want to slide into another discussion about motherhood. 'Look, let me set the table or something? I feel useless sitting here with two arms the length of each other.'

Sorcha turns towards me, oven gloves on and freshly cooked quiche in hand. It smells amazing and I realise that I haven't eaten since yesterday before I uncovered the break-in. Nausea and shock had kept my hunger at bay, but the smell of Sorcha's cooking brings it back with a vengeance.

'I told you,' Sorcha says, 'I'm a control freak. I have it all in hand.'

'What's that?' I hear a voice from the hall, as Esme appears again, this time hand in hand with Joan. A pang of jealousy stabs at me as Esme beams up at her latest companion and Joan bends down to swoop Esme up in her arms. 'Did I hear you, Sorcha Hannon, say you're a control freak? Surely not!' Her tone is one of heavy sarcasm and both she and Sorcha laugh. This is clearly one of their in-jokes and it just reminds me I am on the outside.

Shifting uncomfortably in my seat, I plaster a smile on my face as they embrace and kiss each other on the cheek, Esme still hanging on to 'Auntie Joan' for dear life. 'I picked this up for you when I was in town,' Joan says, handing over a copy of the latest Marian Keyes book to Sorcha. 'You said you hadn't read it yet and I thought maybe you could treat yourself to a few hours in front of the fire with it later.'

Sorcha beams at her and tells her she is so thoughtful, while Joan encourages Esme to get down before she takes two more books from her bag. 'This one is for you,' she says to Esme, 'and this one is for Ivy.' Esme squeals with delight and runs from the room. Joan nods in my direction and mutters a quick hello.

'To what do we owe this pleasure?' Sorcha asks as she leafs through her new book.

'I had a feeling you'd be doing too much instead of recuperating from your stay in hospital so I thought I would arrive over with my best bossy voice and make sure you rest,' Joan says. 'I didn't realise you'd have company.' It's as if it takes all of her effort to cast a glance in my direction.

'Well, Christina here called over for a little chat since we were both afflicted on Wednesday night, and I figured the least I could do after poisoning her at book club was provide some lunch in return. There's plenty here, and you're welcome to join us,' Sorcha says and I will Joan to reveal she is snowed under with plans elsewhere.

Of course she isn't. 'That would be so lovely,' Joan says, 'as long as neither of you mind. And you shouldn't even joke about Wednesday being your fault! That's how rumours start.' She already has her coat half off and her eyes on the cupboards. Without waiting for any further response she gets to work setting the table. It's obvious she knows where everything is in this house and she doesn't pay any heed to Sorcha's protestations that she can do it herself. It makes me feel about two inches tall.

'You're just out of hospital,' Joan says. 'Let people help you out for a change.' I can't help but feel it's a dig at me, sitting and watching Sorcha get on with things, probably getting ready to spread some rumours. At least, that's how Joan seems to see it.

'Joan!' I force myself to say. 'It's lovely to see you. How are you?' In a bid to keep my voice light and friendly, I fear I've erred too far on the side of slightly manic and sound like I'm reciting my lines in the style of a pantomime dame. Of course, Joan doesn't let that pass, and gives me the oddest look, as if I've spoken to her in a different language altogether. It's not a long stare or a long pause but it's long enough to get under my skin.

'Christina,' she says, her voice of course at an appropriate volume and not insanely loud like mine was, 'I'm grand. Can't complain anyway. More to the point, how are you? Have you recovered from your ordeal? You mustn't allow yourself to be embarrassed by it. We just told the others you were feeling under the weather and went home.'

'Thanks,' I say. 'I'm good now. All better.'

She eyes me suspiciously and I can't help but feel unnerved by her. I break her gaze and ask Sorcha once again if she is sure I can't do anything to help.

'Sure Joan here has it all done.' Sorcha smiles. 'There's nothing for you to do but enjoy lunch!' I blush and shift uneasily on my stool. Joan beams as if the teacher has given her a gold star.

'How is poor Ivy doing?' Joan says, turning her attention back to Sorcha now that she has asserted herself as teacher's pet. Sorcha starts to tell her just how 'poor Ivy' has been and how 'poor Ivy' is proving to be a pain in the arse. Joan listens intently, throwing the occasional look and passive-aggressive remark my way. She says I was 'lucky' and 'poor Sorcha' was not – what with ending up in the hospital and all. As if it was my fault. Does she think I got sick on purpose? That I made Sorcha sick? She couldn't think *I* spiked the drinks, could she?

'Oh, by the way, I didn't know you lived so close to town, Christina,' I hear Joan say, pulling me from my mental gymnastics. How on earth does she know where I live? I've certainly never told her – then again, she had said I was being watched.

'Christina's flat is really lovely,' Sorcha adds. 'Very homely. Carla thought so too.'

So Carla has been talking about my flat to Sorcha. About bringing me home. I think of the picture on my nightstand again, the torn letters and notes on my floor... Both women talking about my home now, of all times. Are they trying to tell me something? There's no way either of them could have been involved in the break-in, is there? That's stupid. Sure Sorcha was just getting out of hospital, but if Joan had picked her up and maybe they'd had a key... No! No, I tell myself to stop being a paranoid eejit.

'So handy if you want to take a walk to the shops too,' Joan says. 'I imagine it takes just minutes to be in town?'

I nod, but don't speak. Instead I move from sitting at the island to the dining area where Joan sits directly opposite me, and Sorcha takes a seat at the top of the table.

'I was out in the car the other night, Thursday I think it was, and I swear I saw you powering out of your building and heading towards town at quite the speed. It was a stormy night too,' Joan says. 'I was going to stop and offer you a lift but you seemed like a woman on a mission. That's quite late to be heading out on a walk. You'd want to be careful as a woman out on your own.'

I think of the car that had slowed beside me. Surely that hadn't been Joan?

She spears a cherry tomato and a rocket leaf and looks me

directly in the eye, as if her words are a challenge. She wants me to explain myself. That much is clear.

'I'm not the best sleeper at times,' I say, my own throat dry and my hunger pangs having disappeared. 'So rather than get myself into a tizz about how much sleep I'll get before I have to start work, or drive myself mad pacing around the flat, I find some fresh air usually does the trick. A brisk walk burns off any unspent energy and the fresh air helps me calm enough to sleep.'

'Hmmm,' Joan says, 'I suppose that makes sense.'

It makes as much sense as Joan just happening to be outside my home that late at night, I think. The thought of her creeping around my apartment block, or Carla and Sorcha chatting about my 'homely' little flat, especially compared to this dream home makes me uneasy. I don't suppose I can just ask 'are you stalking me?' or 'were you in the car that followed me?' though. Not without kicking off World War Three.

I force a smile on my face. 'I find it's better to go walking at night. Less traffic means less noise and less pollution. What had you out so late yourself?'

'I was picking my son up from his work. Young people these days,' Joan says, rolling her eyes, 'they want lifted and laid everywhere and of course I'm a proper Derry mammy and have him spoiled. Are you a mum yourself, Christina?' And we're back here again. Why is it impossible for a group of women to get together without a conversation about children starting up?

'No,' I say and this time I don't elaborate. I don't care if it sounds rude because I can't help but feel that Joan is goading me. I'd ask her outright what she's playing at except Sorcha looks as though the conversation is starting to make her uncomfortable and the last thing I want to do is get on her wrong side. Especially not now.

'So,' she says, bright and breezy in the exact same voice she uses when she starts each one of her Instagram videos, 'who's going for a dip tomorrow? I wasn't going to but I feel the sea calling me...'

34

SORCHA

Joan doesn't even flinch when I give her a kick under the table. It's quite clear that Christina is feeling uncomfortable and while part of me thinks it's only what she deserves, another part thinks it's a little cruel.

I still feel delicate after Wednesday night, and I imagine Christina must feel the same. She looks tired and pale. She looks vulnerable and if the truth be told all the teasing makes me uneasy. As does Joan telling Christina she was picking her son up from work and just happened to be outside her apartment.

Joan's son is twenty-six and lives in Belfast. There's no way Joan was picking him up. It strikes me as odd that she would lie about it, so I make a mental note to ask her to explain that one when Christina isn't around. I'm sure she could've come up with something that I would believe too – perhaps she was testing me to see if I would call her out on it. Joan can be a funny creature at times. Fiercely loyal, occasionally possessive but I like to think she has a good heart underneath her bravado.

'I'm not sure I'm up for dipping tomorrow,' Christina says. 'I've had a crazy week at work, and then with being sick I fell behind on my workload and I need to catch up.'

'What is it you do again?' Joan asks, and I glare at her.

'I'm a freelance project manager,' Christina says without missing a beat. I'm impressed, or maybe a little intimidated, by how easy it is for her to lie. 'Basically, I organise things for people in exchange for money. It's satisfying in its own way,' she adds.

'If you say so,' Joan says with a grimace. 'I couldn't work freelance though. I need to have colleagues around me to keep me on track. I need a bit of social interaction. Does it not get very lonely working on your own? How do you make friends?'

Joan is making me angry now. This is not her battle to fight. It is not Joan who has been wronged. I know exactly what she's getting at and I don't think Christina is stupid enough not to pick up on it – if it keeps going the way it is.

'By joining the Soul Sisterhood, of course,' I say brightly. 'Isn't that right, Christina?'

Christina nods back at me. 'Absolutely.'

Poor Christina. She's so meek. It would all be easier if I hated her. But the truth is I just see her as a rather pathetic creature. When I first saw her, the thought that crossed my mind first of all was that it made no sense that Ronan had chosen her, when he had me at home. I'm not particularly vain, but I do know I'm an attractive woman. I've spent a lot of money to make sure I look after myself and present myself to the best of my ability. I don't apologise for that. Ronan had told me he loved my confidence and the way I carried myself.

Christina carries herself like a bag lady weighed down by secrets.

It's quite clear she overthinks every last word that comes out of her mouth and that anxiety is a constant companion. She's a needy kind of a person and Ronan Hannon does not do 'needy'. Yes, my ego was bruised when I saw this dowdy, slightly overweight woman my husband had been sleeping with. But then I came to realise she was *exactly* the kind of woman Ronan would have an affair with.

He might have said he loved my confidence, but the truth was he couldn't compete with that. He couldn't control me. And the more independent I became – the more successful I became – the less I needed him to build me up. My success challenged his sense of purpose and his sense of who he was. He's the kind of man who needs someone to feed his ego and be eternally grateful that he chose her. Someone like Christina – shy and unsure of herself – was the perfect victim.

So, I want to hate her. I want to hurt her. When I first sent her a message to come to the coffee morning, it was because I wanted to make her pay for what she had started because the first time she let my husband into her bed she set us on the path to divorce.

I wanted to call her out on being so arrogant that she'd thought she could just walk into the Soul Sisterhood when she had broken the ultimate sisterhood rule. Another woman's man is off limits. No ifs, ands or buts. I'd planned to stand up at that coffee morning and tell everyone exactly who she was and what she had done. If I'd had to wear my humiliation online to thousands of followers, then I wanted her to at least feel an ounce of that same shame in front of a room of women. It was the very least she deserved, Joan had told me when we talked it over.

But when I saw her, and saw how pathetic she really was, I'd told Joan I needed more time to think about how I wanted to deal with her.

'You're playing with fire,' Joan had said. 'Someone is going to get hurt and I worry it will be you.'

I'd promised her she was wrong. That it was Christina who would have to deal with the consequences of her actions – I just had to figure out the best way to do that and the first step of that plan was to keep her close by. Joan is determined not to let me forget that promise or to forget what Christina did.

35

CHRISTINA

When we have finished eating I find myself wishing I was back in my own space. Messy and all as it is, it would be more comfortable than being in Joan's company.

I know her type. She's the kind of woman who will eviscerate a person and shrug it off with a 'I'm just the kind of person who tells it like it is' excuse. Never mind Sorcha and her beauty, wit and kindness – it would have been Joan who would've been the most popular girl in school and it wouldn't have been because she was the nicest or most helpful. It was simply because she bloody well made sure everyone fell in line with her.

She is a master of saying just the right thing in just the right tone that it sounds like she's being perfectly reasonable when she is, in fact, being a bitch. She is impossible to trip up.

She has proven this afternoon that she isn't afraid to ask questions, and that she is willing to niggle and poke if the answers she gets aren't to her satisfaction. She'd have been right at home during the Spanish Inquisition trials.

I feel sick at the thought of her being 'accidentally' outside my apartment so late at night. Was she telling me that for a reason?

Was she trying to make sure I know she knows where I live? Was she trying to give me a clue about the identity of the person who broke into my flat?

I decide the best way to deal with Joan is to say as little as possible. So, I sit with my head down and my mouth shut as a couple of hours pass and daylight starts to fade away to darkness.

I haven't wanted to appear rude, but once five o'clock rolls around I think about making my excuses.

'I think I should be heading on,' I say, getting up and grabbing my coat from where it has been hanging on the back of one of the stools at the kitchen island. I put it on and swing my bag across my body.

'Are you really sure you have to go?' Sorcha says, but I sense she's just being polite. I've been here for long enough and it's clear she prefers Joan's company.

'I've things to do at home. Just boring old housework but there's no one to do it but me so I might as well just suck it up,' I say with a smile just as I notice Esme, her head through the door and looking at us. She's wearing pale pink fairy wings and sparkly deely boppers on her head. She smiles that same beautiful smile when I look at her. I pull a silly face and she giggles – a gorgeous angelic laugh that makes my heart full.

'Ah, there she is, the little butterfly herself,' Joan says, her voice warm and friendly.

Esme smiles at her but doesn't hurtle in through the door.

'Why don't you come in, pet?' Sorcha says. 'We're nearly done here anyway. Christina is just getting ready to go home.'

With a mournful expression on her face, Esme says, 'No thank you – I don't want to come in. I just wanted to know if Christina would like to see my room?'

'Oh I don't think that would...' I start. Of course, I'd love to go and see Esme's room. Whatever conversation we'd have there would be a hundred times more interesting than Joan's take on the world, but I really don't think it would be appropriate. 'I was just leaving though, sweetheart, so maybe another time.'

Esme sighs in a deep and exaggerated fashion. She's a perfect little drama queen and I already love her for it. 'I tidied my room and everything,' she says. 'Cos I wanted to show you my babies.'

'Wow, you've a fan there.' Sorcha grins. 'It's rare a person gets an invite to meet the precious babies. But God, please don't think you have to humour her. If you have to get on then it's fine, isn't it, Esme?'

Before I can so much as think of a reply, Esme is already pleading with me. 'Please, Christina! It's my favourite thing to show my friends my babies. Just one wee minute!'

My friends. The words soothe me. But is this crossing too far into a territory where I am tying myself up with this family? It was different when it was just Sorcha, but Esme... I already know my battered heart won't survive if I get too close just to lose her.

'I'm sure you wouldn't want to disappoint the child,' Joan says and the feeling that she is goading me once more kicks in, even though there is no way she could possibly know what I've been through.

'Of course not,' I say with a smile. 'Okay, Esme,' I say. 'But it will have to be quick. I really do have to get home and do all my own cleaning and tidying. I bet your room is tidier than mine!' I glance at Joan's reaction, wondering if there will be any tell in her expression about just how messy she knows my flat to be. She's giving nothing away.

Esme is standing with her little hand outstretched towards me again. The pull of feeling it in mine is just too strong to ignore so of course I reach out and take it. 'Lead the way, Princess Esme!' I say brightly.

'I'm a fairy princess actually,' she says, a trace of her older sister's spark about her.

'Well, of course you are. Only fairy princesses have beautiful sparkly wings!'

'And sparkly antennae,' she says. 'I learned that word in my books,' she says as she leads me back up the hall and towards the stairs.

'My mummy and daddy have the biggest bedroom,' she begins then pauses. 'Well, that's not right. My mummy has the biggest bedroom cos she has so many shoes and dresses. Daddy has a bedroom in a different house now and Ivy and me go and stay there sometimes. We have to share a bedroom there and let me tell you, Ivy does not like that. She says she shouldn't have to share with a baby, but I'm not a baby. I'm five, and nearly six. That's definitely a big girl and not a baby. Mummy and Daddy say so. We have bunk beds though and she gets the top bunk, which I don't think is very fair.' The innocence with which she brushes over her parents' break-up and moves on to the important issue of bunk beds sends a shockwave of guilt through me. I wonder, does she harbour hopes of them getting back together? Or does she know this break-up is forever? She was only three when they split. Does she even remember life when Ronan was still here?

'That is the bathroom,' Esme announces as we pass another oak door and then she stops outside the next door, on which a sheet of paper is sellotaped. Esme has clearly made her own sign and just like everything else about her, it is a delight.

Esme's Room, it reads in pink and purple marker. The words are surrounded by glitter, stickers and a large felt flower. 'This is my room,' she says, absolutely vibrating with pride. 'I made that sign myself.'

'No way!' I answer, my eyes wide. 'That's so good! Did you really make it?'

Her smile grows even wider as she lets go of my hand to reach for the door handle. 'I did. My teacher says I'm very good at art but Ivy sometimes says I'm rubbage.' She rolls her eyes dramatically, which just adds to the adorable quality of her mispronunciation, and a part of me feels sorry for Ivy. It's quite clear that Esme doesn't kowtow to her attempts to be the smart-arsed big sister.

'You are definitely not rubbish,' I say. 'I'd love a sign like that for my room.'

She smiles brightly. 'I can make one for you or show you how to make one yourself. It's not too tricky. Just take your time and don't rush,' she says solemnly. 'My crayons and markers are in the playroom cos Mummy says no arts and crafts in our bedrooms.' Looking around I can see why Sorcha would want to keep anything likely to make a mess out of the room. This is a beautiful space. Stunning in fact, but surely choosing a cream carpet for a child's bedroom wasn't the wisest of ideas. This could be in a show house. It's as if every item has been curated specifically to create a dream house feel. A trio of rattan boxes sit on top of a white chest of drawers, little chalkboards hanging by delicate pink ribbon on the front of them – their contents divulged in Sorcha's perfect handwriting. 'Bobbles & Clips' one says, 'Tights & Socks' says the next and finally 'Necklaces & Bangles'. Of course there is a child-sized dressing table, complete with butterfly string lights hanging around it, a glittery-handled hairbrush and a couple of bottles of child-friendly perfume, as well as a few glittery lip balms. The room looks so well styled it's hard to imagine any five-year-old actually plays and sleeps in here. Maybe the playroom is a bomb-site, I think – but then again any time Sorcha has shown it on her Insta feed it has been immaculate.

Looking at Esme as she reaches across her bed to lift one of her dolls, and turns to look at me again, her face a perfect picture of innocence, it crosses my mind that she herself looks as if she has been picked from a catalogue and placed into this perfectly curated life.

I wonder if Sorcha truly knows how lucky she is, with her beautiful daughter in her exquisitely styled room in this dream home. I wonder does she ever stop and truly think about how she has what so many people want but will never, ever have? And yes, I know she'd say it's smoke and mirrors and there is always more to a story than what you see at first glance but I'm here in her actual reality and I'm not seeing any evidence of smoke, and all the mirrors are well lit and sparkling clean.

The reality, I think, as Esme beckons me to come and sit beside her on her crisp white bedsheets, is that Sorcha has a great life and I feel that pang again. It's the one I've been doing my best to push down because I like Sorcha, I really do. I want to be her friend. I want to be a part of this wonderful group she has created. But there's an ugly bitterness in me that is fighting to get out, because this is not fair.

'This is Molly,' Esme says as she climbs onto the bed, the mattress barely dipping as she straightens herself. She's cradling a beautiful baby doll with rosebud lips and a button nose who is dressed in a pink onesie. There is a faint smell of baby powder in the air, the kind toymakers have learned to infuse into the doll to no doubt trigger some sort of hormonal response from cash-rich ovulating women who then buy them for their daughters. Molly is so lifelike she almost takes my breath away. Each crinkle in her tiny, balled fists, the way her rounded cheeks are flushed. This is not just any doll. I know what I'm looking at. Molly is one of those reborn dolls I've read so much about. She looks so realistic that when I reach out my hand and gently stroke her chin, a flutter of disappointment makes itself known in the very pit of my stomach to feel cold plastic beneath my finger as opposed to velvet-soft baby skin.

'She's very pretty,' I manage to croak, my mind drifting to another time.

'She's my very favourite of all my babies,' Esme says, and strokes her doll's cheek, mimicking what I have just done, before gently rocking Molly as if she were the most precious gift in the world. This little girl has so much love to give. 'Do you have any babies?' Esme asks, her pale blue eyes staring directly at me, and my breath catches in my throat.

'No, sweetheart. I don't,' I say, my voice barely more than a whisper. She tilts her head just a little to the side and looks up at me from under her beautiful long lashes. I shouldn't have come here. The inescapable truth is that when I look at Esme all I can think of is the child who should be here now. My baby who I never got to dress in a onesie, or rock to sleep. My baby whose hand I never got to hold. Who I never got to design an impractical but beautiful nursery for with cream carpet and labelled storage boxes. My baby who should be a chatting, laughing, playing almost two-year-old now. Who would probably look up at me with eyes as perfectly blue as Esme's – after all, that baby would've been her half-brother or sister.

36

Esme holds my gaze and I wonder, does she remember? She would've been too young, of course, to really register the first time I met her. It was almost three years ago and it was such a fleeting moment.

I had not long found out I was pregnant – something that was absolutely not planned, even though Ronan remains convinced it was a bid to trap him. No such thought had crossed my mind and it wasn't until my period was a whole seven days late that I even allowed myself to entertain the notion I might be pregnant.

We always used condoms. That was on my insistence. I knew that even though he said his marriage was all but over with Sorcha they still slept together occasionally.

But of course, he accused me of tampering with them, because it absolutely couldn't have been his fault. And it absolutely couldn't have just been bad luck.

I didn't expect him to be happy when I told him – I am not that naive. I knew this was messy and the timing was less than perfect. If this got out, especially at work, it could have serious consequences. One of the bosses getting a more junior member of staff pregnant doesn't look good no matter what way you spin it.

After the initial blow-out, Ronan went quiet. I didn't hear from him. He did not answer my calls or my messages. But I stayed strong. I would give him time to come to terms with our new reality and the reality was that I was going to keep this baby. I didn't need him to be involved. I didn't need anything from him but I knew in my heart a termination was never going to be an option. I didn't want to terminate this pregnancy. I was getting older, and this may well have been my only chance to be a mother.

So even if it meant losing him, I would have my baby. Of course I hoped and prayed that he would come to realise that he wanted me – wanted us – too.

Those days and weeks were torturous – my anxiety grew along with my morning sickness, my boobs and my tummy. I wasn't imagining it. No one else might have been able to see it, but I felt the tightness in my clothes and the thickening in my waist.

I tried to look after myself, making sure I got my daily walk to get those blasted ten thousand steps in. Normally I walked along the riverside, taking in the ebb and flow of the River Foyle. I'd pop my AirPods in my ears and lose myself in dreaming about the future.

That day, however, it was so beautiful. I felt more energetic than I had done in weeks. The sun was beaming down, but there was a soft, cooling breeze that made the heat bearable. I decided to stretch my legs further, walking across the Peace Bridge to the Waterside and then making for St Columb's Park. The park itself has many tree-lined walkways, gardens, allotments and play parks and I just wanted to feel as if I was in nature.

I didn't think Ronan would be there. I was lost in my own world when I got that strange feeling I was being watched. I glanced up and there he was. No more than maybe fifteen feet away, his eyes locked on me. The sight of him set my pulse racing. He was tanned, handsome, dressed in jeans and a sweatshirt and, I then noticed, not alone. Holding his hand was this beautiful little child who I guessed immediately was Esme. She was staring up at her daddy, her eyes wide as she chatted, and chatted and chatted some more, tripping over her words in excitement. I imagine she realised he wasn't responding to her the way he had been because very quickly her gaze followed his and she was looking directly at me.

'Who's dat lady, Daddy?' she said perhaps a little too loudly.

Ronan glanced down to her and back up at me. 'Well this is my friend. She works with me,' he said and I froze, waiting to see what he would say next, which when I think about it was stupid. He was hardly going to announce the true nature of our relationship to a two-year-old.

'Hello Daddy's friend!' she chirped, before shyness got the better of her and she stepped closer to her dad, half hiding her face behind his arm.

I crouched down so that I was at her height. 'And hello, Esme,' I said. 'Your daddy has told me all about you and what a great little girl you are.'

She eyed me suspiciously before casting a look back up at Ronan as if for reassurance I was telling the truth.

'I did,' Ronan told her. 'Because you are the very best girl there is.' When Esme smiled at her dad, the smile he gave her back was unlike any other smile I had ever seen on his face. It was a look of such pure love and adoration that I knew he would not abandon me and this baby I was carrying. Ronan was born to be a father. He loved it. He could never walk away from a child of his own.

I made to speak. Made to tell him it was nice to see him, but he started walking. 'It was lovely to see you,' he said. 'But Esme and I have to be somewhere, and we don't want to be late.'

Disappointment was written all over my face and whether it was because he really meant it, or he was afraid of my making a scene, he called back as they walked on, 'I will call you later. About work.' There was a hint of a smile on his face and I felt as if the sun had just got warmer. That was when I noticed Esme turn and wave at me. As I raised my own hand to wave back I heard her speak. 'Daddy, what's your friend's name called?'

I didn't hear if he answered.

'Do you want to hold my baby?' Esme says, pulling me back from my memories. 'Since you don't have any babies of your own. You have to be careful though. She's like a real baby.'

I'm about to say no, and just make my excuses and leave when I realise I really, really do want to hold Esme's baby. Even though she is not real, I want to feel the shape of a curled-up newborn in my arms. I want to breathe in that fake baby powder scent and pretend it is real. I want to imagine a moment where someone would place my own child in my arms after hours of gruelling labour and I would be lying there, broken, bleeding and utterly exhausted but also incredibly in love with this gorgeous little creature in my arms.

To my surprise the doll is weighted and her body moulds against my arm as if she is a real baby. I've never understood the appeal of these dolls, not until now. It's hard to draw my eyes away from her.

'Molly sleeps up here and not in the playroom because I have to take care of her. I'm not even allowed to cuddle her in bed,' Esme says as I keep staring at this toy in my arms while all these feelings bubble up. 'She has a little teddy bear – I'll go get it,' she adds, and she slides off the bed, landing with a gentle thud before running across to her window, under which is a doll-sized crib. But when she gets to the window, she stops and lets out a little squeal of excitement.

'Daddy!' she calls. 'It's Daddy! I have to run down and get the door,' she says, and she's gone in a flash of fairy wings and glitter and I'm processing the fact that her daddy – Ronan – has just arrived and I am here. In his house. In his daughter's bedroom, having made friends with his ex-wife. I can hear the front door open and Esme's squeals of delight rattle up a notch. I imagine her running to him and throwing her little arms around him. He'll be picking her up and swinging her around as she clings to him, both utterly entranced with each other. Will she lead him to the kitchen like she did with Joan and me? Or will she tell him he absolutely has to meet her new friend?

I need to think. Okay, it doesn't have to be a total disaster. Not unless she does bring him upstairs in which case there is no way I will be able to lie my way out of this one. I will her to drag him through to see Sorcha. That's probably why he's here in the first place, isn't it? Maybe if, just if, Esme does that I can bolt down the stairs and out the door. I can be in my car and on my way home in seconds.

Except for the gate. The fucking gate. How do I open it? Do I need a key code? No one else I know has a security gate at their house so how the hell am I supposed to know how it works? Then I remember Sorcha saying something about leaving it open – please God let her be true to her word! My breath is tight in my chest as I glance out the bedroom window and down the driveway. It's open! Thank God, it's open.

I have my keys and my phone in the bag I have slung across my body. As I hear Esme's and Ronan's voices grow quieter, I realise I have to decide what to do here and now. Yes, there will be questions about why I ran off but hopefully not as many as if I stay. The very thought of dealing with that particular confrontation right now is enough to make my stomach turn. I will myself to make a move and take a deep breath. I'll either make it, or I won't, but if I don't try... I can't even think straight.

Before I know it, I'm running down the stairs and making a beeline directly for the hall. The front door is closed but it's within reach now and I raise my hand to open it when I feel a hand clamp onto my shoulder.

37

I close my eyes and force a breath into my lungs. 'Sorry, family emergency. I have to go,' I say without turning my head. My hand is shaking so violently as I reach for the door handle.

'Why have you got Molly?' I hear from behind me. It's not Ronan. It's not Sorcha or Joan. It's not even Esme. I glance behind me. Ivy is staring at me as if I'm something she dragged in on the bottom of her shoe. 'That's my sister's doll. Why do you have her? Are you some kind of freak or something?'

If only she knew how close to the mark she really is. The truth is I didn't even realise I was still holding the doll, cradling her to me with my free hand. I was just in a panic. I am still in a panic. 'Shit,' I say and catch a smirk on Ivy's face. 'Sorry, I didn't realise,' I stutter in a hushed, rushed voice. 'I got a call about my mum. And I have to go. I'm sorry.' Thrusting the doll in her direction and letting go, I don't even wait to see if she catches hold of it before I have opened the door and am doing my best to keep my footing on the gravel driveway to get to my car.

Of course, Joan has parked in front of me. There isn't much room for me to get round her but I think I can. It will take longer than I'd like and as I throw my car into reverse to create more space, I have visions of the entire Hannon family and smug Joan walking out of their front door to stand in front of me and demand to know what the actual fuck is going on. Tears prick at my eyes as I will my damn foot to stop shaking and to catch the right bloody biting point to get this car to move. I must hit the accelerator too hard as my wheels spin in the gravel and the roar of my engine is deafening.

'Shit!' I shout, fear and frustration pulsing through me in waves. 'Come on!' I tell myself as I slam my car into first and use every ounce of concentration not to spin the wheels again. My car lumbers forward, parking sensors screaming as I narrowly avoid taking the back light from Joan's car. I don't even look behind me as I drive towards the road, terrified the gates will start to close and I'll be caught out. I have visions of them all surrounding me. Ronan horrified. Esme scared. Joan smug. Sorcha hurt and confused. God and Ivy – Ivy will be telling them all I tried to steal the damn doll. And I didn't. I swear I didn't.

Or did I?

I don't even know myself any more. Despite the coldness of the day, I have broken out in a sweat and can feel it bead and slide down the back of my neck, while my hands are slippery on the steering wheel. My heart is thudding in my chest as I make it out of the gates and onto the road before turning right to head back towards town. 'Fuck,' I scream. 'FUCK!' I have just managed to humiliate myself once again.

I pull over into a side street, bury my head in my hands and I cry myself sore for the absolute mess I have become. And I cry for my baby. My poor baby. Who never even had a chance at life. Who has never even been acknowledged. I'm just very, very sorry.

38

SORCHA

'I was wondering how you were after your little incident and I was passing by so thought I might as well call in and use this as a chance to see the girls. You don't mind do you?'

Ronan is all sweetness and light as he walks into the room carrying Esme, who is clinging to him as if she hasn't seen him in a month, even though it's only been two days. He knows he has me over a barrel, just as he knows I will mind him calling in unannounced. We've talked about this before. We've talked about this through solicitors. This isn't about checking in on me, or even about seeing the girls. This is about control and refusing to let go. But he knows I won't want to make a scene in front of Esme, and Ivy – who has just walked into the living room carrying Esme's precious 'Molly Dolly'.

My youngest daughter's eyes widen at the sight of her sister, and arch nemesis, carrying her favourite doll which, quite frankly, gives me the heebie-jeebies.

'Why have you got Molly? I don't want you to play with Molly!' Esme cries, pushing away from her dad and planting her feet back on the ground.

Ivy, very much at that stage in life where she seems to taunt her little sister for sport, rolls her eyes. 'As if...' she says. 'Mum's creepy friend had her... and then she just ran out the door...'

I'm about to scold Ivy for calling Christina my 'creepy friend' when I register the second part of her sentence and simultaneously hear an engine turning over outside. The skid of wheels on gravel as an engine revs and tries to find purchase on the slick, wet stones comes next.

Joan and I exchange glances.

'Who? What?' Ronan asks. He looks to me first, then to Ivy. Probably because he knows that while I'm likely to tell him to go take a running jump, his first-born daughter will spill whatever beans she can with abandon.

'Just one of Mum's creepy cult members,' Ivy says and I, only too aware that Joan is sitting just feet from me, feel my face colour. 'She said to tell you she got a call about her mum or something...'

Poor Christina. She must have nearly had a stroke when she realised Ronan had arrived.

'Well, that's quite rude, young lady,' Joan says with the same icy tone she had used on Christina earlier. If I could frame the look on my elder daughter's face at being called out by her Auntie Joan, one of the 'creepy cult members', believe me I would. I will take my wins wherever I can get them these days.

I will my daughter to apologise spontaneously – to show me that I actually do parent my children correctly and teach them that manners are important. I will her to treat Joan, who she has known all of her life, with an ounce of respect. Of course, she doesn't and just as I'm about to demand she say sorry, Ronan speaks.

'With all due respect to you, Joan, I don't think people should just be calling by the house whenever they feel like it,' he says, with not one hint of self-awareness. 'This woman was trying to take Esme's doll – if that isn't a red flag I don't know what is, and after what happened on Wednesday...'

'One, she was invited round unlike some people,' I say, glaring at him. 'And two, she wasn't trying to take Esme's doll!' Ronan will be giving his daughters nightmares at this rate.

'I showed her my baby and asked her did she want a cuddle,' Esme pipes up. 'I like Mum's friend. She was kind and funny and she brought us a cookie.'

The look on Ronan's face as he looks from her to me is enough to make my blood run cold. He drops his voice to little more than a whisper. 'So, now you're letting a stranger give our children food? After what happened at your book club? Now tell me this, was your "kind and funny" new friend here on Wednesday too? In charge of drinks or food perhaps?'

'You're being ridiculous,' I snap. 'She's an ordinary, lovely woman and here you are accusing her of being Lucrezia Borgia!' My voice is louder than I would like it to be but I can't help it. Ronan brings this out in me and that annoys me more than words can say. They say the opposite of love isn't hate, but indifference. I long for the day when I can think of my ex-husband with nothing more than sheer indifference.

'Who's Lucree-see-ah Borka?' Esme asks, her eyes wide. 'Does she bring cookies too?'

There's a cough, and I turn to see Joan on her feet. 'I think maybe I should be on my way. Unless you need me to stay?'

I shake my head. 'No, you go on. It was lovely to see you,' I say, painting a bright smile on my face. I don't want to end up refereeing Joan and Ronan on top of everything else.

'Thanks for having me over for lunch, Sorcha. It was very kind of you to host a creepy weirdo like myself.' She gives me a sly wink and a smile plays on her lips. I can't help but smirk back.

'And maybe I'll see you tomorrow? The wild Atlantic coast again or maybe closer?' I say.

'That would be lovely. Some vitamin sea would do the trick right now. I'll be in touch,' she says and hugs me, the scent of her perfume filling my nostrils. 'Call me later if you need me,' she whispers in my ear as she gives me an extra squeeze. I squeeze back in acknowledgement, and she pats my arm as she turns to leave. 'And young Ivy, give your mother a break. You don't know how lucky you are!' she says. Ivy nods without rolling her eyes, and I'm grateful she doesn't bite back with some spoiled-brat response.

'I'll walk you to the door,' Esme says with authority. 'That's my job! And Molly will come too!'

'Well, aren't I lucky getting a grand escort from two lovely young ladies,' Joan says, as she takes the hand Esme has offered her. My heart swells. Part of me wishes I could freeze time and keep Esme this size, this innocent, for as long as possible. I remember the days when Ivy would delight my heart with her cuteness in the same way. But that was before she hit the 'tween' years – or maybe it was just that it was before her precious daddy moved out following the implosion of our marriage.

'And Ronan, for your information, the creepy friend who left in a rush was the other woman who fell sick on Wednesday night too. I don't think anyone would be mad enough to be wandering about spiking their own food and drink, would they?' Joan adds before she and Esme walk out of the room.

Once we hear the front door open and Esme shout her good-byes, Ronan visibly relaxes. Even though he knows this house is no longer his – that I have bought out his share – he still likes to make himself at home here.

'I wasn't intending to accuse your friend of spiking your drink, never mind her own,' he says. 'I just think it's odd that she would leave so fast and without so much as popping her head around the door.'

'She's very shy,' I tell him, thinking again she must've seen her life flash before her eyes at Ronan's arrival.

'Maybe she is shy,' he says, 'but look, I'm only worried because I care about you, and our girls.' This is him changing tack again. This is the tried and tested Ronan Hannon charm offensive. And it works – with the girls anyway. Me? I know better.

'It's hardly a crime that I want to take care of you all,' he says. 'And you can't really be cross at me for wanting to spend some time with you. One thing you can never accuse me of is being a dead-beat dad,' he says. 'I'm here for them. And for you.'

Ivy snuggles beside him on the sofa and curls her legs up on the sofa, resting her head on his shoulder. I watch as he strokes her hair with the gentlest of touches and kisses her softly on the top of her head as if she is the most precious and fragile thing in the world. She smiles back at him, and then takes his hand. I know he will surreptitiously be giving her hand a squeeze and she will squeeze back. It's their little thing. Jealousy nips at me and it's not because I want Ronan to be squeezing my hand. It's because I want to be on the sofa with our eldest daughter snuggled up beside me. I want her to reach out and take my hand. I want her to look up at me with the same expression of adoration she is currently giving her father.

'There's no need to worry,' I tell him. 'We're fine. All of us.'

He raises one eyebrow in that condescending way he does so well. 'If you say so,' he says.

'I do,' I say, growing impatient for him to leave. Esme trots back into the den with Molly still in her arms. Ronan spent a small fortune on that doll for Esme the year he left. It was typical Ronan. Over the top and completely impractical. It's not even a child's doll – it's the kind of doll collectors buy, that people use to help them overcome the loss of a child. She is scarily lifelike. Ronan had her made to order and ensured she looked and weighed exactly the same as Esme did when she was a newborn – I think he hoped that when I held the doll in my arms I would connect it, and him, with happier times. Instead, it just gave me the creeps.

'Mummy, was Christina really going to take Molly with her?' she asks, her bottom lip petted, and brow creased with concern. 'I told her Molly was my very favourite baby, but maybe she wanted her to take home because she doesn't have any babies of her own.'

The petted lip starts to wobble again and Esme brushes tears from her eyes with the back of her sleeve. I can see the inner battle to be brave playing out on her little face.

'No, darling,' Ronan says and pulls her into a hug, dislodging Ivy temporarily from her limpet position by his side. 'I don't think she was going to take Molly. If she had to leave in a hurry she was probably just distracted. That happens with grown-ups sometimes because we have so much to try and remember in our old, cruddy heads.' He pulls back from her and tickles her on her tummy, causing her to peal with laughter.

'Hmmm, I suppose. Mummy can be very forgetful sometimes,' she says and while I don't like that she'd sell me down the river for her father's approval, I still smile because this fun, jokey way of being together is nice – regardless of the circumstances. This is the only thing I really miss about my life with Ronan. The feeling of being in this together. That we were a team because of the girls.

'Sweetheart,' I say, crossing the room to sit beside my ex and pull my youngest daughter onto my knee. 'I promise you... no, Daddy and I promise you... that we would never, ever let anyone take Molly away. If anyone ever tries, they'll have to answer to us,' I tell her, scrunching my face to fake an angry expression. Ronan follows suit and makes an angry growling sound, which causes Esme to laugh even more, and Ivy to declare she's disgusted.

Grown-ups, it seems, are 'cringe'. I wonder when to break it to her that she'll be a grown-up one day too.

'No one would dare try and get in our way,' Ronan tells Esme. 'Isn't that right, Mummy?' he asks.

I nod and reach over to kiss the top of my precious daughter's head. 'That's absolutely 100 per cent correct,' I say. And I mean it.

39

'How about we order some pizza and watch a movie?' Ronan asks the girls without so much as a look to me to gauge my reaction, never mind checking with me first that I don't mind. 'We can even get ice cream.'

Of course, the girls squeal with delight, while I'm left wanting to squeal for another reason. I'm absolutely okay with fighting to protect our girls but Ronan seems to have taken my statement of solidarity as a green light to play happy families again, and of course it's me who will look like the big bad witch if I call him out on it now.

'Ronan,' I say, keeping my voice as measured as I can, 'have you thought maybe I've plans already for dinner?'

'Whatever they are, they can't be as important or exciting as pizza and movie night with our girls,' he says, pulling both Ivy and Esme back into him for a hug and a tickle. Ivy laughs so loudly and without any self-consciousness that I feel my coldness thaw a little. For that moment I have my little girl back and not just the demon pre-teen and it feels great.

'Please say we can, Mum,' she says. 'I really miss family pizza nights! Please!' Ivy, it seems, is equally adept at piling on the guilt. I want to tell her I miss family pizza nights too, but I wasn't the one who destroyed our family. I'd have been perfectly happy to have family pizza nights every Saturday from now until forever if I hadn't discovered Ronan was a cheat. If he hadn't left me on my own to clean up one huge mess of his making – a mess that he had the audacity to blame me for in the first place.

'Don't be a party pooper, Sorcha,' Ronan pleads, his hands in a prayer pose. Esme follows suit, batting her eyelids and giving me her best angelic look. 'Pretty please, Mummy,' she says and I see the three sets of eyes stare at me, all mirror images of each other, and I know I'm fighting a losing battle.

'Okay!' I say. 'But one movie and that's all. I have work to do tonight and I'm sure Daddy has plans back at his own house.' I give Ronan a glare Medusa herself would be proud of. 'And I've content to upload.'

My darling eldest daughter rolls her eyes and once again declares me 'cringe' but very quickly moves on to discussing what she would like on her pizza.

'I'll just tidy these few things up,' I tell my family, 'and then we can choose a movie.' I glance at the clock and see it's gone half past five. 'I will order pizza after six, okay?'

'Can we watch *Encanto*?' Esme shouts and even though her oldest sister starts to protest that it is babyish we already know that's what we will end up watching. Esme Hannon rules the roost. She has done from the moment she was born.

I nod and lift the coffee cups left behind by Joan and Christina to carry them through to the kitchen. Ronan will order for me. He knows what I like. Ronan has always known me better than I know myself, which is why he was able to deceive me. I genuinely think he thought he'd get away with it. That I would forgive him, or at least give him time to re-ingratiate himself into my good books. He thought I wouldn't want the bad look of a marriage break-up – not when my brand was centred around family and selling the dream of a happy home, a handsome husband and two beautiful little girls.

But on that score, he had me all wrong. What I would not have, as an influencer who women looked up to, was a husband who made a fool of me, allowing the whole world to laugh at me behind my back. I load the coffee cups in the dishwasher, wrap the remainder of the quiche in cling film and pop it in the fridge before feeling my phone vibrating in my pocket.

I smile when I see Joan's name flash up on screen. I'd been expecting this call and it's not one I want to have in front of Ronan, so I walk through to the utility room and close the door behind me before I answer.

'Hi,' I say. 'I was wondering how long it would take you to call and check in. Look, Ronan has very kindly invited himself for a pizza and movie night and I'm expected back at ground zero soon to play happy families,' I say, leaning back against the worktop and taking in my perfectly organised laundry shelves. Glass storage jars, bottles, a cute little rustic peg box and one of those boards looking to pair single socks with their matching partner. I'd got it on Etsy because I thought it was cute at the time. 'Lonely socks,' it reads, 'seeking sole mates.' Now that I fight my own loneliness I don't find it nearly as cute.

'He's still there? And he invited himself to stay for a movie?' Joan asks, and I can hear from the exasperated tone of her voice that she thinks I should be booting him out the door.

'He used Ivy to get me on side, of course,' I say. 'He knew I'd be persona non grata to her if I said no and to be honest, after the week that's just been, I have adopted a choose your battles approach to this weekend. I don't have the strength to go head-to-head with Ivy, or Ronan for that matter.'

'Hmmm,' Joan says. 'I get that, but you know Ronan. You give an inch, even one, and he'll take a mile. You don't want to let him get into a habit of spending his Saturday nights at yours. I'd be putting my foot down if I were you.'

I know there's truth in what she's saying but I bristle all the same. It's okay for her – she isn't the one who has to deal with Ivy going off on one, or Esme breaking down into hysterical tears. It doesn't seem to matter how much time passes, they still don't seem to fully accept that their daddy and I aren't getting back together. It still hurts them if they sense any tension between us. Her tone has me on the defensive.

'Look, there's no harm in it,' I say, as I spot a white ankle sock beside the dryer that matches one of the needy socks on the board. 'He is their father after all and we are a family at the end of the day. He should be able to enjoy that quality family time too.'

'And he does! He gets to have them come stay with him every second weekend and enjoy as much family time as he wants. He shouldn't be eating into your time too,' Joan retorts.

But the truth is, Ivy aside, I think a part of me feels obligated to agree to him staying. Especially after we'd summoned him over in the early hours of Thursday morning to deal with our emergency. I can't pick and choose when he's allowed to be a part of our family, can I? 'It's only one night,' I say.

'Until it's more,' she replies. 'You'd think he'd have enough to keep him busy. A single man like him. I'd have thought he'd be out on the town.'

'Please,' I say. 'Can we not have this conversation just now? It's been a long week and I don't want us to fall out.'

There's a pause as she ingests what I've said and perhaps more importantly, my tone when I said it. Sometimes the only way to get through to Joan is to be firm. Her heart, I think, is in the right place but sometimes she can be a bit too much. I don't need her to question my every decision or to act as my one-woman security team. I'm a big girl and I can look after myself – yes even when it comes to dealing with Ronan. She doesn't have to insert herself into every part of my life.

'You do know I'm only watching out for you,' she says. 'That I just don't want you to get hurt again.' Her tone is brusque. I can imagine the look of hurt on her face. After all, she saw me at rock bottom when my marriage went south. She saw what Instagram didn't see. The blooper reel of depression and heartache that was my life. Without her I'm not sure I'd be where I am now. I'd probably still be in my pyjamas crying over our wedding album like a complete saddo.

'I know,' I say. 'And I love you for it. Just as I love you for calling to check in, but I'm fine. Honest. Now I'd better get back to them all before they send out a search party.'

'By "they" you mean Ronan?' she says and I sigh.

'I'm going to go now, Joan. Love you. Bye,' I say, hang up and slip my phone in my pocket as I'm walking out of the room. I don't even see Ronan standing staring at me.

'Were you on the phone? Who were you talking to?' he asks, making me jump.

'Jesus, Ronan. You almost scared the heart out of me,' I say and try to walk on past him. I've no intention of telling him it was Joan on the other end of the line. It would only invite his well-worn tirade on how she has stalker qualities and is no good for me.

'Are you not going to tell me?' he asks, his voice stern. 'We didn't realise you'd gone to take a phone call. We weren't sure where you'd gone.'

'Well it wasn't as if I was likely to leave the country,' I tell him.

'It was all very secretive, hiding in the utility room like that. I heard you speaking in a hushed voice.' His eyes are set on mine.

The same pale blue I find so beautiful in my daughters' eyes looks positively menacing in his. Cool. Steely. Sharp.

My ire is up. Who does he think he is to demand to know who I was talking to?

'Maybe you did, Ronan, but I don't think I need to remind you that it is absolutely none of your business. Nothing about my life – outside of those two girls who are waiting for us to walk back into the room smiling and playing at being happy and functioning co-parents – is any of your business any more. It hasn't been for more than two years now and it's about time you all started to get used to the idea.'

'Who was on the phone?' he repeats, his voice low and menacing. 'What are you keeping from me? Do you think I don't know something is going on here?'

'Oh, go to hell, Ronan,' I tell him and push past to walk back to the girls. I immediately switch to a light and happy voice even though it feels as if my heart might just burst out of my chest. 'Okay, ladies. Is the pizza ordered? Are we ready to talk about Bruno?' I grin.

'Mummmeeeee!' Esme squeals. 'We don't talk about him!' she declares, just as Ivy rolls her eyes once again. I can feel Ronan's eyes burning into my back.

Joan's warnings ring in my ears.

40

CHRISTINA

I don't think I've ever downed a glass of wine so quickly. I don't think I've ever understood the need for a medicinal drink so much until this moment. Not even when I lost our baby.

God, how I hate that expression. I didn't lose our baby. I didn't leave it somewhere or forget about it. I wasn't careless. I could never have done anything that would have risked losing that which was most precious to me. I did not *lose* our baby.

My hands are still shaking as I top up my glass, filling it to the brim with lukewarm white wine, which I bought in the off-licence on the way home. I can't tell you anything about it other than it was white wine and it was on a shelf beside the till.

I haven't even taken the time to chill it. Truth told, it took all my strength not to open it in the car and take a few slugs before driving on home. It tastes like sour, warm piss and I gag on it, but drink anyway. I need to feel anaesthetised. I did not buy this wine to savour it. I bought it to get obliterated.

I have fucked up this time. Hugely. I shouldn't have gone to Sorcha's house today. I don't know how I ever thought it would end well. I don't know if I ever really did think it would go well.

I should've made my excuses and left as soon as Esme had answered the front door with that smile, and those beautiful eyes. I should never have allowed her to take my hand.

And I most certainly should not have allowed Esme to bring me up to her room, or show me her favourite doll. I should've left and told her I'd see her room the next time I visited, but of course I didn't. Instead, I stirred a hornets' nest of memories and they just keep coming – hitting me again and again and again.

I tip the contents of my nightstand out and find the envelope just under the picture of Ronan and me. Inside it is the grainy image of an ultrasound, which proves that for a while at least, my baby was real. It's the only picture I will ever have of my child. I remember the two pink lines on the pregnancy test and how nervous I was to tell Ronan. Him being a walking cliché and telling me I needed to 'get rid of it' and he would give me the money to go to England and 'get it sorted'. The horror I felt at how coldly he spoke to me – how it just didn't seem to make any sense whatsoever. Seeing him with Esme in the park. Hearing him talk to her. Seeing how beautiful she was and knowing that deep inside me was a child who would no doubt resemble her. I looked at her beautiful blue eyes and I could see a future where my child had those same gorgeous eyes and it would be my child's hand that Ronan was holding as we walked to the playpark with our child.

Every time I have thought of the baby that died inside of me, I have thought of that beautiful little girl. Coming face to face with her today was like seeing a ghost of a child who never got to be.

I shouldn't have allowed myself anywhere near Esme. I should've known that was too much. I'm so stupid.

I've proven that beyond all doubt by being caught making a run out of the door with Esme's precious baby doll, before hurtling down the driveway like some modern-day Thelma or Louise, my heart in my throat. I hadn't meant to take it. Not consciously anyway. Everything went a bit blurry as soon as Esme announced her daddy had arrived. It was panic that drove me down the stairs with the doll still in my arms.

The look on Ivy's face as she saw me heading for the door will stay with me for a long time. It wasn't fear, or confusion, it was simply disgust. This mess of a woman hyperventilating as she tried to escape must've made for quite the sight.

I'm afraid to look at my phone in case there are calls from Sorcha, or Joan, or worst of all from Ronan. What if he saw me? What will he be thinking? What will he be saying? Will he out me to Sorcha, and will I become a figure of hate for every Soul Sisterhood devotee in Derry and beyond? Will I be cast out as a slut and a girl-code breaker? She who let the side down and got into bed with a married man? And not just any married man but Ronan Hannon! I imagine the dissections of that juicy morsel. Dissections of my looks. My size. My personality. How could a man like *him* see anything in a woman like *me*? Why go out for a burger when you have steak at home – or some other such rubbish.

And it will be easy for them to hate me. Because it's always easier to hate the other woman. Men get forgiven by society, eventually. It's always easier to portray the other woman as the needy, desperate, bunny-boiling one. And God, haven't I given them the material to do that with. I can imagine Sorcha now, uploading a new video, talking about her stalker horror. Her face pale and tired and her voice heavy with emotion. 'Hey, everyone,' she'd say. 'This isn't going to be the same as my usual content. I've not spoken about this before but I think now it's time that I opened up about what has been going on in my private life. How there is a woman who wasn't just content with sleeping with my husband but who then tried to wheedle her way into my family...'

I log in to Facebook and immediately leave the newly re-activated group. I block the page from my account. I unfriend everyone associated with it and block them too and I delete the WhatsApp chat and group from my phone.

I am done. I am not putting myself through this any more. None of this is worth it. I can't live under this fear of being discovered.

I neck the rest of my glass of wine and fight the urge to vomit it back up. The slight fug of inebriation starts to curl its way through my brain and body, giving everything a blurry, hazy feel. I'm not a bunny boiler. I never was. I was never a temptress. I was never a slut. I was just lonely and naive and if I could turn back the clock I'd change it all because the pain from what has happened has broken me. And the tears come again, sliding in fat droplets down my cheeks before plopping into my wine. I can't believe I still have any tears left to cry but yet, here I am in this flat that is still upside down, halfway towards being pissed and having landed myself directly in the middle of a fucking shitstorm and I've no idea how to fix any of it.

I drink again from my glass, and am surprised to see I need another top-up and then even more surprised when my top-up leaves the bottle itself empty.

The sound of the door buzzer jolts me from a fresh flood of tears, and immediately a fight-or-flight reaction kicks in, with the primary urge being flight. I cover my ears with my hands, squeeze my eyes closed and hope that whoever it is goes away. I imagine Sorcha or Ronan, or maybe the pair of them together, standing outside the flats debating whether or not to press the buzzer again. I do not want to talk to either of them. I don't have it in me to deal with their criticism, or their anger.

The buzzer goes again. Even with my hands over my ears I can hear it. It cuts through my thoughts as it sounds a third time. Something inside me says I have to face this head on if I'm to face it at all. I climb off the floor and get to my feet, the room spinning just a little. I tell myself it's because I stood up too fast but the reality is that it is more than likely down to the wine I have just necked. Drying my face with the cuffs of my cardigan, I lift the handset and say hello in a croaky voice, still thick with tears, bracing myself for a storm of abuse from whoever is on the other end. I'm not sure who I'm most afraid it could be. The voice that echoes back to me though is not one I immediately recognise. The image on the screen is grainy – a figure with their back to the camera.

'Hello,' a female voice says.

'Yes, hello. I'm here,' I reply. This is probably someone looking for one of my neighbours but who has tapped in the wrong number. It happens much more often than I'm happy with. 'Can I help you?' I ask, noticing a slight slur in my words.

'Christina,' the woman says and I stiffen. There's something recognisable in her voice but it's slightly muffled by the traffic from the street and the static on the line. Before I can place her, she speaks again.

'It's Joan. I think we need to talk. Don't you?'

My mouth dries instantly.

41

SORCHA

The girls are lost in a Disney haze. I've even caught Ivy mouthing along with some of the songs. Ronan looks like the cat who got the cream, with his two girls on either side of him. He's pulling out all the stops on the daddy of the year routine and the girls are lapping it up.

Meanwhile I'm sitting on the armchair by myself, unable to concentrate on a single word. I barely managed one slice of pizza, anger making it taste like sawdust and stick in my throat.

I'm angry with him, of course, but angrier with myself for letting him wheedle his way back into this house – even if just for the evening – because once again he's manipulated his way to being the number-one parent. Once again, he's trying to insert himself into our home life. To gain access to every part of my life, of *our* lives. If the girls only knew the truth about their darling daddy, I don't think they'd feel so enamoured of him. But telling them would make me a bitch, wouldn't it?

Ronan poured me a glass of merlot when the pizza arrived but I still can't bring myself to even look at it, never mind taste it. I know what his plan is. It's not the first time he's arrived all sweetness and light to cosplay at happy families. I fell for it last time. I let him ply me with wine and tell me that losing me was the biggest regret of his life. I allowed him to tell me how beautiful he thought I was. To remind me of some of our happiest times. I let him because it was nice to hear.

I've not dated in the two years since our marriage imploded. I've not had the time, patience or emotional energy for it. I've not wanted to even *think* about trying to trust someone again since we broke up, and as much as I'm okay with that, I do sometimes miss being kissed. I miss being touched and wanted. I miss someone telling me they love me. I miss having someone I have a shared history with talk to me about things only the two of us know. Above the door to our utility room there is a sign that says 'Team Hannon'. And while the girls and I are still a team, the sign was bought at a time when Ronan was included too. I miss my team mate.

So the last time he did this, four months ago, I didn't argue when he asked to stay for pizza and a movie. I allowed myself to indulge in a little fantasy where he hadn't done anything wrong and we were still together and still in love. It couldn't hurt, right? To forget the bad stuff that had happened for one evening with our girls?

Once they were in bed and he had helped me clean up the pizza boxes and put the empty ice cream bowls into the dishwasher, he had suggested 'one more drink, for old times' sake' and I had been in that fuzzy in-between stage of not quite sober but not quite drunk – just relaxed and pliable – so I agreed. He topped up our wine and we sat in the den together and we talked. We talked until he reached across and pushed my hair back gently from my face and moved closer so that all I could see were his blue eyes. The smell of his cologne whisked me back to a time when it was all so much simpler. When he moved closer still and brushed his lips ever so gently on mine, every nerve ending in my body screamed in recognition of an old familiar touch, of what it meant.

I should've pushed him away but I didn't. I let him place his lips on mine once again, firmer this time, needier as he pulled me closer to him. My mouth opened just a fraction and I could taste him. I hadn't realised just how hungry I was for him until that moment. Or maybe I was just hungry for intimacy and he was simply the nearest person.

A small, low moan escaped his lips and I was done for. There was no turning back.

But this time I see it for what it is. He may well want back into my bed, but this is more. This is about winning to him. About knowing he can pull my strings and get what he wants from me. This is about owning me and my freedom.

But I'm not that slightly drunk and slightly needy person I was four months ago. It's amazing really – how one message popping up on my Facebook Messenger could change everything. How meeting one person could cement my belief than Ronan is irredeemable. And that I don't want to be sucked into his mess again. Ronan Hannon only comes knocking when he wants something, and he isn't happy until he has it all. He wants what he can't have. The wife he lied to, the house he lost, and the life he threw away without caring about the mess he left in his wake or the people he hurt.

I think it's likely that he senses he is not going to break down my barriers so easily this time and that's why, with me at least, he is starting to show his true colours.

He tenses every time I so much as glance in the direction of my phone. It's killing him that he doesn't know it was Joan I was talking to in the utility room; and that he doesn't know what I was talking about. He hates that I have a life now that exists outside of the bubble the two of us had once been in – and yet he doesn't seem willing to acknowledge that it's all his fault. I can see anger pulsing in him every time he looks at me and it's frightening how quickly he slips between acting the loving, happy father singing Disney songs to an ex-husband glowering at his ex-wife because I won't let him win.

It's ironic, really, how he hates that I have secrets of my own when his entire life revolved around keeping secrets from me.

By the time the movie has ended, Esme is tired but of course protesting to anyone who will listen that she is not. 'I'm not tired at all!' she says, before yawning loudly and widely.

'I think you might be, sweetheart,' Ronan says.

'And it's past your bedtime anyway,' I reply. 'So no arguing young lady! Run upstairs and change into your PJs and I'll be up in a minute to help you with your teeth and to read you a bedtime story.'

'Can Daddy read my bedtime story?' Esme asks, as she scooches onto Ronan's knee and wraps her arms around his neck. 'He does the best funny voices.'

'No, darling, Daddy has to go home now. But I'm sure he'll read you an extra story next week when you stay with him to make up for it,' I quickly interject. While Esme is, thankfully, easily pacified with the promise that I will read her two stories tonight, Ronan is not quite so happy.

Once the two girls have disappeared upstairs to get changed he glares at me. 'Was it too much for you to let me read my daughter a bedtime story?' he hisses.

'Was it too much for you not to have an affair with the mousy accountant from your work?' I bite back. I'm past playing nice, just to pacify him.

'There's no need to bring Tina into this,' he says. 'I told you that was a mistake. I've told you a million times. A stupid one-night lapse in judgement and I think I've paid dearly enough for it already, don't you?'

The righteous indignation in his expression leaves me wanting to laugh at his shameless bullshit. If only he knew his precious 'Tina' was here earlier. That I know more about him and her than I have ever told him before. That I know, and Joan knows and if I wanted, everyone could know him for the liar he is.

I take a deep breath. 'Stop with the lies, Ronan, please. We both know it was a lot more than a one-night stand,' I say, my voice steady. 'And, I think you'll find "Tina" prefers to go by *Christina* these days. You can go and ask Esme if you don't believe me – since her new friend, and my new friend, Christina was here earlier playing house with that creepy bloody doll.'

42

CHRISTINA

I should be ashamed of the mess my flat is in. I should be ashamed that I'm drunk and my face is tear-stained and make-up-streaked. But I'm not. I think I've gone past shame. I only have room in my head for so much self-hatred and at the moment embarrassment and fear are vying for top spot. Joan is on her way up and she will likely read me the riot act for running out of Sorcha's and trying to steal a stupid doll.

She won't have bought the story that I had a call from my mum and had to run. I don't think she would buy anything I tell her. I get the feeling Joan sees through everyone's bullshit – and especially mine. She's had my card marked from that day on the beach, and no amount of playing nice has been able to hide her abject suspicion and dislike of me.

I stiffen as I wait for her to appear, wringing my hands together, tighter and tighter, until the automated light flicks on in the hall to indicate someone is on the way. Sucking air into tight lungs, I feel the friction burn of skin on skin intensify. My nervousness is showing, threatening to spill over into abject panic. I'm as close as I've ever been to feeling utterly, totally overwhelmed. Maybe I should just tell her everything. Tell her before she calls me out on it. Maybe everything would stop then.

'Christina,' Joan says as she approaches, but I can't bring myself to look up. I'm scared of what the expression on her face will tell me. I'm scared to see her glower at me with a mixture of hate and disgust on her face, so instead I step back to allow her the room to come inside.

It only takes seconds for her to clock the aftermath of the break-in, and to take in the empty bottle of wine, the disarray all around and my scattered memories on the floor. 'What on earth...'

'There was a break-in,' I stutter. 'Yesterday. I've not had the chance...'

'And what did the police say?' she asks in her authoritative, no-nonsense way.

'I... I didn't call them.'

'You didn't call them?' she asks, incredulous. 'Why on earth not?'

'I didn't think there was any point,' I tell her.

'Your home was violated,' she enunciates slowly. 'Of course there was a point!'

'I can manage without their help,' I say and even though I don't want to see the pity and judgement that will be in her eyes, I force myself to lift my head and look her directly in the eye.

'Can you?' she replies, gesturing around the room before bringing her gaze back to me. Her features are sharp, harsh. Resting bitch face taken to the nth degree.

Emboldened by the alcohol swirling in my bloodstream, I steady myself and speak. 'Joan, as you can see, I have a lot going on right now so if there is any particular reason for you being here, can we just cut to the chase? Otherwise, as lovely as this has all been,' I say, gesturing my arms widely around me to indicate the very sorry state of my flat and my life, 'I'd really rather you left.'

'I'll cut to the chase if you will,' she says. 'I think we both know why you didn't call the police. Could it be because you want to avoid their attention yourself? I hear stalking is a crime these days. And on that note, I think we both know why I'm here.'

'I can assure you that I have absolutely no idea what you're talking about,' I say, my voice slightly less confident this time. Stalking? Does this woman, who was outside my flat late at night, have the nerve to accuse *me* of stalking?

She raises one eyebrow. 'So we're going to play it this way, are we?' she asks, and before I have the chance to answer she adds, 'How's your mother, Christina? You had to run off to help her with something very urgent earlier. I do hope it's nothing serious.'

I feel heat rise in my cheeks. 'She's fine. She was ill but she's okay now. She panics sometimes.'

'Hmmmm,' Joan says. 'It's actually impressive how easy lying comes to you, but then again, you've had a lot of practice I suppose. A new name, a rewriting of your history to pretend you're lonely and looking for a friend. God, the effort you must've gone to with your social media accounts...'

I freeze. So she knows. Or at least, she knows enough. I wonder how, and for how long and who else she might have told. I'm willing myself to speak but I have no idea what to say. She's right, of course – except about my pathetic social media accounts. It didn't require much effort to hide evidence of my half-lived life. That stings.

'Maybe we should sit down and talk this out,' she says, as she moves some of my belongings to one side and sits down on my sofa, making herself comfortable as if this is the kind of conversation she has every day in life.

Frustration bubbles inside me. I don't want to 'talk this out'. I don't owe Joan my time or any right to talk about my life with me.

She's just some woman I barely know who has no business imposing herself on me in my own home.

'Look,' I say, my whole body trembling. 'I'd rather you just leave. You've got me. I lied about my name. Clearly that means I'm the worst person in the world. Don't worry. I've already extricated myself from the group, and I've deleted all your numbers and details. I'll just disappear back under this rock. So if you just leave, we'll call it quits at that. I'm sorry I didn't get your message that day on the beach. I thought it was a friendly warning, not a declaration of war, but you've won, Joan. I'm done. I'm just not the right fit and that's okay.' I've barely registered that tears have started to fall as I describe myself as 'not the right fit'. It's how I've felt my entire life. I'm always just a little bit too big, or too small, too loud or too quiet to fit in anywhere. I look like I do fit in for a little while. Until I start to feel as if I might finally belong and allow myself to relax enough to be the real me. That's when people start to slip away.

Maybe they think I don't notice, but I do. It always starts with how they look at me. A kind of 'you're a bit weird' expression they all adopt, and then they don't chat so much or message so much any more. They make plans and exclude me. They find other friends. They find excuses. They find the idea of a life with me in it so completely untenable that it always happens. It always fucking happens.

'Christina, sit down!' Joan says, her voice authoritative and cutting through my spiral into self-pity. 'And stop it. Stop pretending this is all on us not finding you the right fit for the group. It's not that. You know exactly what it is and I can't believe you ever thought we wouldn't work it out. I tried to warn you. Before this all went too far. I don't understand why you didn't listen. I tried to be nice. I really thought you'd get it when I told you that you were being watched. That you'd realise your scheme, whatever was behind it, was stupid. You didn't get it. So I tried again. On the phone.'

I gasp. This woman in her fifties. This professional, well put together woman who bakes scones and helps run book club meetings was behind the hateful, childish nicknames and threatening phone calls.

She simply shakes her head. 'Don't look so surprised,' she says. 'We all do things we shouldn't when pushed, don't we? I'm not particularly proud of it but remember, I know who you *really* are. I know where you work and we know what you did. What I don't really know – and this really does throw me – is why? Why try and be a part of the Sisterhood? Have you not done enough damage to Sorcha? Why did you feel the need to come back for second helpings?'

Again I'm at a loss for words; there is nothing I can say in this moment that will make any of this better.

'She's one of my very best friends,' Joan says. 'I'll do whatever it takes to protect her.' If she is the person behind the phone calls, then just what else is she capable of?

I slump back onto my armchair, Joan's words registering in my brain.

'Did you break into this flat?' I blurt.

She gives a short, sharp laugh. 'You think I broke into this flat? No, Christina. I did not break into your flat. Don't be ridiculous!'

'You said you would do anything to protect Sorcha,' I offer.

'Well, I would,' Joan says. 'But I'm not a burglar! Maybe you've made enemies elsewhere, or are you going to try and tell me that Ronan was a one-off mistake? Just what was it about someone else's husband that appealed to you so much? Do you like a challenge? Were you after his money? Because I can assure you there isn't much on that score. Ronan has always lived beyond his means. It's Sorcha who has the money in that duo or maybe you know that now and that's why you're creeping around her so much.'

I shake my head. 'No. Just no. It's nothing like that. You don't understand.'

'You're right,' she says. 'I don't. But try to explain it to me,' she says.

'I don't owe you an explanation or anything else,' I say, humiliation fuelling a degree of fightback.

'That's true enough. But you do owe Sorcha one. Maybe I should give her a call and invite her over? She might have been too polite to challenge you about it, but I'm not.'

Sorcha knows? My heart sinks like a stone. She knows it was me. Has she always known? I think of the conversations we have had – of the lies I've told about my last relationship, my work, my life and wonder if all that time Sorcha has known I've been lying to her. Joan had my number from that first day on the beach. Who else?

43

'Look, Christina, or Tina... actually what would you prefer I called you?' Joan says, cutting through my thoughts.

'Christina,' I mutter, shame pushing all fight out of me.

'Okay,' she says and to my surprise she reaches her hand across and grabs my hand. The gesture makes me flinch and I pull away from her and fold my arms around myself. I don't trust her. I don't know who to trust any more.

She laughs at my reaction. 'You don't have to be scared of me,' she says. 'I'm only watching out for my friend. I'm not some sort of enforcer or hit person sent to rough you up a bit. Sorcha recognised you when you first messaged the group.'

'But Ronan said he never told her who I was. He said he wanted to make sure I didn't get in trouble,' I say.

Joan rolls her eyes dramatically. 'Ronan says more than his prayers. I wouldn't believe a word that comes out of his mouth. He could come in from outside soaked to the skin and I'd still want to check the weather if he said it was raining. Let's just say he told Sorcha a version of events that we know wasn't true. He maintains to this day what you and he had was nothing more than a one-night stand.'

Humiliation flushes through me and I feel tears prick at my eyes again. I'm not crying for me. He can deny what we had for the rest of his life and it won't hurt me more than it already has. But with his lie he is denying that we made a baby together. That I was, for the briefest of times, a mother.

I shake my head. 'It was more than that.'

'It always was with him. He liked to keep his other women around for a while – generally until they got a little too clingy,' Joan says.

My stomach turns. His other women? The words land heavy. He'd told me he'd never cheated before. That I was a one-off. That he had never met anyone who made him feel he had no choice but to pursue despite being married. And I'd believed it. Even right up to this moment, I'd believed it. I have been so very stupid.

Joan must see the realisation written all over my face. 'Oh... pet. You didn't think you were the only one, did you? You're not that naive, surely? Men like him have a pattern and you were caught up in it. For that I feel sorry for you. I really do. No one deserves Ronan in their lives.'

Of course I wasn't the only one. Of course I wasn't special.

But Joan isn't done. Not yet. 'And here's the thing, not everyone deserves a Sorcha in their lives either. She's a good person and not everyone has the right to benefit from her kindness. You should've just left her alone. That's what I don't understand. What have you been trying to achieve? Why would you think it's in any way appropriate to try and wheedle your way into the life of the woman whose marriage you played a role in destroying? Why would you think it was in any way okay to want to spend time with her children? To try and befriend her and get her to take you into her confidence? Is this some sort of twisted game to you? Because let me tell you, I'm tired of playing now. Just what is it going to take to get rid of you once and for all?'

With every word her voice has risen in volume or maybe it's just that each word hits harder than the last. There's nothing I can say in this moment that will make this sound any better than it does. I should never have even contemplated joining in but I was just so fucking lonely. I *am* just so fucking lonely. A sob, loud and gasping, escapes from my lips. Because ultimately Joan doesn't care that I'm lonely or that I just wanted a friend who could understand on some level the pain of being betrayed by the man she loved. Joan only cares that I hurt her friend and then lied about who I was. I can't deny it. I can't excuse it. I slept with a married man knowing that he was married, and that he was a father to two beautiful children.

And I was, at that time, so insanely jealous of Sorcha. She got him every night. She woke up with him every morning. She could proudly stand beside him and claim him as her own and tell the world about the father of her children. And I could not. Even though I loved him more deeply than I had ever loved anyone before.

'It's not like that,' I eventually say. 'That's not what it was about.'

'Well then, what *was* it like? I'm listening,' Joan says, not taking her gaze from me for even one moment.

44

SORCHA

Ronan stares at me, his mouth gaping open as he takes in what I've just told him. Christina was here. In this house. With his precious Esme.

It's quite glorious, to be honest, to see him at a loss for words, realising he's not quite as smart as he thinks he is. I can see his expression change as the full realisation of what I've just told him sinks in.

Eventually he, red-faced and just a little clammy, splutters, 'I don't know what she's told you, but I'd put money on it being nothing but lies.' He can't look me in the eyes as he spins this rubbish. As far as liars go, he's pretty rubbish. A good profiler would have him bang to rights in minutes. I laugh at his histrionics and the muscles tense in his jaw as his anger starts to simmer. Well, he can be angry all he wants. I'm not going to go out of my way to make him feel less guilty about what he did. It should be more than enough for him that I haven't told his daughters what a useless creature he turned out to be. If that makes him angry, he'd better be ready to deal with the consequences.

I shake my head slowly, amazed that in this scenario he is trying to make me out to be the villain. 'You know *you* lied to *me*, don't you?' I ask him, incredulity dripping from my every word. 'You know you've lied to me so much that I can't trust a single word that comes out of your mouth any more. Not one. I doubt you even know what the truth is yourself.'

His fists clench with the effort of holding in his anger but I don't want to stop. I have so much to say. 'It's a shame she ran off so quickly. I reckon the three of us could have had a lovely chat,' I say.

'You're some bitch, Sorcha Hannon,' he hisses. 'What the hell are you playing at?'

'I'm not playing at anything, Ronan,' I tell him, keeping my voice low but firm so the girls don't hear. 'I'm not the person who lies and cheats their way through every situation, remember? That's your specialty. My problem was that I believed you for a long time – too long. When you told me each one of them would definitely be the last time. Even when you told me she – this Tina – was a one-off who meant nothing – I believed you at first. Because I wanted to believe that deep down there was a good man inside you.'

'I *am* a good man,' he says, walking towards me, his hands raised, palms forward as if he is trying to placate me but I'm not the person who needs to be placated. I am fully in control of my emotions right now.

'No,' I say, taking a step backwards. 'You're not. You might like to think you are but a good man does not do what you did. He doesn't cheat and he doesn't lie.'

'I didn't...' he mutters. 'Please, Sorcha. I've made mistakes but this Christina, she's not right in the head. She lives in her own bubble – in her own version of reality. She switched to working from home because it's too much for her to communicate with other people properly. She gets too attached. Much too attached. And now, you're telling me, she's joined your little happy-clappy group of super fans? Maybe you're just her next target. She has form. She likes to take people down and this – getting involved with you – well this kills two birds with one stone, doesn't it? It gives her someone with influence to cling on to, and she manages to get back at me – again. She's living her best life with this carry-on.' He looks so impressed with himself – that he's come up with a response so plausible that maybe, just maybe, I'd believe him if I didn't know he was utterly full of shit.

'So first it was Joan who is a stalker, and now it's Christina. And you're the innocent victim in it all? If what you had with her was only one night and it meant nothing, why would she have any cause to get back at you?' I ask. 'And how on earth do you think her going for a swim or coming to a coffee morning is going to exact a terrible revenge on the man who wronged her?'

'Have you even considered that she might be behind your drink being spiked on Wednesday night?' he asks.

'Don't be so ridiculous. She was sick too, for goodness' sake. You heard Joan say it. Carla had to take her home early because she was so unwell,' I tell him.

He stares at me for a moment and shakes his head as if he's thinking of possible scenarios then discounting them one by one. 'But you ended up in hospital and she just ended up going home early? It's almost as she might have given herself a smaller dose. Enough to get sick but not enough to end up needing a middle-of-the-night ambulance? She was always, always bitterly jealous of you, Sorcha. I wouldn't put anything past her.'

'Oh for goodness' sake, Ronan. Carla says it was more than likely something gastric and some doctor or other is running away with conspiracy theories in the hope he'll end up Insta famous. I'd

say that's a damn sight more believable than a phantom poisoner.'
I say this even though I don't know what to believe any more. If it
was gastric, wouldn't more people have become sick?

'Carla said that?' he asks and I nod. I kind of expect him to
accuse her of being some sort of obsessive too. I don't have long to
wait for him to speak.

'You're so determined to believe in them, aren't you? To believe
they don't mean you any harm and it's only me – the big bad wolf
in all this – who could possibly be at fault. As long as you have
your horde of sycophants telling you how amazing you are, you'll
choose to believe them every time when I'm the one who was there
for you for years!' he hisses.

'You were there for me?' I ask, incredulous at his victim
complex. 'Was that when you were sleeping with Christina, or any
of the others who came before? When you were shagging someone
else while I was caring for our daughter, or pregnant with Esme?' I
am doing my best to keep my voice quiet because I do not need my
daughters to hear this, but rage is bubbling inside of me. 'And as
for my horde of sycophants as you so delicately put it? Do you
mean friends? Because that's what these women are. Not that you
would know what real friendship is. Every relationship you've ever
had in your sad little life has been transactional and nothing
more.'

He rolls his eyes. 'You tell yourself they're your friends but they
wouldn't want a thing to do with you if you weren't Sorcha Hannon
– Influencer. They're not your friends, they're your stalkers. Joan,
for God's sake, she's nearly old enough to be your mother and she
swans about like your minder. It's creepy as fuck – surely you can
see that? But no, you're so blind you ignore it and say she's your
friend and then invite Tina into our home even though I've told
you she's unhinged?'

'Ronan, you think every woman is unhinged. It's never you that's the problem, is it? It's us crazy women doing crazy things. I bet you've told everyone I'm not right in the head too. The thing is though, Ronan, when you start to amass a lot of people who you call crazy around you, the problem might be you and not them.'

He stands and stares at me and I am suddenly overcome with tiredness. I'm growing tired of this back and forth now, of listening to excuse after lie followed by these preposterous allegations. Nothing ever changes with him. It is always, always all about how he feels, what wrongs have been done to him. I have two beautiful, precious if sometimes precocious girls who are all that really matter. The fight is going out of me for today. I just want to tell Esme she can sleep in with me tonight. I want to curl up with her and read her a bedtime story. If I'm lucky then Ivy might wander in and lie at the bottom of my bed pretending not to listen while I read.

I am too tired for Ronan.

'I want you to go now,' I say, picking up his jacket and his keys and starting to walk towards the hall. 'I'm asking you nicely this time because upstairs there are two little girls who we both love very much and who I think we'd both be loath to upset.'

I stop at the doorway, turn and watch him still standing in exactly the same position as he had been when I started walking. 'If you don't leave now, I will call the police and have them remove you – and you know that will mean you end up back in the family court. And I will sit down and explain to our girls exactly why Daddy can't come visit any more.'

His face blanches and it's his turn to shake his head slowly. 'You are the worst kind of bitch, Sorcha, and you'll live to regret this. When you have to come back and apologise to me because you discover I'm telling you the truth. When Joan goes too far with her overprotective, vindictive ways, or when Tina shows her true colours, you'll know. Does Joan know about her? About us? Because if she does, you know she's not going to let that lie. She never lets things lie. That's when you'll come running to me for help, but you won't be able to have me because I'll have stopped caring. I'll have moved on.'

'You had already moved on while you were still sleeping in our bed,' I say, with no bitterness, just honesty. 'It was over two years ago. It's still over. Please move on again. Now.'

He shakes his head in disgust, but at least he moves this time. I don't speak as he crosses the room, takes his jacket and his keys from me and walks to the front door. When he's gone, and when I hear his car drive away from the house, I close the door and double-lock it before tapping in the code for the alarm. I make sure the electric gate to the driveway is closed. I do a quick scan of the den, grabbing my phone and my bottle of water and I'm just switching off the lights when I spot Molly Dolly left on the sofa. I'm surprised that Esme hasn't appeared looking for her, so I lift her to return her to her designated spot in the crib in my daughter's room. As I walk up the stairs, I think of Christina running for the door with the doll in her arms.

Of course I understand why Christina bolted when Ronan arrived. I'm glad she did. I can only imagine the consequences if she had come face to face with him in front of the girls. It also reassured me that my instincts were right – Christina doesn't want to be around Ronan any more than I do. Perhaps she's even frightened of him – and that's something I can relate to. I wonder if I should call her just to check if she is okay. I should come clean, really, and tell her that I know who she really is and that I've known for a long time. Yes, if you'd asked me two years ago did I want revenge, then I would have said yes. I absolutely wanted to make her suffer for what she did to my family. I still want to hate her and hurt her, but I can't. Not now I know her in real life.

She has been as much of a victim in all this as I have been.
Maybe even more so. And it doesn't matter that my friends tell me
I'm being naive, and too soft, or that I'm playing with fire having
anything to do with her. I know what I'm doing. I'm not as naive as
people might think.

45

CHRISTINA

I have never been as mortified in my life as when I tell Joan my truth but I know I have to do it. I'm done being scared.

'I was just so lonely,' I say, aware how pathetic that sounds. 'And yes, I followed Sorcha at first because of who she is – but I watched how she coped with her break-up, how she grew the Soul Sisterhood and I read all the posts about your meet-ups and how you supported each other, and I just thought I wanted that. I wanted support and friends. I wanted to be less lonely.'

'But there are other ways to meet people – why Sorcha? Knowing what you did – were you trying to make a fool of her? You couldn't have genuinely thought she'd want to be your friend?'

I shake my head. 'No... I don't know... I wasn't trying to make a fool of anyone. If anything I felt a kinship with her. Both of us know what it's like to lose Ronan...'

'Both of you had a lucky escape,' Joan replies.

'He said she didn't understand him,' I tell her, but even as I speak I know he was lying to me. Every word that he uttered was a lie, and I fell for it like the fool I am. He didn't even try to be original about it.

'He's a compulsive liar. It comes as naturally to him as breathing,' Joan says just as the buzzer to my apartment sounds again. My first thought is that it's Sorcha and she's come to have her own heated conversation with me about this whole sorry mess. Joan must read the panic on my face because she rests her hand on mine. 'Do you want me to see who it is?'

I shake my head. 'I'll get it.'

The buzzer goes again. Whoever it is clearly must be impatient as it sounds a third time, this time in one loud, long buzz.

'I think that's probably my cue to be going, then,' Joan says, and I immediately want to ask her to stay. This woman who not that long ago I was terrified of – who maybe I should still be terrified of. This woman who I have no right to ask for anything, so I just nod and get up to answer the door. When I see the pixelated face of Ronan Hannon staring directly into the camera, all semblance of bravery leaves me. Here I am between the devil and the deep blue sea and not sure which is worse.

I turn to look at Joan, but see that she has already spotted the face on the screen. 'You don't have to let him in,' Joan says. 'You owe him nothing.'

'He knows I was at her house, doesn't he? He knows it was me with Esme?' I ask, my heart hammering in my chest. That's the only reason I can think of as to why he would be here. Because he knows I've been in his house, with Sorcha and the girls.

'I'd say that's likely,' Joan says.

'Then I need to face him. I need to deal with this all head on. I made my bed et cetera,' I tell her, not feeling an ounce as brave as I'm trying to sound. Maybe I want the chance to have him here in this flat one more time. Maybe I want the chance to break him the way he broke me, the last time we were in this very room. Or maybe I feel the very least I deserve right now is for him to hurt me again. It would be a penance of sorts for how I treated Sorcha.

'You don't have to face him alone,' she says and I watch the screen as he presses the buzzer over and over again in quick succession, frustration written across his face. My stomach twists as I think of him here, in this flat again, for the first time since that awful afternoon. 'I can stay,' Joan adds. 'Even if I hide in the bedroom or something... just so you know you're not alone?'

'Please,' I blurt as I lift the handset and press the door-release button. I suppose I have no choice but to trust Joan.

46

It's amazing how quickly you can sober up when you need to. I am stone-cold sober the moment I open my door to Ronan. My heart is in my throat and my hands are clammy as I see his thunderous expression in person. He towers over me – the height I once found so attractive now completely intimidating. His body is radiating anger – just as it was the last time he was in this room. The last two years just melt away as he steps into my safe space and overpowers it with his presence. I might as well be that same pathetic creature crying on the floor that I was back then. When I told him I was sorry.

I was sorry for losing his baby. I was sorry for loving him. I was sorry for making him feel smothered. I was sorry I had angered him with my emotional neediness. I was sorry, sorry, sorry. How was it that I thought I was the one who needed forgiveness?

Seeing him now, in front of me, his eyes steely, his jaw clenched, I have a moment of clarity like no other. It shouldn't have been me on my knees begging for one more chance.

Still my heart thuds, blood rushes in my ears and flashes of that day, and of the days that came before when I wished that my heart would stop just like my baby's had, flood my memory.

Jesus, but he'd been a cold-hearted bastard. When I'd called him, weeping from the hospital, he'd sighed as if I was an irritant and not a woman losing her baby. 'I need you,' I'd pleaded, sure that there had to be a trace of humanity there somewhere in him. That he would hear how desperately I needed someone to hold my hand. He'd known Shaunagh had moved, that my parents didn't know about the baby and wouldn't understand. He'd known I'd loved him. He'd known I'd had no one else. He didn't come, though. 'I told you if you were insistent on continuing with this then you were in it alone,' he'd said coldly before hanging up.

I'll never forget the look on the face of the nurse who was with me when I called him. How she'd taken my phone out of my hand before I dropped it and how it was she, a complete stranger, who held me while I cried and not the man who had fathered my poor, dead baby.

'Why are you here?' I ask, my voice shaking – but this time my fear is being replaced with something else.

'As if you don't know!' he says. 'What the fuck are you playing at, you absolute psychopath? Coming to MY house? Becoming all pally with Sorcha? Going into my fucking daughter's bedroom and... what... stealing her doll? What is wrong with you?'

He barges his way into my flat, pushing me out of his way so that my back slams against the wall, forcing the air from my lungs. I suck in a deep breath as he storms through to the living area.

'It was two years ago, Tina! You need to drop this and stop behaving like some sort of demented stalker! What are you trying to achieve? What the hell do you think you're doing? And Jesus, look at the state of this place! You're living in a fucking dump – have you no sense of dignity about you at all?' His words drip with scorn and I let him speak knowing better than to interrupt Ronan Hannon when he is on a rant. Something strange is happening though – instead of feeling mired in shame, I feel anger. I feel hate towards him. I feel emboldened and empowered knowing that Joan is in the flat and is listening in. Joan who I know, despite her loyalty to Sorcha above everything else, will be here to protect me.

'What are you trying to make me do?' he shouts. 'Do you want me to take out a restraining order? Do you want me to get Sean to sack you because I will do that without thinking twice, Tina. I'd have got rid of you a long time ago if it had been up to me. It was bad enough that I have to see your name on emails, and worry about bumping into you at work. But now I find you're BFFs with Sorcha? And this... this I really can't believe... you really had the brass neck to come to MY house? Not just today, but on the day someone poisoned MY wife? At a book club? Jesus Christ, you couldn't make it up! You're unhinged.'

Flecks of spit fly from the mouth I once thought I'd want to kiss for the rest of my life and they hit my face. I wince, disgusted at the feel of them. But I don't speak. And it's not because I don't have anything to say. There's so much I could, but because I suddenly realise I don't owe him an explanation. I don't owe him an apology. Yes, it was foolish of me to join the Soul Sisterhood and befriend Sorcha. And it was definitely foolish of me to put myself in the precarious position I did by following Esme up to her room – but that's all it was. It was foolish. I didn't do anything wrong. I didn't wilfully hurt anyone and I don't owe him an explanation of my comings and goings, or an apology. The only person I have ever needed to apologise to in all of this sorry mess is Sorcha.

I can see the anger flare in his eyes as I stand, mute, my breath steadying after his push. He wants me to reply. He wants me to answer back and to fight him. He wants me to prove his theory that

I am unhinged because that will give him all the ammunition he needs to completely annihilate what is left of my life.

'Have you nothing to say for yourself?' he barks, like he's some sergeant major and he has the right to order me to respond.

I shake my head. And I know it will enrage him further but even though my very body is thrumming with nervous energy, I don't want to give him the satisfaction of winning. Because that's all it has ever been about with Ronan. He wants to win. He wants to be the best. The biggest. The loudest. The richest. He is never happy, I realise, and he'll never be happy. He had the beautiful wife, and he wanted more. He had the gorgeous home – one that looked like it fell out of the pages of an interior design magazine – and still he wanted more. He had everything that should've made him happy but it wasn't enough. Nothing, I realise, will ever be enough for him. The realisation that I was not the problem in our relationship hits me and suddenly I see him for the pathetic nothing that he is.

I can see him tense as he takes in the shake of my head – his frustration growing that I'm not pleading for forgiveness. I will never cry for Ronan Hannon again. That realisation makes me feel almost euphoric with relief.

'Say something!' he roars. 'Explain yourself.'

But still I stay quiet. I'll let him shout and rant until this storm within him is spent. Nothing he says can hurt me now. Not the way he hurt me in the past. That's the thing – once you've been through the most painful experience imaginable, everything else can be managed.

'Jesus Christ, Tina!' he yells, his anger spilling over as he swipes his arm along my sideboard sending my belongings – my lamp, framed photos, candles – scattering to the floor. 'Are you really that pathetic you can't even defend yourself? You can't explain why you would use a five-year-old child as some sort of weapon? How dare you go anywhere near my children!'

At those words, I decide there is something I want to say after all and it's what I've wanted to say to him all along.

'You had another child, Ronan. You didn't give a damn about that one. You wanted it dead. So don't play father of the year to me when you took joy in telling me how relieved you were when your baby was dead inside me!'

The force of his hand slamming into my throat, gripping it tight, causes an acrid mix of wine and tea to try and escape from my stomach. Only his tight grasp around my neck stops me from being sick and as I try to gulp air back into my lungs, I swallow the vomit, choking on it.

'I'm glad that baby died. Imagine having you for a mother. I only wish you'd died too!' he screams, and I can barely hear his words over the rush of blood in my ears and the awful gurgling sound coming from my own throat. 'You stupid fucking bitch.' I'm waiting for Joan to come out, but do I really want her to get in the middle of this? Haven't I done enough damage without putting her in the firing line too? Dark spots start to dance in front of my eyes and while I try to pull his grasp loose, my arms are tiring. His face is close to mine, twisted in anger. 'That bastard was nothing more than a mistake just like its mother.'

My knees start to buckle, my lungs burning through lack of oxygen and I see Ronan's eyes widen in shock, and just like that his grasp releases and it his him and not me who crumples to the floor.

As I gasp for air, my bruised throat swollen and my head spinning, I see Joan standing behind Ronan, my lamp, the base smeared with blood, in one hand. Our eyes meet. She drops the lamp to the ground and reaches out for me, pulling me across Ronan's splayed body on the floor, and guides me to the sofa where she rocks me like a baby, while telling me the police are on their way – an ambulance too. 'You're okay,' she soothes. 'You're going to be okay.'

My eyes fix on Ronan, watching for any signs – any at all – of movement and, despite my abject hatred of him, hoping that he wakes up because I don't want to see Esme broken by the loss of her father. Enough people have been hurt.

SORCHA

47

SORCHA

I am reeling as I try to take in the events of the last twenty-four hours. My mother has come to pick the girls up and take them away for a short stay with their granny. I desperately want them near me, but I know this is the best thing for them. I am no good to them as I try and process what has happened and what I have learned.

Joan had called me to break the news about Ronan. She didn't want me to find out via the arrival of sombre-faced police at the front door in the middle of the night. She wanted to tell me she had no choice – and on that score, I believe her. Joan may well be fiercely overprotective, but she would not wilfully cause physical harm to someone.

She couldn't stay on the phone long. She was being taken into police custody for interview. I have never felt so useless. I could do nothing to help except tell the police about the kind of man Ronan really is. And the kind of friend Joan is.

Did I care that he was on his way to hospital? That he had sustained a head injury? Not really. I know that sounds cold-hearted but he's lucky it wasn't worse. He deserved worse. Besides, he had regained consciousness by the time the paramedics were wheeling him out of Christina's flat and it was looking as if the worst he had sustained was a bad concussion.

I was more worried about telling the girls why their father had been struck in the first instance. I'd considered keeping it from them, just as I'd kept so much from them. But I had finally come to realise I was doing them no favours by hiding his truth. It was likely he'd be spending some time at His Majesty's pleasure. Whether that would be for GBH or attempted murder was yet to be determined. Either way, no matter how painful, that was the kind of thing that children need to know about their dad, in an age-appropriate manner, of course. My girls need to know that men who seem decent and good can also be men who are violent and manipulative. I have protected him for long enough. It's time I protected my girls.

But I'll wait a little bit longer. Let them have time with their grandparents enjoying the kind of things that girls of their age should enjoy. Let them have their innocence a little longer before I break the news to them. I dread to think how they will react, but I know I'll have the right people around me to help me navigate them through it.

And those same people will help me. Joan and Carla are sitting opposite me at the kitchen island drinking tea. Joan is pale and tired-looking. She might be quite the ballsy woman but clearly the events of last night have left her shaken. She spent the night between a cell and an interview room in the custody suite as she gave her statement and the police tried to piece together what had happened. Frankly, I'm amazed she's still standing and hasn't taken to her bed to try and get over what she has been through.

I want to wrap her in a blanket and pamper her, but the best I can do is supply tea and scones and tell her she is the best of people and I love the bones of her. She nods, but I see her eyes fill with tears.

'I'm not sure I am,' she says, her usual confidence gone. 'I was so determined to think the worst of Christina. So suspicious of her. I'm so suspicious of everyone and that's no way to live. And that flat of hers? It was just an awful mess. She says someone broke in and trashed the place but I'm not sure it wasn't just a sign that she wasn't coping with life. I was giving her such a hard time and she was struggling daily.'

'You were trying to protect your friends,' Carla says, her own face pale and drawn. She'd been working in the ED last night when both Ronan and Christina were brought in. She said she got the shock of her life to see them both. While she didn't treat either of them, they were very much the talk of the hospital. I wonder how long it will take before that talk does the rounds on social media – if it hasn't already.

I've decided that once I've had a chance to talk to my girls properly, I'll upload a video to address what has happened. I don't want it to be a spectacle, but I want to stop the rumours running away with themselves. It doesn't take very long for a story to grow legs in this part of the world.

I've also decided I need to go and see Christina and talk to her face to face. I've already messaged her to tell her I'm sorry for what happened and that I'd like to talk. I can't push her now – not with everything she has been through – but I can see the message hasn't been delivered. It's possible she has blocked me from contacting her. I don't blame her, but my need to make things right as quickly as possible is strong. I should've been open with her from the very start.

When Joan says there is something else she needs to tell me, I feel my heart sink. What else could there be? Just how big is this mess of our making?

My first instinct is to say: 'No more! I can't cope with hearing any more.' But I know she wouldn't tell me something unless she really feels it is something I need to hear.

She runs her hands through her short, grey hair and looks up at me. 'This won't be easy to hear,' she says and I almost, *almost*, laugh. As if anything in the last twenty-four hours has been easy to hear.

'I don't know all the details. I think that's a conversation you need to have with Christina. But... when they were together... Christina fell pregnant, but she had a miscarriage. It wasn't a planned pregnancy, but losing the baby utterly devastated her.'

I hear a gasp and look up to see that Carla has her hand to her mouth. My eyes flicker back to Joan. 'He didn't want the child. He made that very clear – said he was glad the baby had died. Called it a bastard,' she says.

The tea I have just drunk curdles in my stomach. I think of Ronan and how much he dotes on our girls. Of how he always has – from the very moment he knew about both pregnancies. How he'd cried at both their births, insisted on being the first person to hold Esme. How those days, even though I'd been exhausted and in pain, had been the happiest of my life because we had been the ultimate team and I had seen this man cry with pure joy at being a father. And I try to marry that with a man being so cold and brutal to a woman who'd had a miscarriage.

I am stunned into silence.

'Oh God,' Carla stutters. 'That's... that's awful. I can't...'

She gets up from the island and goes to get a glass of water. Joan wipes a tear from her eyes. 'God, Sorcha, the pain that girl went through. I know that she knew he was married and that's unforgivable, but she has a vulnerability and he took advantage of that just as he did with you. The way I saw him speak to her – as if she was nothing...' There's a beat. 'And she wanted that baby so much. I could see it in her. She might only have been a few months along but that baby was as real to her as Esme and Ivy are to you.'

That baby, I realise, would've been a brother or sister to Esme and Ivy. And there was their father celebrating the fact it had never had the chance to take even one breath.

'He's a monster,' Joan says and I can't argue with her. 'The look on his face when he had his hand clasping around her throat. He was going to kill her, Sorcha. I know that. It's like he lost every ounce of humanity and he was actually going to kill her.'

'I feel sick,' Carla says – and she's not the only one.

48

CHRISTINA

This is not how I expected to make friends. Proper friends. But the Soul Sisterhood has been there for me these last few days – ever since Ronan stormed into my flat and choked me so hard that even now it hurts to swallow. My voice is returning, slowly. The livid purple bruises are starting to fade to green and blue.

By the time I got out of hospital the following day, I came home to find that Joan and Carla had cleaned and tidied my flat, having borrowed my keys. There were fresh flowers in a vase on the table. Scented candles were lit in each room and soft blankets and pillows were on the sofa so that I could relax and recuperate in comfort. The remainder of the mess from the break-in had been tidied away and despite what happened here, it felt more like home than ever.

Joan had left a large pot of home-made soup, which would be easier for me to eat on the stove, and had filled my freezer with ice cream. I had never had anyone take care of me in this way and when I saw what they had done all I could do was cry.

Carla had sent a text offering to sleep over. She wondered would I be nervous on my own, but I knew I had to get used to being in the flat all by myself. I had to reclaim it as my safe space or I feared I'd never go back again, and this is my home. I am not going to let Ronan take that from me as well.

I still don't know who broke in, or what they were looking for. I believe Joan when she says the only things she was responsible for were the phone calls... 'And being a complete bitch,' she'd added. But I tell her I'm glad for her bitchiness in particular. If it wasn't for that she would never have been in my flat when Ronan arrived with his temper flaring.

Maybe I will never know who broke in. Ronan has sworn to the police that it wasn't him and that he would have no reason to. Given that he didn't know about my involvement in the Sisterhood at the time of the break-in, I can believe that. The police have told me a fingerprint sweep would be pretty pointless at this stage. There have been too many people – police, paramedics, Ronan and Joan in my flat since – all of them leaving their own marks.

I'll also probably never know for certain if someone spiked my drink, or Sorcha's, at the book club. It seems such a ridiculous notion, I'm happy to put it behind me as just a stomach bug because in reality I might not have many friends, but I also don't have enemies. Not outside those who are now standing with me.

Sorcha, for all her confusion and upset, doesn't hate me. We have to build on our trust again – and we have to get to know each other, properly this time. At least now we understand each other. More than anyone else. I know she didn't walk away with everything. I know that there were more smoke and mirrors at play in her life than even she had admitted to herself, never mind anyone else. She says she knows I was manipulated by the master manipulator himself. It's an incredibly generous take from her and one I'm very grateful for.

What we have agreed on is that we'll put it behind us. I

suggested the best way to start anew is to do what we love, to cleanse ourselves of this horrific chapter in the wild Atlantic itself.

Call it what you want – a baptism, a rebirth, a cleansing – we've agreed to do it at the next full moon. The four of us have planned to go to our beloved Tullagh, at night when the moon is high in the sky. We'll build a fire first on the beach, to warm us when we come back out of the water. I'll bring hot chocolate and marshmallows for toasting.

And we'll walk into the water illuminated by the stars, wearing LED lights on our beanie hats to guide the way. I know that by the time we come back out we will all feel stronger for it and, God knows, I'm going to need that strength for what is to come. Ronan is planning quite the defence and I know he's unlikely to play fair. Luckily, I have Sorcha on my side, and on top of that we both have Joan and Carla with us. And the rest of the Soul Sisterhood waiting in the wings, of course.

Nerves fizz in the pit of my stomach as I slip on my fleecy joggers and my softest hoodie over my swimsuit. My bag is packed – with my towel and clean underwear. With my neoprene boots and gloves and my beanie hat with LED torch. I put on my fluffy woollen socks and stuff my feet into my Ugg boots. I just have to make up the hot chocolate to fill my flask – this time with enough for four people – and I'll be good to go.

Of course, being the kind of person I am, I'm ready much too early. Sorcha isn't due to arrive for another forty-five minutes but I've been like a cat on a hot tin roof all evening. I just want to get this over and done with – I feel as if I can't move on until I have cleansed myself of all Ronan brought into my life.

Apart from my baby, naturally. My baby who I can finally talk about. My baby who in my heart I thought was a girl and who I hoped to call Grace. Joan says I should use that name when talking about her from now on. That every baby, no matter how small, or how long their heart beats for deserves a name. I like that. I like that I can talk of her and that short time she was alive and inside me and not feel shame, or fear, or guilt. Sorcha and I have cried together about her. I even admitted that in my mind she looked a lot like her big sister Esme, and perhaps that's why I had felt a special bond with Sorcha's youngest child.

Maybe one day – in the very distant future when they are better able to understand and when the confusion and pain over the last few days has eased, we will tell both Esme and Ivy about the sister who never was. Then again, perhaps that's too much to expect.

I don't think I'll ever be able to apologise adequately to Sorcha for what I did with Ronan, even if she tells me there is nothing more for me to apologise for. I'm hoping when we walk into the water tonight, and as we walk back out, I will feel cleansed enough to believe her.

The thought of a moonlight swim, on this late October night when the wind is high, is a little scary. But I've been through worse and survived. This will be easy in comparison. I'm sure of it.

I mix the chocolate powder into the warm milk and whisk it. The smell is deliciously sweet and I remember to pack both big marshmallows for roasting and small ones for sprinkling and stirring into our drinks. I'm just screwing the lid on the flask when my phone starts to ring.

Carla's name lights up the screen, and I hope she's not cancelling. She needs this as much as I do. She hasn't been herself since the night I was wheeled into the ED. She said the shock of seeing me, my face pale, my neck already purple with bruising has really shaken her up. She's become much more withdrawn, quiet even and not her usual self.

'Hey, Carla,' I say as I answer. 'Is everything okay? I've got enough marshmallows here to sink a small ship so please tell me that you're still coming.'

'Oh, don't worry,' she says, her voice cheery. 'I'm still coming. Wild horses wouldn't drag me away! But there's been a wee change of plan if that's okay? Sorcha's running a bit late. Esme has a bit of a temperature – nothing serious – but Sorcha's waiting for the miracle dose of Calpol to do the trick before she leaves. Anyway, since I'm driving past yours anyway, I said I'd pick you up and save a bit of time. There's rain forecast for later and we really want to catch the moonlight if we can.'

'Is she sure she's okay to leave Esme?' I ask. 'We can do this another time if that suits better?' I say, eyeing the flask on the worktop and my dryrobe hanging over the back of my sofa. I'll be disappointed but of course I'd understand that Sorcha would want to stay with Esme if she's sick.

'She's says she's fine to come. She wants this great big cleansing experience as much as anyone, I think,' Carla says, 'but there is one more thing. Apparently there's some community event on down at Tullagh, so Sorcha has suggested we try Kinnagoe Bay instead. She doesn't want to attract any attention to herself, so she fancies a quieter beach.'

I haven't been to Kinnagoe Bay in years, but it used to be one of my favourite spots. It's definitely more remote than Tullagh Bay and you need nerves of steel to drive down the winding road to it, but I'm not the one doing the driving.

'Sure,' I say. 'As long as we can all get in the water. And Kinnagoe is gorgeous too. Although it might be a bit creepy on a dark night like this,' I say, adopting a spooky voice. 'Maybe the ghosts from the sunken Armada ship will join us in the water!'

Carla lets out a loud laugh. 'Stop it! You'll give me the heebie-jeebies! I'd forgotten about that ship,' she says, of the Spanish galleon that sank more than four hundred years ago just outside the bay.

'I'm only teasing,' I say, thinking I've enough ghosts of my own to lay to rest, never mind worrying about phantom Spanish sailors. 'None of them would be stupid enough to mess with us anyway. Joan would put them right in their place.'

Carla laughs again and tells me she'll be outside in five minutes. A frisson of excitement runs through me – the longing to let go of the past is strong and the need to feel the endorphin rush that only the bitter cold water can bring even more so. I gather my things together and tap a quick message into my phone to Sorcha. I'm trying not to be too much – but I do want to say I hope Esme is okay, reassure her that I'm absolutely fine with the change of plan, and I'm looking forward to seeing her at Kinnagoe.

Message sent, I slip my phone into my bag along with my keys and my purse and head out to where Carla is just pulling into one of the parking spaces outside my apartment block.

As soon as she has brought the car to a stop she jumps from the driver's seat and pulls me into the tightest of hugs. 'It's so good to see you,' she says. She grabs my bag and the flask from me. 'Get in the car. I'll put these in the boot and we'll get going.'

It feels nice to have her look after me – to see the concern on her face – and to feel the concern radiating from her. When she gets into the car beside me she gives my hand a squeeze. 'I suppose we better do this!' she says with a tight smile.

I can sense she's nervous. It's hardly a surprise. I'm nervous myself but I remind myself that my new philosophy in life is going to be: 'Feel the fear and do it anyway.'

49

SORCHA

My phone pings just as I'm about to leave the house with Joan. It's a message from Christina telling me she hopes Esme is okay, and she's okay with the change of plans. She's looking forward to seeing me at Kinnagoe?

I'm baffled. I wasn't aware there was a change of plans, or that there was anything wrong with Esme. As far as I know Esme is perfectly well and being spoiled to within an inch of her life by her granny. How would Christina know if there was something up anyway? My stomach tightens. This doesn't make sense.

'Hang on a minute,' I say, raising a finger to Joan. 'I need to make a quick call. I've just had the strangest message. It's ringing,' I tell her as I put my phone to my ear.

'Hello,' my mother's voice answers. 'Is everything okay, Sorcha? Are you wanting to talk to the girls? They're currently making their way merrily through all my make-up.' She's put on a voice to sound like she's annoyed when it's quite clear she is having the time of her life. I already feel my body sag with relief – but that doesn't explain the message Christina just sent me.

'So Esme is fine then?' I ask.

'Well, she looks like she belongs in an eighties pop video right now, but apart from that, yes. Why would you think she isn't?' my mother replies.

'I just got a strange message. It's probably nothing.'

'No. Jesus, Sorcha, you're starting to worry me now. What's going on?'

I can hear the panic in my mother's voice, followed by a: 'Granny, what's wrong?' from Ivy in the background.

'Nothing, dote,' my mother tells her.

'The message I got. It was from Christina – you know the woman who...'

'I know who *Christina* is,' my mother whispers, hissing her name, and I can hear a door close. 'I've just gone into the bathroom. Right, what was this Christina saying?'

'She said she hoped Esme was okay and she was all right with changing our plans. I was supposed to be picking her up shortly to go swimming,' I say.

'Is there actually something wrong with you?' my mother scolds. 'That woman slept with your husband, she stalked you and now you're going to pick her up to go swimming on a Saturday night? Tell me you're at least planning on going to an actual swimming pool and not one of your mental walks in the ocean.'

I see Joan raise her own phone to her ear.

'Mum it's complicated with Christina. You know that. But the main thing is – Esme is perfectly fine?'

'Correct,' my mother says.

'Okay,' I reply. 'I'll explain later,' I say. 'It must be a misunderstanding or something.' I end the call before my mother can launch into the second round of her lecture. Of course, I know she means well, and I can absolutely understand why she would not trust Christina but as long as I know my girls are well and safe, I'll worry about everything else later.

'It's just ringing out,' Joan says, looking up at me. 'Christina's phone. It goes to her voicemail.' She holds her phone out towards me and I hear Christina's voice telling me to leave a message and she'll get back to me as soon as she can.

'That's very strange,' I say. 'Did you speak to her earlier? Discuss going to Kinnagoe Bay instead of Tullagh?'

'Absolutely not,' Joan says, shaking her head. 'As far as I was aware everything was happening just as we discussed.'

'I'll try calling again,' Joan says and I scroll through my phone in case I've missed an earlier message that offers more of an explanation but there's nothing. As Joan shakes her head I start to feel uneasy. There's something about this I don't like but I can't put my finger on it. Maybe it's just that I know she's vulnerable, or maybe it's because the police never got to the bottom of the break-in at her flat or what, but call it instinct or a gut feeling, I just don't like it.

I remind myself it can't be the case that Ronan has got to her. He's still in custody as far as I know, and the investigating officer had promised someone from his team would let me know if that changed. I couldn't see that the wheels of the justice system would move on a Saturday evening. Unless, perhaps, he's accessed some way to contact her from the inside. It wouldn't surprise me if he already had the inside track on the black market. Could he really be that hateful or stupid a man that he would threaten her or try to wrongfoot her from his prison cell? I couldn't see it.

I hear Joan leave a message asking Christina to call as soon as she picks up the voicemail. That there's been a little bit of confusion and we were just getting ready to come and get her.

'Should we drive over to hers – just to check she's okay? Or if her car is there?' Joan asks, but the truth is I don't know. I'm not sure what we should actually do, but I do know I can't do nothing.

'Maybe call Carla?' I say. 'See if she's heard anything from her?

She might have spoken to her and have an explanation for all of this confusion?'

'Good idea,' Joan says, as I lift my coat and put it on – one ear on what Joan is doing. I can hear the echo of Carla's phone ringing down the line before it too goes to voicemail. Carla never lets her phone go to voicemail unless she's on shift and I know she's off today.

'Tell me I'm catastrophising,' I say to Joan. 'That the events of the last few weeks have left me paranoid and reading drama into things when there is no need.'

Joan lifts our bags and starts to walk towards the car. 'I'd like to say you are,' she says, 'but I have a bad feeling about this. Carla hasn't been herself since all this happened. I've tried to speak to her a few times but she's not been very accessible. It's just...'

'Just what?' I ask.

'I'm not sure how to say this...'

My patience is now wearing thin. It's not like Joan to be so reticent with anything she has to say.

'I should have said this at the time, but I figured Carla must've had a good reason for keeping quiet and I didn't want to be a tout,' Joan says.

'A tout? We're talking about a sisterhood of women here not the bloody IRA.' I laugh, even though with every second that passes this feels less and less like something to laugh about. I take a deep breath. 'Just tell me,' I say. 'Whatever it is, it can't be that bad.'

'You're right,' Joan says. 'It's probably nothing and it's probably just me being a drama queen... But when I admitted to making those phone calls to Christina, I wasn't acting alone. Carla was in on it too.'

'Carla? Our Carla?' Just when I thought the world couldn't surprise me more.

Joan nods. 'She could be quite nasty. The second call... the one where Christina was called a bitch et cetera. That was Carla. She wanted to make more calls and I talked her down. But it was Carla who had the burner phone we both used when Christina was kicked out of the group. Carla was the person who did it. I thought she was just being more protective than I was. I know the pair of you are very close. But from the way she acted after Ronan and Christina were taken to the hospital, I'm not so sure.'

'What do you mean?' I ask. We were all upset after the incident in Christina's flat. We all seemed shocked and disturbed by it. What made Carla's reaction any different?

'So, you know the police took me to the hospital to be checked over for shock before they took me in for questioning?' Joan says, her face blazing at the memory. I can only imagine the shame she would've felt as one of the Health Trust managers being walked into the ED department with police, possibly in handcuffs.

'No! You didn't tell me that,' I stutter.

'I've told as few people as possible,' she says. 'And some of my ED staff are keeping it quiet for me. I've no need to tell you that if it gets out my job is at risk, regardless of why I was arrested in the first place.'

I can't believe she has been carrying this weight on her own.

'Well, while Carla said she got the shock of her life to see Christina and Ronan brought in, it was Ronan she reacted to most of all. Her face went sheet-white and she ran straight to him, took his hand. One of her colleagues told her to step out – it was against hospital policy for staff to treat their own family,' Joan says, her face pained.

'Family?' I ask. 'Yes, she's known him a long time. But they're not family. Still I suppose when we were together...'

'Sorcha,' Joan interrupts me. 'I can't prove it, and that's why I haven't mentioned it to you. I was trying to find out more and then

I was going to confront Carla myself, but I suspect from how she reacted that night, there's more to them than just friends.'

No. My mind immediately screams no. Not Carla. I'd have known. I always knew when he was up to something. There's no way he'd have been able to hide an affair with my best friend from me. Unless it was now, after the split? But even then... Carla knows what he's like. She knows what he's capable of.

I run over countless interactions between them over the years, raking my memories for signs I might've missed. How they would laugh together. How they'd gang up on me and tease me. There were occasional touches that maybe weren't as fleeting as they should've been, or shared looks that might've been more but which I'd ignored because this was Carla, and Carla would never. Would she?

'She wouldn't do anything stupid?' I ask, almost afraid to give a voice to fears that are starting to gather in the very pit of my stomach. Carla and hateful phone calls. Carla and the look on her face when Joan told me about Christina's baby. That was more than just surprise, I realise. And dear God, Carla and the drink spiking. The doctors had wanted to run more tests. They'd talked to me about spiking and it had been Carla who had insisted the doctors were being overcautious and that it just had to be a stomach bug.

'We should get going,' I say. 'Let's get straight to Kinnagoe.'

'I think that's the best idea,' Joan replies, as I punch in the alarm code and pull my front door closed. I have a very bad feeling about all of this.

50

CHRISTINA

I hear the faint ringing of my phone and curse myself for not taking it out of my bag before Carla put it in the boot of her car. I should've waited until we reached the beach before I put it away for safekeeping, but then I'm not usually inundated with calls so there's never usually a problem with me packing my phone away before I leave the house.

Carla must spot me turning my head in the direction of the ringing. 'Oooh! Do you have a mystery caller?' she asks. 'Some handsome gentleman, maybe?'

I laugh. 'Chance would be a fine thing. No, it absolutely definitely will not be a gentleman caller,' I say. 'If I never have a gentleman caller ever again in my life it'll be absolutely fine with me.'

'I hear that,' she says with a roll of her eyes. Her love life, it seems, is as disastrous as mine. 'It's probably some scam call. I've been getting so many of them recently, and they're getting clever too. They've been using mobile numbers more and more so I answer thinking it might be something important. It's never anything important.'

I've noticed that too and I tell her of the times I've had my work interrupted by someone trying to talk to me about the account I allegedly hold with some bank I've never so much as darkened the door of never mind opened an account with.

She tells me of a nursing colleague who lost four hundred pounds to a hoax caller who managed to convince her that her electricity would be cut off unless she paid up that very day.

'I can't believe someone who is smart enough to work as a nurse – and a bloody good nurse at that – could fall for such an obvious scam,' she says. 'She doesn't think she'll be able to get any of the money back. That's the worst part.'

We drive on in companionable silence, out along Lough Foyle, crossing over the border from the north to the south of Ireland at Muff and onwards to Kinnagoe. It's thankfully a dry night, and the sky, for now, is clear. Of course, that does mean the temperature is dropping quickly and I wonder just how cold the water will be when we reach the shore. A shiver of anticipation runs through me. A part of me is craving the bite of the first wave washing over my feet and ankles.

'Nervous?' Carla asks.

'Yes,' I say, 'but in a kinda excited, good way, if that makes sense? I feel like I need to let go of everything that's happened and move on. It will be cathartic.'

'And freezing.' She laughs. 'But yes, I agree. I think it will be the perfect way to wipe the slate clean and start over. Life has become so messy, don't you think?'

'Absolutely,' I say, taking comfort that I'm not the only person who feels that life with all its twists and turns has become over-whelming. 'Hopefully Sorcha and Joan will get something from it too. I can't help but feel responsible for the stress they've been under lately. If I hadn't wandered into their lives, everything would have continued just as it was.'

Carla nods, but she doesn't speak for a moment. It's as if she's trying to think of the right thing to say and the right way to say it. 'It will be hard for her, you know, to tell the girls. They must be wondering where Ronan is. It will be heartbreaking for them to hear what she's going to say about their daddy. And for them not to see him if he goes to prison. I don't see Sorcha taking those two girls to visit him in Maghaberry,' she says. She's not wrong, and to be honest I wouldn't blame Sorcha for not wanting her girls anywhere near Northern Ireland's largest prison.

'They have a right to know though, don't you think?' I ask, my hand moving instinctively to the bruising that has faded to shades of yellow and green around my neck.

Carla shrugs. 'I don't think children should be weaponised in a battle between parents. I worry about the damage it will do to them to have a father in prison.'

I stiffen. This is hardly a battle between parents, nor is it something Sorcha should shoulder the blame or responsibility for. This is Ronan paying for a crime he committed and Sorcha letting her daughters know the truth about what happened. I know she's a sensible woman; she'll tell the truth in an age-appropriate manner. She'll probably temper what she says because she won't want to destroy their faith in their father, but they do need to know that he did a bad thing and he has to make amends for it. In the adult world, that means facing time in prison.

I don't say this though. This is supposed to be a positive, life-affirming evening. I don't want to argue the rights and wrongs of the justice system. I just want to wash myself clean and start again.

So, I stay quiet – as does Carla as we start to wind our way down the treacherous country road to the shoreline. She taps her nails on the steering wheel, and it feels to me that there has been a distinct change in atmosphere. Maybe she just didn't realise quite how dark and remote this little bay is.

As we turn into the small car park at the bottom of the hill, the sweep of Carla's headlights illuminates the beach and I see the swell of the water rushing towards the shore. The moon is high and bright, and the glow it casts over the choppy waters is nothing short of breath-taking. It's quite clear that there is no one else here though. Hopefully Sorcha is on her way. I suppose we can always use the time we have to wait for them to build the fire and set out our small picnic.

'Shall we make our way down to the sand?' I ask Carla and she gives me a small tight smile.

'Yes,' she says and unfastens her seatbelt.

'I wonder if Sorcha and Joan will be much longer?' I ask as I get out of the car and walk back to the boot.

'Maybe we should give them a ring and find out?' Carla says as she opens the boot, and I reach in to grab my bag and fish my phone out. Of course, I see a couple of missed calls registered on my screen and when I open the notifications I see they were from Joan.

There's a message indicating I have a voicemail but when I try to access it, my phone won't connect. Squinting at my phone screen, I register I have no signal.

'Do you have any bars on your phone?' I call to Carla who is pulling on her dryrobe. She looks at her own screen and shakes her head. 'Not a one, but hang on, I've a couple of missed calls.'

'Me too,' I say, 'from Joan. I can see she left me a voicemail, but I can't get through to it.'

Carla swipes at her screen. 'Joan has been trying to call me too,' she says. 'But she didn't leave a voicemail – not that I'd be able to access it either. Oh, but hang on. There's a text from Sorcha.' She holds her screen closer to her face to read the message and pulls a face that screams 'disappointed'. 'Shit,' she says and looks up at me. 'Esme started throwing up, so Sorcha decided she didn't want to leave her. She apologises and says maybe we can do it at the next full moon.'

Disappointment courses through my body and while I understand – of course I understand – I can't help but feel sad that our moonlight swim isn't going to happen. I know it's stupid of me to have tied so many feelings and so much meaning to tonight but I really felt it could mark the birth of a whole new me. Not only that but it would seal my friendship with Sorcha, Joan and Carla. To my embarrassment my eyes fill with tears and I turn my head to wipe them away.

'Oh, Christina,' Carla says as she pulls me into a hug. 'Don't be sad, darlin'. It will happen, just maybe not tonight.'

I sniffle and try to hold back more tears from falling. 'I know. I'm being silly. I was just all hyped up and ready for it.'

'Me too,' Carla says as she hugs me again. 'Me too. Wait, here's a thought... how about we do it anyway? Just you and me? There's no reason why we can't. Just a quick in and out and we can go home feeling like absolute champions?' She pulls back and looks me in the eye, smiling encouragingly.

She's right, of course. There's no reason why we can't do it tonight. Just the two of us.

'Okay,' I say. 'Let's do it!'

51

SORCHA

Joan and I have barely spoken a word to each other. We have tried to get through to Christina and Carla but have had no luck. Our calls are going straight to voicemail now, which makes us think they must be out of range.

Kinnagoe Bay is breath-taking but it's not a location I would choose for a swim – especially not at night. The lack of phone service there makes it impossible to call for help should an emergency happen, not to mention it's not very accessible to emergency vehicles. Like Tullagh, the sea floor shelves off not too far from shore so it's important to be extra cautious in the water. The current can be insanely strong. We've swum at Kinnagoe once or twice but only in the daytime, and only ever when there have been a large number of us so we can take care of each other. We've certainly never done it when the tide is at a full moon, or when the water is likely to be choppy as it is tonight.

'Do you think they're waiting for us?' I ask Joan, although I already fear that Joan and I are not meant to be part of tonight's plans. After all, Carla didn't contact either Joan or me about a change in plan.

'I think the best we can hope for is that they've driven down separately and maybe only one of them has arrived,' Joan says. 'Then we can be sure nothing bad happens.'

God, I can barely get my head around it. I can't believe I'm even considering that Carla could be capable of intentionally hurting someone.

I can see Joan's jaw is tense, her face serious. I'd feel so much better if she didn't look worried too. I take a deep breath and have to focus as I start to drive down the winding hill to the beach. I can see the glare of one set of headlights up ahead, illuminating the shoreline. It's hard to tell for sure but it really doesn't look as if there is anyone on the sand. That has to be a good sign. There's either just one of them there, or both are waiting in the car. We might just have made it in time to stop Carla making a mess of the rest of her life.

'Wait,' Joan says and I look to where she is pointing to the water. Two small lights are moving towards the shore. 'They're in the water!' she shouts.

I know I can't rush down this hill, not at night, but the urge to hit the accelerator is strong. My heart is drumming in my chest. This is all I need to confirm my worst fears that something bad is about to happen.

52

CHRISTINA

The first bite of the icy water always stings, I remind myself as the waves rumble towards the shore and over my neoprene-clad feet. I gasp, let out a strangled, nervous laugh and look across to Carla whose face is stony in concentration.

'Just breathe,' I say out loud, for myself as much as Carla. We'll be so proud of ourselves when we walk back out, I remind myself as the bitter cold of the salt water causes every blood vessel in my body to constrict, making it feel as if my lungs are being vacuum-sealed. My breath is coming in quick, shallow puffs, through my quivering lips and I have to force myself to breathe long and slow, sucking as much air into my lungs as I can before letting it go.

'Are you okay?' Carla calls, as we continue our walk into the water hand in hand, holding on to each other for moral and physical support. The water's now lapping at our knees, and the swell of the waves pushed and pulled by the wind make me fear they might knock me over. The small LED torches on our hats illuminate the rushes of foam heading our way. There is power in the sea tonight.

The blood in my veins is already chilling. The numbness will come in time. I can't wait for the dissociation that comes with the drop in body temperature. That's what I want – the feeling of not being in my body for a while, only to return again with a new, refreshed look at life.

'Are you okay?' Carla repeats, her voice now firm and loud over the noise of the waves and wind. I feel her grip on my hand tighten – so much its uncomfortable.

I try to answer but my body is still trying to adjust to the cold as the water hits my middle, the force of it almost bending me in half. I look to Carla. Her eyes are focused dead ahead. I force myself to call her name, and when she turns her head to look at me I see something that chills me more than the water we're walking in. It's the expression she's wearing, the darkness of her eyes.

The energy between us has shifted. Maybe it was the conversation on the drive down that did it, but even with Carla's reassurance that we can do this – just the two of us – I don't feel like we're in it together. I want to look away from her gaze but at the same time I'm scared to. I feel as if something bad – something really bad – will happen if I don't keep my eye on her.

'Carla, are *you* okay?' I ask.

She blinks at me but doesn't speak for a moment. Then she turns her head forward again. 'Let's keep walking,' she says and she holds on to my hand tighter again.

A high wave forces me to my tiptoes to avoid the water washing over my head, my feet slipping on the moving sand below. I'm trying to find my balance and so I try to pull my hand from Carla's so I can use both my arms to centre myself. She does not let go.

We're out further than we would normally go. I feel panic start to build. It would be mad enough to do this on a beach we're familiar with but we don't know this one. And it's dark. The Atlantic tides can move fast – they can knock you off your feet and pull you under in seconds. Especially on nights like this when the water is choppy and the wind is up. It just takes one big wave. A surge of water douses me, and I splutter while the light on my hat starts to flicker.

I try to stop walking, to pull my hand from Carla's once again. 'I think we're out far enough,' I shout, my teeth chattering, but Carla ignores me and I find myself trying to kick my feet and move my one free arm to stay afloat.

My heart is thumping now, only just distinguishable from the roar of the water and the wind. A voice in my head screams over and over – this is not safe. I am not safe.

My feet bob up and down off the seabed and I'm buffeted by the waves. A mouthful of salt water makes me gag. Again I try to pull my hand free, try to tell myself I am panicking for no good reason. But Carla just stares at me with that same cold, dead look in her eyes and holds on tighter as rain starts to fall – water on water until it feels like the world is turning upside down. Rain falls in fat, heavy drops, like icy bullets pummelling my skin, and I'm not sure if I noticed it before now but the moonlight has dulled, lost behind the sudden influx of clouds and cold rain.

I shout as loud as I can, 'I think maybe it's time to get out?' But my voice is carried off on the wind and Carla appears to be doing her best to pull me deeper into the water. I don't know why. Carla knows I'm not a confident swimmer. I glance to the shore to see if there is anyone there, anyone at all, but even if there was, would they hear my calls for help? Would they know this was not just two friends enjoying a swim?

Panic rises in me as I feel my arm twist back, pulled upwards by Carla.

'What are you doing?' I scream, though it comes out strangled. 'Let go!'

And that's when I see it. The anger and the fury as Carla's illuminated face comes into focus. I finally recognise the expression on her face for what it is. It's the same as the one I saw just as

Ronan wrapped his hands around my throat and I realise something – only one of us is going to make it out of the water alive.

I blink through tears as I try to understand why Carla is doing this and I see her face twist in fury. 'You're going to ruin him. You're destroying his life! You're taking him away from me. You fucking bitch!'

With that I feel the weight of her hands on my shoulders, forcing me downwards into the freezing water, and I try to gulp in a lungful of air but manage it just a moment too late and swallow a mouthful of acrid sea water, before I bend my knees, and push my heels as hard as I can into the seabed to force myself back up and out of the water, choking as I gasp for air in the cold night and bracing myself for another onslaught as Carla's face burns with fury. 'He's mine. He was going to be mine and you... and that stuck-up bitch... you couldn't leave it,' she screams and my legs burn with the effort of not bending to the pressure of her body pressing into mine as I try to scrabble towards the shoreline. With the light on my hat extinguished and the rain and wind, I can't see which way to go or which direction to turn.

'Why did you come back? You should've let it go,' Carla screams over the sound of the crashing waves. 'When we killed your baby. That should've been it...' Her words cut through the noise, and the fear, and the cold. My baby. My Grace. When *they* killed my baby? I stop trying to fight. I stop trying to run. I want to see this monster's face as she admits what *she* did. I want to see her face as I reach back and force her murderous head under the water and hold it there until the life is gone from her body. A primal, maternal anger swells within and in that moment I know I can kill her. I know it wouldn't take much effort. And most of all I know she deserves it.

She must see the shock on my face, and she seems to relish it. 'A couple of pills in your drink and that bastard wasn't a problem for us any more...' She sneers, as water crashes into us. I lunge towards her, arms flailing, legs kicking, words of hate streaming from the very back of my throat even as I splutter and choke from the icy, dark water. I fight and push, and I manage to push her head beneath the waves – her eyes wide in anger or terror just as they are submerged. I feel her fight below me, thrash about and claw for air. I wonder did my baby feel the same fear and pain?

My tears mix with the rain and the sea water and I have never felt rage or grief like it and I want this woman to die. I want her to die. I want to kill her.

Only the feeling of arms grabbing mine, pulling me back, hauling me to the shore, stop me from seeing this through to the end. I am crying. Screaming. Roaring with pain. 'She killed my baby! She killed my baby! She killed my baby!' I feel the hands that pulled me away wrap themselves around me in a hug.

As I watch Joan drag Carla's body onto the shore, I feel Sorcha shudder and shake along with me as she hugs me. 'It's okay,' she says. 'You're okay. It's okay.'

53

SORCHA

I'm not sure which of us is shaking more violently now. Is it Christina, who I have dragged from the water and who is howling about her dead baby? Or is it me, my wet clothes icy cold against my skin, chilled further by the wind and the rain on the shoreline. I grab for my coat, which I'd thrown on the sand as I'd rushed into the water, and try and wrap it around me but I'm shivering so violently – adrenaline surging through me – it's a struggle. I cling to Christina for warmth as well as for comfort. I have no doubts about what I just saw as we drove into the car park and my eyes were drawn again to the lights in the water. I could hear indistinguishable screaming and see Christina disappear under the surface.

Joan and I had abandoned the car, the engine still running, and had bolted towards the sea, discarding our coats and shoes as we ran. I can barely remember the bite of the cold as we forged our way through the waves, the shouting getting louder and the scene in front of us coming into sharp focus.

Carla's face was grim, determined, as she reached up and grabbed at Christina, pushing her down under the water. Her expression, illuminated by the torch on her hat was cold and as terrifying as I had ever seen and I tried to quickly piece together what was unfolding. This was Carla. Carla who has been my friend for years. Carla who was godmother to Esme. Carla who spent Christmases with us after the break-up of her marriage. Carla who I would have trusted with my life. But I did not recognise the Carla in front of me now.

As we got closer I could hear her shouts amplified by the water and surrounding hills. 'You're ruining his life. You're taking him away from me.'

The shock stopped me momentarily in my tracks, just in time to be buffeted back by the waves and to lose my own footing momentarily, plunging myself into the darkness of the stormy waters.

Spluttering, salt water streaming down my nostrils, I managed to get back on my feet to hear Carla – my Carla – shout about killing Christina's baby, and watch as she tried to force Christina under the water again and to watch Christina fight back with renewed energy and anger, and grief so palpable I could feel it in my very core. I could understand it even though I was tiring and cold and gasping to get air into my lungs. I knew I had to get to them both. I needed to save Christina from the damage her grief would do, no matter how justified it was.

As I reached her from behind and pulled her arms back, I felt her kick and buck under me. I barely registered that Carla hadn't resurfaced, as I pulled a still-fighting Christina back to the shore.

She's sobbing in my arms now, gulping air as she cries about her dead baby and Carla and pills and how Carla was angry because Ronan was in jail. I feel my world spin on its axis once again. With my fingers almost too numb with cold I manage to get my phone from my pocket and try to call for help to come to this small cove where four lives have just been changed forever. But as predicted, there's no signal. I'll have to leave them and drive to the top of the hill.

A short distance away I see the light from the torch still on Carla's head illuminate her pale white face as Joan crouches over her, pumping on her chest with the palms of her hands, before she stops and tries to breathe air into Carla's mouth. I hear a sob rise from Joan's throat, and despite the exhaustion that is now setting into my ice-cold limbs, I discard my coat and crawl to where she is, stilling her hands and telling her I'll take over, grateful for the first-aid course I took when we started our wild swimming group. She slumps back as I pump my hands over Carla's heart, willing her to come back to us and not because I care about her – but because I want to know the truth, the whole truth and nothing but the truth. Eventually, with a convulsion that expels seawater and vomit from her mouth, Carla chokes and gasps in lungfuls of air. I put her into the recovery position and tell her to stay there and that help is on the way.

With burning limbs, I make it back to the car, grabbing what towels and blankets I can, along with the hot water bottles Joan and I both filled to bring with us for after our swim. I give one of the hot water bottles to Carla, who is now shivering violently as she lies on the sand, and cover her with towels. I order Joan to take off her wet clothes and put on her dryrobe, and I notice that Christina has started to do the same but her expression is now blank as she goes through the motions. Shock, I realise, is setting in – but I shake with cold and feel nausea rise in me and realise Christina is not the only person trying to come to terms with what has just happened. But I can't rest yet.

Jumping back into the driver's seat, I set off for the top of the hill, my whole body shaking. God knows how I make any sense when I call for help but I'm told it is on its way so I drive back to the beach where finally, defeated, I slump to the sand, just about finding the energy to wrap my coat around me once again.

My hands and face are numb from the cold and I heave as my stomach unloads itself onto the sand in front of me. I'm crying now too and I feel as if I might never stop. But I feel the presence of someone beside me, and it's Christina – her face still pale, her hands still shaking and she is trying to pull my coat away from me. 'You... n-need to get out of... t-hose wet cl-othes...' she stutters, as she tries to peel my sweatshirt off. 'H-hypotherm-mi-a,' she warns and I allow her to help me, and to wrap me in my much warmer dryrobe. As Joan hands me a cup, the sweet smell of hot chocolate hits my nostrils. I relish the warmth of the plastic cup on my hands and though my stomach is still sick, I sip the chocolate to try and warm my body from the inside.

In silence broken by occasional muffled sobs we four sit looking out to sea, watching as the clouds clear and the moon once again shines brightly and we wait for blue lights to illuminate the hillside to bring help. When I turn to glance at Carla, her head is bowed but she must sense my gaze. As we hear the sound of approaching engines, she turns her head to me just long enough to mouth: 'I'm sorry.'

EPILOGUE

CARLA

It could have been so different. It should've been. Ronan was mine. He loved me. He still does love me. I'm sure of it. I'm the person he turns to when he needs comfort. I'm the person who takes him in whenever everyone else pushes him away.

I've been loyal to him for so very long. From the first night we kissed, a quick shared moment at a party to mark his thirtieth birthday, while his pregnant wife sat po-faced drinking water for fear of 'hurting the baby' with anything else.

She didn't even dance with him, claiming her pelvis hurt and she was having Braxton Hicks; she was making the entire evening all about her. And look, yes, she is my friend and I love her but God above, I've never known anyone so utterly self-obsessed as Sorcha Hannon. She could've given him that one night. His birthday. But she didn't and it was me he kissed in the dark corner of a deserted smoking area. It was me he kissed again, more deeply, at the end of the night when she had gone home early to bed.

It was me who was his dirty little secret on and off for almost as long as they stayed together, and even now he still comes and knocks at my door when he wants me. So he's mine, you see. Not

Sorcha's. Or Christina's. Or anyone else's. I have earned him and I know it's only a matter of time before we are together properly. I totally understand why he wants to put a respectable distance between his divorce and us officially coming out as a couple. I do. And I didn't want to lose Sorcha as a friend – boring and self-obsessed as she is – so I agreed to wait. But how long is reasonable?

God knows I've been understanding. Even when I didn't want to be.

When he confided in me that he'd got that dowdy accountant from his work pregnant and, worse still, that she was intending on keeping the baby, I'd done what any decent girlfriend would do. I stepped in to help him.

I was sure that every time I helped it would bring us closer to our eventual happy ever after, you know?

Anyway, it was relatively easy to procure the abortion pills through my network of connections. I managed to get them sent to me by a women's rights organisation who were aware that obtaining an abortion in Northern Ireland was still nigh on impossible despite the 2019 change in the law to decriminalise it. I'd just needed to lie and pretend I was in need of them for my own use.

'Pop this first one in her drink,' I'd told a grateful Ronan. 'And within forty-eight hours, pop the second one in. That should do it. It's not foolproof, given that she's a little bit further on than we'd like, but it's the best chance you have.'

I'd hoped this selfless act would show him again that I had his back. That I was his partner in crime – literally now. Maybe that's in poor taste, but who cares? I was a woman on a mission. Surely it was only a matter of time before he would realise he owed me.

But of course, Ronan Hannon never feels like he owes anyone anything, and I went back to pretending to be okay with that. Because maybe the next time, it would be different.

The first time I saw Christina at the Soul Sisterhood coffee morning there was something familiar about her. I couldn't put my finger on it at first. Truth told, I quite liked Christina. Just as she quite liked Sorcha. This wasn't about whether or not I liked them – this was simply about how much I like... no, how much I love Ronan.

It was a chance conversation with Christina that triggered something in me though. I know people overuse that word these days, but that's what it was. A trigger. We'd been driving to the beach, chattering, and Christina mentioned something about her accountancy job. Until that point when asked, Christina had always referred to herself as a project manager. Later, when I thought about it, I remembered a 'dowdy accountant called Tina' who I had procured abortion pills for. Poor Tina who suffered a 'miscarriage' a few days later. But it couldn't be? Could it?

Of course, I didn't want to ask Christina outright if she worked with Ronan. It was clear she was hiding that for some reason. Then it crossed my mind. Was it possible that Christina and Ronan had rekindled their old romance in secret? Was Christina trying to ingratiate herself into the Hannon family so that when they went public she would be accepted by Sorcha and the girls more easily? Is that why Ronan hadn't gone public about us yet?

And yes, I could've asked Ronan outright, but he gets so angry when I ask him about his life. It was, he said time and time again, 'none of my business'.

And then I realised that Christina wasn't just content with sleeping with the man I loved – she also wanted to take one of my best friends away from me too. I saw the way she and Sorcha were getting all pally-pally. Soon I wouldn't count any more.

So I'd taken matters into my own hands. A small dose of ketamine in her drink at book club and it should make her ill but not too ill. I could swoop in, offer to take her home and maybe get a little look around her flat and see if there were any clues that would point to an ongoing romance with Ronan. It was foolproof.

Except that interfering busybody Joan had beaten me to it and handed Christina a drink before I'd been able to swoop in with the laced glass. And that wasn't the worst of it, because then Sorcha lifted the laced drink from my hand and started drinking it! Thankfully, she had nursed it all night. She was still the same lightweight she'd always been but this time it worked in my favour. If Sorcha had necked it, and fallen into a vomiting heap early in the proceedings, the whole evening would have been for nothing.

As it was, I was able to get a little – okay a lot of – ket into Christina's second drink and that was enough to set my original plan in motion. Sadly, as I couldn't be sure how much of the drug Christina had actually ingested, I was on edge, afraid to get caught snooping around her flat properly. So when I found a bunch of keys in the drawer of the hall table I checked to see if one of them worked on Christina's front door. I was delighted and knew if I was clever, I could come back another time and have a really good look. And that's exactly what I did – I pulled that flat apart looking for signs that Ronan was still visiting. That they were an ongoing thing. When I couldn't find anything, beyond that awful photo which I knew was old, I decided simply to leave a little warning message for Christina instead. I'll be honest, it was extremely therapeutic to cause such destruction to her flat. And best of all, I was able to slip the spare key back into the drawer before I left so there was no sign of a forced entry.

I wouldn't use the phrase criminal genius as such. But I am clever. And I don't have any regrets. You all heard what she did, right? How she lured him to that horrible, grotty flat and with busybody Joan at her side they beat him around the head. Self-defence my arse! I know my Ronan. I know my Ronan wouldn't hurt a fly.

They've locked him up, you know. And me too, but not in the same place. I'm in the madhouse undergoing 'assessment'. I wonder, do they know that I know better than anyone how to play the long game?

I've waited years to get what is rightfully mine, and I'll wait as long as it takes and do whatever it takes. That's what true love looks like.

ACKNOWLEDGEMENTS

The Affair is my first thriller to be published by the incredible team at Boldwood Books who have welcomed me with open arms to the fold. I'd like to thank the entire team for the faith they have shown in me. In particular, thanks to my editor Rachel Faulkner-Will-cocks whose guidance and support has been invaluable. It has been a pleasure to work with you and learn from you on this book. Thanks to Amanda Ridout and Caroline Ridding who sold their publishing approach to me so enthusiastically. To Claire Fenby and the marketing team for the absolutely tireless work they do, to Helena Newton for her attention to detail and guidance during the copyedit and Candida Bradford for a superb proofread.

Thanks as always to my agent, Ger Nichol, the world's greatest cheerleader and strongest advocate. I know that my career is safe in your hands and I am eternally grateful for the journey we have been on.

Thanks to the writer friends who have encouraged and supported me – and in particular when it came to writing this book, thanks to Sharon Dempsey, Emma Heatherington, Brian McGilloway and, of course, the best writing friend a woman could ask for, Fionnuala Kearney.

Thanks to my family and friends – to my parents, my brother and sisters, for encouraging me when I felt my well was empty. To the Caravan Survival Club members for being brilliant and also having the ability to make me laugh until I cry. To Fiona – who is a one-woman hype team who always understands the tougher days.

And to Lesley, bookseller extraordinaire, who is always there with a frankly offensive cup of tea, encouragement and funny memes.

When writing this book, I offered customers of Bridge Books in Co. Dromore the chance to win the opportunity of naming a character in this book. All they had to do was support their local independent bookstore on World Bookstore Day. The character of Una Doyle, Christina's therapist, is named after the winning customer.

To all the Twitter (I will NEVER call it X) followers and friends who entertain and distract me.

To my husband, who has helped me to live my writing dream and to my children – to whom this book is dedicated. No matter your age, you will always be my babies and I will always be inspired by you.

To the library workers, the booksellers, the book clubs, the people who write reviews – thank you.

Most of all thank you to every reader who picks up my books and allows them into your world. Every single one of you is appreciated beyond words.

ABOUT THE AUTHOR

Claire Allan is the internationally bestselling author of several psychological thrillers, including *Her Name Was Rose*. Boldwood publish her women's fiction under the name Freya Kennedy and will continue to publish her thrillers.

Sign up to Claire Allan's mailing list here for news, competitions and updates on future books.

Visit Claire's website: www.claireallan.com

Follow Claire on social media:

f facebook.com/claireallanauthor

X x.com/claireallan

instagram.com/claireallan_author

BB bookbub.com/authors/claire-allan

THE *Murder* LIST

**THE MURDER LIST IS A NEWSLETTER
DEDICATED TO SPINE-CHILLING FICTION
AND GRIPPING PAGE-TURNERS!**

**SIGN UP TO MAKE SURE YOU'RE ON OUR
HIT LIST FOR EXCLUSIVE DEALS, AUTHOR
CONTENT, AND COMPETITIONS.**

**SIGN UP TO OUR
NEWSLETTER**

BIT.LY/THEMURDERLISTNEWS

Boldwood

Boldwood Books is an award-winning fiction publishing company seeking out the best stories from around the world.

Find out more at www.boldwoodbooks.com

Join our reader community for brilliant books, competitions and offers!

Follow us
@BoldwoodBooks
@TheBoldBookClub

Sign up to our weekly deals newsletter

https://bit.ly/BoldwoodBNewsletter

Printed in the USA
CPSIA information can be obtained
at www.ICGtesting.com
LVHW032251080824
787784LV00046B/1659

9 781835 334225